THE FIRST KISS

He opened his eyes and saw tears in her green eyes. This wonderful, sensitive woman was crying over his pain. And that wasn't right. He couldn't move his gaze away from her eyes, her lips, that pert little nose that he wanted to kiss.

And why couldn't he? Abigail didn't want him any longer, if she ever had wanted him. Right in front of him stood a beautiful woman who openly flirted with him, teased him, and seemed to desire him.

Slowly he lowered his head toward hers. He paused barely an inch away from her lips. If she moved, he would let her go. But she did not.

He curved his hand around her neck, bringing her closer, until their lips met. Shock and desire soared throughout his body as they kissed. All he'd wanted was a little comfort from her. Something to make him forget his pain. And now, all he wanted was to lay her down on the sofa and make love to her all afternoon. He wanted to leisurely explore her body and kiss every freckle, wherever they might be.

He let his tongue glide across her lips, hoping she would open for him. And she did. But he never expected the all-encompassing passion as her tongue touched his, met him, and caressed him. He moved his hands to cup her face.

She tasted sweeter than he ever imagined. A combination of honey and cinnamon, and it drove him mad. He trailed his hands down her back, pressing her closer to him, to his rising erection. Damn, how he wanted her . . .

BOOK YOUR PLACE ON OUR WEBSITE
AND MAKE THE
READING CONNECTION!

We've created a customized website just for our very special readers, where you can get the inside scoop on everything that's going on with Zebra, Pinnacle and Kensington books.

When you come online, you'll have the exciting opportunity to:

- View covers of upcoming books
- Read sample chapters
- Learn about our future publishing schedule (listed by publication month *and author*)
- Find out when your favorite authors will be visiting a city near you
- Search for and order backlist books from our online catalog
- Check out author bios and background information
- Send e-mail to your favorite authors
- Meet the Kensington staff online
- Join us in weekly chats with authors, readers and other guests
- Get writing guidelines
- AND MUCH MORE!

Visit our website at
http://www.kensingtonbooks.com

SOMETHING SCANDALOUS

CHRISTIE KELLEY

ZEBRA BOOKS
KENSINGTON PUBLISHING CORP.
http://www.kensingtonbooks.com

ZEBRA BOOKS are published by

Kensington Publishing Corp.
119 West 40th Street
New York, NY 10018

All Kensington titles, imprints, and distributed lines are available at special quantity discounts for bulk purchases for sales
promotion, premiums, fund-raising, educational, or institu-
tional use.

Special book excerpts or customized printings can also be
created to fit specific needs. For details, write or phone the
office of the Kensington Special Sales Manager: Attn. Special
Sales Department. Kensington Publishing Corp., 119 West
40th Street, New York, NY 10018. Phone: 1-800-221-2647.

Zebra and the Z logo Reg. U.S. Pat. & TM Off.

ISBN-13: 978-1-4201-0876-7
ISBN-10: 1-4201-0876-X

First Printing: April 2010

10 9 8 7 6 5 4 3 2 1

Printed in the United States of America

ACKNOWLEDGMENTS

This book would never have been, if not for the wonderful people in my life. To my writing friends, Kate Dolan, Kathy Love, Kate Poole, Janet Mullany, and Sheryl Fischer, thanks for letting me call and whine about my characters and plot.

A special thanks to Allison Lane who assisted me greatly with answers on British citizenship. And more thanks to the Beau Monde Chapter, whose members can answer all my silly questions faster than any reference librarian can.

To the Romance Bandits, thanks for being such wonderful friends and understanding when I forget to write my blog!

Finally, to the men in my life, Mike, Stephen, and Tommy, thanks for understanding when I need to be alone in my office with the door shut. I love you all!

Chapter 1

London, 1817

As the door to Elizabeth's home slammed shut, she braced herself for the inevitable confrontation. They hadn't even waited for the butler or footman to open the door and announce them. Loud footsteps preceded their entry. Her heart raced as she attempted to rein in her emotions. Glancing up from her needlework, she watched Richard enter the salon with his wife Caroline following behind him.

"Elizabeth, we have given you six months and still you have refused to comply with my—our simple request," Caroline said as she sank to the sofa with a deep sigh.

"You have no claim here." Why must she have this conversation with them every month? And worse, why did it distress her so terribly each time? He had no claim here . . . at least not yet.

"Actually, I just might," Richard said, and then sat in the chair across from his wife.

"You are not the duke, Richard."

"Not yet," he added softly.

Her attempts to keep the greedy couple from taking over her father's house had only made them more determined. They only wanted the house and the estates in the country for their ambitions. Mostly, Caroline's ambition. Without her, cousin Richard would have been happy with his manor home in Dorchester. But Caroline wanted more. She would never be satisfied as the wife of a baron. She wanted the duchy and all that went with it, including Kendal House.

Only the house didn't belong to them . . . or her.

"Do you have any new proof that Edward is dead?" Elizabeth asked, staring at him. "Don't forget he had at least one son who would inherit over you."

"It has been ten months since your father died," Richard said harshly. "The solicitor sent several missives to Edward, but received no reply. And he has yet to arrive. Everyone knows about those heathen savages they have in America. Edward and his family were probably killed by them."

"Edward has been in Canada for the past five years." Elizabeth inhaled deeply, trying to keep her patience. "And until you know for certain about his death, you have no right to live here. Kendal House and the estates belong to the duchy until such time as his death is confirmed."

She prayed she was right. Richard and Caroline would squander the income from the estates on gambling, gowns, and balls. Neither appeared to have an interest in putting forth the effort to ensure the tenants were cared for and the lands remained profitable.

"That is where you are wrong," Caroline said with a tight smile. "Our solicitor is drawing up the paperwork right now."

"That shall be nothing but a waste of his time—and your money. It means nothing. This is the duke's residence, and Richard is not the duke."

"Edward refuses to return and claim his rightful inheritance," Richard added.

"That still makes no difference," Elizabeth explained. "*He* is the duke, whether he chooses to return home or not. Besides, ten months is no time at all. He most likely had to pack up his entire house in York and arrange passage over here. Plus the voyage time. I have heard the winters in Canada are dreadful, so they might not have been able to leave as expected."

"Then he should have sent a missive to that effect. Something acknowledging his inheritance," Richard replied.

Caroline shook her head. "For all we know, Edward is dead."

"Then his son would inherit." Dear God, they were driving her mad. It seemed as if they were far more determined than in previous months.

"Ah, yes," Caroline drawled. "But if he and Edward are both dead, then Richard inherits."

"True enough. However, if they were both dead then someone else in his family would notify the family solicitor here." Elizabeth clenched her fists in frustration.

"Unless the entire family was wiped out by those savages they have over there. Besides, it really should not matter to you," Caroline commented. "You will either be a burden on us or the new duke."

A fact not lost on her. Elizabeth had only the very small allowance left to her from her fath—the late duke. "I realize that, Caroline. I suppose I shall live with one of my sisters once the duke is installed."

"As if they want you," Caroline sneered.

"It is nothing to concern yourself over," Elizabeth snapped. Her sisters were so much older that she barely knew any of them, save Jane. And none of them had ever taken the time to invite her to stay with their families for more than a week.

"And I don't," Caroline retorted with one brown eyebrow arched. "But if I were you, I would be looking at all the eligible gentlemen."

Self-serving Caroline would only be looking for the richest and highest titled gentleman she could hope to snare. Elizabeth didn't want that. If she found herself in a position that required marriage, then she wanted to find a man who would love her for who she was . . . or who she wasn't.

"Nonetheless, Elizabeth," Richard started in a slow, warm voice, "we only want what is best for the estates. Your late father's steward could be robbing the family blind, for all we know. Someone must take over things until we hear from the new duke. My solicitor will petition the prince so that I may oversee the estates until such time as Edward either makes an appearance here, or is deemed deceased."

Elizabeth stared at Richard. With gray hair and tired lines creasing his forehead, he looked every bit his sixty years. She released a long sigh. "I have been checking over the books from each estate every month, Richard. My father's steward is an honest man."

Caroline gave a quick shake of her head. While her husband looked on the verge of elderly, Caroline was only six years older than Elizabeth's twenty-six years.

"You are looking after the books?" Caroline asked in a high-pitched tone. "I thought you were a lady."

"I am quite competent when it comes to mathe-

matics. Unlike either of you, I grew up on the estates.
Who better to know what they need?"

"Of course, cousin," Richard said quietly.

Elizabeth knew she was defeated. Unless she peti-
tioned Prinny himself. But she doubted the prince
would even listen to her. He would want what was best
for the estates, and that meant a man controlling the
lands, not her. She was a bit surprised the prince
hadn't managed the situation before now.

"If your sisters refuse to take you in, I suppose you
could stay here," Richard said.

"Richard!" Caroline's voice pitched higher. "In a
few months, there won't be room in the house." She
rubbed her rounded belly.

Richard shook his head and rolled his eyes. "This
house is large enough for a parcel of children, Caroline. I cannot have my cousin on the streets."

"But—"

"Enough, Caroline."

Elizabeth might have felt a spark of hope, except
Richard's tired tone was scarcely convincing.

"And yet, we all know she isn't truly your *cousin*,"
Caroline muttered before standing to leave.

Before Elizabeth could think of one decent retort,
the couple left. It wasn't surprising that they knew about
her past. The rumors regarding her lack of inheritance
had been the talk of the *ton* for months now. Most assumed it was due to a disagreement with her father over
a suitor—a rumor she had started and encouraged.

But a few might have guessed the truth.

Silence finally filled the house as Elizabeth sat on
the brocade sofa with a sigh. She couldn't remember

the last time she had felt this tired. Picking up her small glass of sherry, she took a sip, letting the fruity essence rest on her tongue a moment before swallowing. Her head lolled back against the fabric as she stared at the ornate ceiling of her small salon. She closed her eyes and listened to the sound of horses clomping past her home.

Only it wasn't her home any longer.

She had to do something, but at this point, her options had just about run out. Tomorrow, Richard and Caroline would return. This time with a solicitor in tow, no doubt. Elizabeth understood their desire for the house—greed and position. Nevertheless, the house wasn't theirs, and she would do everything in her power to make certain it stayed that way. She'd never trusted Caroline, and lately, Elizabeth questioned Richard's reasonableness. In the past four months, he had been spending more time at the gaming hells, and according to the gossips, losing serious amounts of money. Money she knew he didn't have.

Some days, she even wondered if the new duke had ever attained notice of his inheritance. Her father had died ten months ago, and she had never received one word from her distant cousin, Edward.

Of course, he wasn't truly her cousin.

Elizabeth opened her eyes and stared at the empty fireplace. She had to find her mother's diary before Richard and Caroline found a legal way to have her removed, or Edward arrived from Canada. Her mother had kept several diaries, and none held the information Elizabeth desired. After finding those journals in drawers, she discovered none contained anything too personal. However, one book made a mysterious reference to a hidden diary, and that was the one Elizabeth needed to find.

She had to uncover the truth.

After all this time, she wondered if the diary even existed any longer. Her father might have found the journal and burned it. Or her mother might have given the diary to a close friend to keep it away from Father. Elizabeth doubted both ideas. Her mother had died quickly following a carriage accident. She would have had no time to give the diary to a friend, and her father never seemed to care enough to look for it. Perhaps he had no need and had already learned the name of her mother's lover.

Elizabeth had only five rooms left to recheck. It made the most sense that the diary had been stashed somewhere in this house, since her mother rarely traveled to the estates. After checking every room in the townhome, she'd performed a thorough inspection of the other estates and uncovered nothing. Not one clue to her real identity.

Furiously, she blinked away the tears welling in her eyes. She refused to cry one more tear over something as silly as her real father's name. In the eyes of Society, she was and would always be Lady Elizabeth Kendal.

There had to be something she was missing in her search. Perhaps there was a secret compartment in a desk, or a hidden room that she had overlooked.

"Lady Elizabeth?"

She turned at the sound of the footman. "Yes?"

"Miss Reynard is here to see you."

Why would Sophie be here at this late hour? "Send her in and bring some tea and cakes."

"Yes, ma'am."

Elizabeth sat up and composed herself while waiting for her dear friend.

"Elizabeth, thank goodness you are here and not at Lady Tavistock's ball." Sophie rushed into the room and flopped to the sofa. Black tendrils clung to her forehead as she removed her damp hat.

"Why?"

Sophie shook her head. "Lady Tavistock would never have invited me to her ball and then I wouldn't be able to speak with you. I do apologize for the lateness of the hour, though."

"Is something wrong?"

"I am not certain. I had a vision and needed to see you immediately." Sophie picked up Elizabeth's hand and clutched it tightly in her own hand. Closing her eyes, she went still. "I was right," she whispered.

"Right about what?" Elizabeth pressed her friend for an answer.

"Something is about to happen," Sophie started, then paused and frowned.

"What?"

"A man is going to enter your life," she said softly.

Elizabeth smiled. Sophie had gained quite the reputation as a medium and matchmaker in the past year. She had even matched Elizabeth's dearest friends, Avis and Jennette, with husbands. "Are you certain?"

Sophie glanced away from her and shook her head. "Not in that way, Elizabeth."

The serious tone of Sophie's voice made Elizabeth say, "Oh?"

Sophie shook her head again. "I cannot be sure but I feel there is something dreadfully wrong. This man will upset your entire life. I fear he will bring you great pain."

Great pain? "How do you mean?"

"Oh, how I wish my visions were clearer." Sophie looked back at Elizabeth. "This man comes with children. Many children."

The duke. Elizabeth's shoulders sagged. She'd heard the stories that Edward had numerous children and stepchildren. Obviously, he was on his way here. Once he arrived with all those children, she would have to find other accommodations.

"Elizabeth?"

"It must be the new duke, Sophie." Elizabeth pulled her hand out of Sophie's grasp. "Do you have any idea when he will arrive?"

Sophie shrugged. "I really have no way of knowing. With Jennette, it was that very evening. However, with Avis, I knew in advance. My visions don't give me schedules."

"I understand."

"You don't think he would ask you to leave here, do you?"

Elizabeth waited while the footman brought in the tea and cakes on an ornate silver tray. After he left, she poured tea for them both and then rested back against the sofa.

"I don't believe I ever met Edward, the new duke. My father never had a pleasant thing to say about the man. Then again, he rarely had a good thing to say about anyone."

"You know my home is always open to you," Sophie commented. "My aunt would say that it lends credence to our social position to install a duke's daughter in our home."

Elizabeth blew on her tea before taking a sip. "Thank you, Sophie. I am praying it won't come to that."

She needed time to perform a meticulous inspection of the remaining rooms. It shouldn't take too long, a few days at most. Then she would be happy to leave the house to the duke. Not that she had any ideas on how she would survive. She only had a small allowance to live on, and despised the idea of being a burden on anyone.

"What will you do if he asks you to leave?" Sophie asked quietly before sipping her tea.

Elizabeth sighed. "I suppose I could find work."

"Elizabeth, you shall do no such thing."

"I won't be a burden, Sophie."

"You have some income from your father."

Elizabeth shook her head slightly. "It's not enough to survive on my own."

"You cannot even think about working. It is beneath you," Sophie said with a nod.

"Not any longer," she answered. "Besides, I have quite a talent for gardening. Perhaps I can find work taking care of someone's flowers."

"True. But do you think anyone would hire a woman gardener?"

"Perhaps not," Elizabeth said flatly. "I suppose there is always a governess position."

"Yes. But the lady of the house might be suspicious that the daughter of a duke needs to look for work. She might even believe her husband is installing you as his new mistress."

Elizabeth slammed down her teacup. The hot liquid spilled over the edge, just missing her fingers. "Then what am I to do?"

"Marry?"

She barely kept from rolling her eyes at the ever romantic Sophie. "I do not need a man."

Sophie giggled softly. "Of course you do. Just not for what you're thinking."

This time she did roll her eyes. "Now you are as bad as Avis."

"A good man in your bed cannot hurt," Sophie replied with a slight shrug. "Think about what I said. My aunt and I would love to have you stay with us." She stood and reached for her damp hat. "I should take my leave now."

"Very well."

As Sophie left, her words remained with Elizabeth.

The last thing she needed was a man interfering in her business. Most men liked nothing better than to stick their noses, and other parts, where they didn't belong. Therefore, until she uncovered the truth of her parentage, she refused to suffer through any man's attempt at courtship. Even then, Elizabeth doubted she would desire any man.

It just wasn't in her.

While she found some men attractive, mostly she found them annoying. Sometimes she wondered if there was something wrong with her. After watching two of her dearest friends fall madly in love and marry, she thought she might feel as if something was missing in her life. Yet, the only thing she yearned for was the knowledge of her background.

Not knowing her father's identity seemed to be eating at her more and more lately.

Perhaps because she knew her time in this house might soon end. Even if her cousin took over control of the house, she couldn't stay. She wasn't one of them.

Her heart constricted with pain. All her life, she'd been Lady Elizabeth. The daughter of the Duke of Kendal. Since the duke had never disowned her in public, no one knew the truth, except the few people who might have guessed. Even Richard and Caroline couldn't know for certain. All they had were the obvious clues—her father had left her barely enough to survive, and with her red hair and freckles, she looked nothing like her sisters or late brother.

Elizabeth reached for her forgotten sherry and sipped a bit of the liquid. She had to come up with a plan for her future. There had to be something she could do with the little money the duke had left her.

Her only skills seemed to be mathematics and botany. Neither proficiency would bring her any income unless she taught them to young ladies. Perhaps that was the answer. Find a school for gentlewomen and teach. It would not be an exciting life but she'd had the glamour of the *ton* for the past eight years. Society became more tedious with each passing Season.

The small mahogany mantel clock chimed eleven times. Elizabeth rose to retire for the night. Most of the servants had already departed their posts for bed, but she could hear a footman in the hall. She kept one man on duty all night to protect her and her aunt.

Thankfully, her aunt had left last week for a visit with her ailing sister. That had given Elizabeth the opportunity to search her aunt's room. Aunt Matilda had become quite impatient waiting for the duke, and wished to leave and live with her three sisters in Kent. Of course, Elizabeth would be welcome to stay with the cantankerous elderly women—a thought that made employment sound very attractive.

She walked into the hall and smiled at the tall footman. He turned and unlocked the front door.

"Is everything all right?" she asked.

He looked back with a smile. "Nothing to worry

about, Lady Elizabeth. I just heard a strange noise out on the street, and thought to investigate."

"Very well, then. Good night, Kenneth." Elizabeth stepped on the first marble tread and remembered she'd left her book in the parlor.

"Is everything all right, Lady Elizabeth?"

"I forgot my poetry book."

"Did you leave it in the salon? I shall fetch it for you immediately," he said before she could even reply.

She walked down the hallway behind him but stopped as the front door hurled open.

"Unbelievable," a huge man said at the threshold. "They just leave the place unlocked at night."

Elizabeth screamed as the strange man and several others walked in the house. "Kenneth, we have intruders!"

"Intruders?" the stranger said, shaking his head. "Lucy and Ellie, take the children upstairs and find rooms for everyone."

"Of course," said one of the women.

Elizabeth shouted, "Kenneth, where are you?"

"Right here, my lady," he said from behind her. "I'm going to need some help with all of them."

"Go wake the others," Elizabeth said quickly. What was wrong with everyone? She walked closer to the huge man with dark brown hair and a scraggly beard wet from the rain. She stepped back quickly when she smelled him. "Get out of this house!"

Instead, the children followed the two women up the stairs.

A few of them glanced down at her and giggled. One dark-haired boy of about ten looked down at her and whispered, "Will's gonna have to let her go. She's just mean."

Elizabeth glared at them all and then turned her stare to the man leaning against the banister. "You had better get those children and leave the premises before I call the night watch."

"Call whoever you damned well want." He took a step toward her. "Is this not the Duke of Kendal's London residence?"

"Yes, but certainly you're not . . ." her voice trailed off. No, it was inconceivable. This ruffian was far too young to be Edward.

Finally, she heard the loud stomping of footmen coming upstairs like a herd of cattle. She leveled the thug a smug look. He raised an eyebrow at her and smiled. His smile took her completely by surprise. With even white teeth and small crinkles by his eyes, the man's smile made her heart pound.

"Get this man and his children out of my house," she ordered the footmen.

"Yes, ma'am."

Two of the burliest footmen in service came forward and walked toward the man.

"Your house?" he said with a stifled chuckle.

"Yes."

"I thought this home belonged to the Duke of Kendal," he said as the two footmen pulled his arms behind his back. "Not so rough, boys. At least not if you wish to continue to serve in this household."

"What are you blathering about?" Elizabeth asked.

"This is the home of the Duke of Kendal. Allow me to introduce myself. William Atherton, at your service."

Elizabeth grabbed for a baluster of the handrail. Hearing the giggles of children, she glared up at them. At her hard stare, they ran toward their rooms. All but the two eldest women, who held her glare.

William Atherton was indeed Edward's son. His only natural born son. Edward's heir.

While hard to determine his features with his hair to his shoulders, a beard that desperately needed a shave, and a stench that would make a seaman proud, she didn't doubt his claim. His dark brown eyes were almost black, the exact shade of the former duke.

"Where is your father?" she asked softly.

"The good Lord took him nine months ago."

She breathed in deeply in an attempt to gain some measure of control. Finally, she stepped away from the stairs and curtsied to him.

"Welcome home, Your Grace."

Chapter 2

Will finally broke away from the footmen's tight hold. "Thank you . . ."

The woman's face flushed pink. "Elizabeth, Your Grace. I am the former duke's daughter," she replied in a halting voice.

"I see. A cousin of mine, then."

"Very distant, but yes."

"Wonderful." The last thing he needed was one more mouth to feed. The past two years had been a struggle as he attempted to keep his family from falling apart during his father's long illness.

"Those children," she started, glanced up the stairs, and then paused.

Watching her freckled face cringe, he almost laughed. "Yes? The children?"

"They can't all be . . ."

"Mine?"

"Well, yes. I had heard you were eight when you left for America, and that was only twenty years ago . . ."

He walked toward a large room as she attempted to determine the source of all the children. Glancing around the room, his gaze focused on the gilt furnishings. He remembered very little of his life in England, and this was one part he must have forgotten. The opulence of the room astounded him. Red silk wallpaper lined the walls of the room, vast gilt frames with oil paintings and portraits hung from the walls. He had only heard of such wealth. Not even Abigail's family had this much.

God, he missed her already. He had to get this nasty business completed as quickly as possible.

"Your Grace?"

"Oh, yes, the children. Perhaps I had an early start," he said with a smile. His innocent cousin's eyes widened.

Slowly, her lips tilted upward. "That must have been an extremely early start."

"Considering Ellie's nearly twenty, I do believe eight is just a bit young."

"Your siblings, then?"

"All seven of them, plus Alicia, who stayed behind with her new husband." Will walked farther into the room and ran his hand over the soft velvet of a wingback chair.

"Nine children? And they all survived infancy."

He only nodded at the sound of amazement in her voice. He chuckled softly. "They include four stepbrothers from my father's second wife."

"Would you like something to eat, Your Grace?"

He turned back toward her and frowned. "Why do you keep calling me that?"

"Your Grace?"

"Yes."

"Because you are the duke. If you were an earl, I would have addressed you as 'my lord'."

He shook his head. "Well, stop. I will never understand this country and its odd penchant for titles."

She stood upright and quickly brushed a red lock back from her forehead. "It is not an odd system of titles. How long did you live in Virginia before moving to Canada?"

"Ten years. Then my father was reassigned to another diplomatic position in York near Lake Ontario, just before the war broke out."

"I think you must have forgotten how English Society works. After all, you lived in that heathen country where no man needs a title."

"Perhaps. But at least there, every man has the chance to better himself without needing a title to get ahead," he said before sitting in the wingback chair.

"Your Gr—" She halted abruptly when he glared at her. Throwing up her hands in the air, she said, "Then what do I call you?"

"William, or better yet, Will."

"Very well, William. Would you like me to awaken the cook for a quick meal?"

"I wouldn't wish to disturb the servants."

"The servants are here for your every convenience. Besides, I must wake the maids to make up the bedrooms. Mine is the only one ready."

"Then yes, I would love a little something to eat. The food on the ship was not the best."

She smiled and two small dimples creased her freckled cheeks. The woman was quite pretty with her red curls and green eyes, but when she smiled, she became absolutely radiant.

"I will return in a moment," she said.

As she left, her slim hips swayed under the muslin of her amber gown. Listening to her give orders to the footmen, he smiled. She was obviously used to assigning tasks for the servants.

God, he hated the idea of being back in this country. If he had only surrendered his citizenship and moved to America before his father's death. Then he would not be here. He wouldn't be eligible for the title. Instead, he would be in Virginia with Abigail, enjoying the warmth of a late May evening.

Being an American, his stepmother had ingrained in him the ideals of freedom from tyrannical forces. How no man had the right to call himself king. The people had the right to choose their leaders, and titles should mean nothing.

While she preached to him about the importance of freedom, his father continued to speak of the duchy and their responsibility to it. Or more importantly, the opportunity it would give them financially. Once the title fell to either of them, they could give their family wealth and respect. In order for that to happen, Will had to keep his British citizenship. He'd only done it to make his father happy. What Will wanted remained in Virginia.

For the past five years, he and Abigail had faithfully written to each other monthly. Every six months, he would propose to her again, telling her that he would give up everything for her. Each time, she had another reason he shouldn't give up his citizenship for her. During the war, their correspondence had been sporadic, but she had told him of her love for him. When the war ended, Will had begged her to come to Canada, but she told him she could not disregard her father's feelings. After losing his only son in the war with the British, he could not lose his only daughter to an Englishman.

Not that any of that mattered. Now that he was the duke, he could do what he wanted. He was here for only one thing. Once finished, he and his siblings would be on the first ship out of England forever.

After telling the footman to awaken the servants, Elizabeth quickly walked up the stairs to organize the children. In the first room, she found the two oldest women, and a young girl who couldn't have been more than five. The little girl gave her a shy smile.

"Good evening, ladies."

The two older women folded their arms over their chests in unison. "Good evening," the woman with blond hair said.

"I am your cousin, Elizabeth."

"I'm Sarah," the littlest girl said excitedly.

Elizabeth walked over to the girl on the bed and said, "It is a pleasure to meet you, Lady Sarah."

Sarah giggled. "I'm not a lady yet."

"Oh, but you are, at least I think you are. Will is your half brother, right?"

Sarah shrugged, but the other two nodded.

"Well, since your brother is now the duke, that makes you a lady," Elizabeth replied with a smile.

The little girl giggled again and looked over at her sister. "See, Lucy. I am a lady."

"You won't be a lady for a very long time, Sarah," Lucy retorted.

Elizabeth turned toward the young woman named Lucy. "And it is a pleasure to make your acquaintance, Lady Lucy."

"Thank you, Elizabeth."

"I think she must also be a lady, Lucy," the woman with blond hair stated.

"Are you Ellie?" Elizabeth asked.

"Yes, Lady Elizabeth."

"Well, it is a pleasure to meet you all. I have to admit, I'm a little confused about who is related to whom."

Ellie smiled. "It is a little difficult. Will, Alicia, Lucy, and I are from the same parents. James, Michael, Ethan, and Robert are my stepbrothers. Sarah is the youngest, and she is my half sister."

"That clears it up a little. The servants are on their way to make up the beds for you. Tomorrow we shall see about setting up a nursery for the younger children, which will free this room for you both to share."

"You mean we don't have to make up the beds?" Lucy whispered.

Elizabeth smiled at the sound of awe in her voice. "No, Lucy. We have servants here to attend to our needs."

All three girls gave each other amazed looks.

"We don't have to help cook?" Ellie asked.

"We don't have to wash the clothes?" Lucy said at the same time.

"No. We have several servants to do all those chores." It finally dawned on Elizabeth that they were used to doing these chores themselves. She had assumed her cousin Edward must have had money, but perhaps he hadn't.

"Good night, ladies. I shall see you tomorrow morning." Elizabeth walked slowly toward the door.

"What time is breakfast?" Ellie asked.

"Whenever you want it," Elizabeth replied. "Just let the maid know if you will eat in the breakfast room, or if you want a tray in your room."

"We can eat in our bedroom?" Sarah exclaimed.

"Yes, I do most mornings," Elizabeth commented.

"Good night, Lady Elizabeth," Lucy said.

Elizabeth walked out of the girls' room and toward another room. Hearing loud voices, she knew before she opened the door that the boys were inside. She walked into the bedroom and found two of the younger boys investigating a bug in the corner of the room. They both turned as she entered the room.

"What are you two about at this hour?" she asked.

"There's a spider," the younger of the two answered. His hair was sandy brown and he had large blue eyes.

"And you are?"

"Robert, ma'am."

Glancing toward the older boy with blond hair, she asked, "And you?"

"Ethan, ma'am."

"I see. Have you two decided which bed will be yours tonight?" She walked over to where they still stood in the corner. Spying the spider, she lifted her skirts and stomped on it.

"I can't believe you did that!" Ethan said. "It was a poor little spider. He wasn't going to hurt anyone!"

Elizabeth inhaled deeply. She had no idea how to deal with children, especially boys. "That spider might have bitten you. And that is no way to speak to an elder."

"Yes, ma'am," they muttered together.

"Now, tomorrow we shall settle everyone into their permanent rooms, but for tonight, you will have to make do with the beds that are in here."

"It doesn't matter about the beds," a sullen voice from the doorway said.

Elizabeth turned and looked at the older boy. "Why is that? And who are you?"

"I'm Michael. And it doesn't matter about the spider

or you or the beds or anything else." Michael moved toward one of the beds and flopped on it, facedown.

Elizabeth stood there, unsure of what to do. Should she call for William? She had never been around young boys before now.

"Michael, we're not going anywhere," said an older adolescent from the corner.

Had he been in the room the entire time? She was in completely over her head. "What do you mean, Michael?"

He turned his head slightly from the pillow. "As soon as Will sells off everything, we're moving back to America."

"What did you say?" The boy had to be wrong. William could not sell off everything and then leave. The estates were entailed and he had responsibilities to attend to here. If he left, who would care for the tenants? Who would care for the lands?

Michael rolled onto his side and stared at her. "We're going back. Will is going to sell off everything."

"Oh, no, he is not," Elizabeth said, striding toward the door. "The servants will be up in a moment with bedding. Good night."

She slammed the door on the way out. Picking up her skirts, she raced down the marble stairs. Did the man know nothing? He couldn't sell off the estates and return to America.

She strode into the parlor to find the duke with his feet on the mahogany table and his head tilted into the corner of the wingback chair, with his dark brown eyes shuttered and his breathing even. Her anger should have dissipated at the sight of his obvious exhaustion, but it did not.

"Get your filthy feet off my table!"

One dark brown eye stared at her. Slowly, the other eye opened and one brow arched. "*Your* table?"

She swatted at his feet. "Yes, my table."

He placed his booted feet on the floor and sat up straight. After folding his arms over his chest, he continued to stare at her.

"Last I checked, I was the duke," he said in a low tone. "I believe that means this house and everything in it belongs to me."

"Hah! You are incorrect on that matter. Some of the things belong to the title, not to you."

"It's all the same to me," he said with a dispassionate shrug.

"Well, you would be wrong."

"Perhaps I am. I may have been born in this country, but it isn't my home and never will be. For all I care, some other cousin can inherit this damned title."

She glared at him as her anger rose higher. "But they cannot."

"Oh?" He arched one eyebrow slightly.

"As long as you are alive, *you* are the duke. Whether you like the idea or not," she retorted.

How dare this man think he could dismiss centuries of family history? Did he have no idea of what his relatives did to gain that title? The battles fought over land, the marriages brokered over money and land. All done to increase the family's position and fortune. All done to give them the wonderful and secure life they had now.

Meeting him almost made her wish Richard had inherited the duchy. At least he would have respect for the title and the history that went along with it. Although, he would gamble away the money. The situation was bewildering. She had one cousin who would gamble the estates to ruin, and another who would sell off everything. Well, she wasn't about to allow either of those things to happen.

"But again, I am the duke," the arrogant, uncivilized man stated. "Therefore, I can do as I wish with the assets."

"You might be the duke," she replied, balling her hands into tight fists. "But you cannot sell off this family's properties and belongings."

He leaned his head back into the corner of the chair and smiled. "I don't believe you have a say in the matter."

She smiled sternly at him. "Perhaps not. But I do know you cannot sell off any entailed property."

Watching his eyes widen and his mouth drop slightly, she knew she had caught him off guard. He knew nothing about the laws of inheritance in England. She could use his ignorance about the subject to her advantage.

"What can't I sell?"

Ignoring his demanding question, she walked toward the door. "Good night, *Your Grace*. Pleasant dreams."

Chapter 3

Will watched the aggravating woman walk out of the room as frustration seeped into his bones. What did she mean? Not everything he owned could be entailed. Could it?

All his plans hinged on his selling some of the properties and finally returning to America. It had been his dream for the past five years. Without the money, he was no better off than he had been in Canada.

He combed his fingers through his long hair. He desperately needed a shave and a haircut. Nevertheless, that could wait until tomorrow. He would question the little shrew about her comments then.

The idea of staying in this godforsaken country for more than a moment necessary bothered him terribly. He had to get back to Virginia before Abigail's father married her off to another man. A wealthy American man. Something Mr. Mason was certain Will was not. While many would consider Will wealthy now, in no manner would Mr. Mason consider an English duke an ally to the United States.

"Your supper, Your Grace." One of the footmen

who had attempted to throw him out of his new home stood at the threshold.

"Thank you . . . ?"

"Kenneth, sir."

"Thank you, Kenneth."

The footman set down the tray on the table where Will's feet had previously been settled. "Your Grace, I must apologize for earlier. I was only doing as Lady Elizabeth requested. She had no idea who you were."

"I understand, Kenneth."

"It's just that . . ."

Will glanced up at the footman's terrified face and understood. "You will not be turned out."

Relief washed across the young man's face. "Thank you, Your Grace."

The man hurried from the room as if he feared Will would go back on his word. What a rigid society. Everyone concerned about not insulting a man because of his title. A rush of homesickness came over him. He hoped Alicia and David were doing well. His sister had always had a tough exterior but was a sentimental, soft-hearted woman. She would miss them all dreadfully.

Almost as much as he missed her already.

He reached for the bowl of stew and sighed. The aromas floated past his nose, bringing back memories of his stepmother's wonderful cooking. She would have hated the idea he was here, but would have enjoyed the thought that he planned to sell off as much as possible. After he finished the delicious stew, he walked to the stairs, determined to find his room and finally sleep in a nonswaying bed.

"The maids just finished in your bedchamber. Your room is the first door on the right."

"And the children?"

Kenneth smiled. "They are on the third floor. Good night, Your Grace."

"Good night, Kenneth."

Will walked up the stairs and opened the door to the first room. Peering inside, he found the girls soundly asleep. Thank God. He wanted no more conversations for the night, only his soft bed. He departed the room and walked farther down the hall to the next room on the left. The boys were all asleep, except Michael.

"Are you all right, Michael?" he whispered.

"Go away, Will."

Will smiled. When Michael told him to go away, it meant come talk. Will sat on the edge of the bed and glanced about the room. "Nice to have a bed again?"

"I suppose."

Will reached out and rubbed his stepbrother's head. "We won't be here for long."

"James said that once you see all the money you have here, you won't wish to leave."

"Your brother is a fool."

"I know that."

"What I want is in America," Will said, thinking of Abigail's sweet, innocent face. "Selling off everything will enable me to have what I want, and give you all a better life. So chin up, boy. I just need a couple of months."

"James said you could have all that here, and more. Being a duke is a really important thing."

"I thought we already established that James is a fool."

"We did," Michael replied with a giggle.

Will still hadn't become accustomed to the lower register of Michael's voice. At fourteen, Michael was a gangly jumble of half boy and half man.

"Many of your elder siblings have idolized the idea of what England is truly like," Will whispered.

"I haven't."

"No, you haven't. But James, Ellie, and Lucy certainly do. That is why I insisted that all of you come with me. You need to see the England I remember. The poverty, the class system, the fact that people don't get ahead here without a title . . . like your father, and mine."

"But you *have* a title, Will."

Will sighed and rubbed his stepbrother's hair. "And if I didn't, I would be nothing here, which is why I cannot stay."

Michael nodded. "Good night, Will."

He walked back downstairs, reached for the doorknob, and stopped. Had Kenneth said the second door on the left, or on the right? Will was so beyond tired he couldn't remember. He opened the door to the left and a light, feminine gasp sounded from near the fireplace. She turned around and glared at him.

"What are you doing in my bedchamber?"

The small fire behind her displayed the shadows of her modest curves, and the glow flamed her long hair into beams of crimson. Her heart-shaped face, while covered in freckles, was completed with a pert nose and lips that were not too full and not too thin. Perfection. Her green eyes looked like emeralds shimmering in the dim light.

He truly hadn't taken an account of her beauty this evening when he'd been too preoccupied with other things. Or perhaps her irritable behavior had been the only thing he noticed.

"Your Grace?" she squeaked.

"I apologize, Elizabeth. I was looking for my room."

"It's across the hall. The duke's bedchamber is a full

suite." She crossed her arms over her chest as if to hide the fullness of her breasts. Instead, it only seemed to plump them.

Desire flared but he attempted to tamp it down as quickly as it had fired. He was not attracted to the shrew. No matter how her lush body seemed to call to him. His heart had settled on Abigail.

Not that his body seemed to note that fact. His erection pressed against the cotton of his drawers, desperate for release from its cloth prison.

"Your Grace!"

He swallowed hard, attempting to gain a measure of control of his sudden yearning. "Good night, Elizabeth."

He forced his feet to move toward the door, when all he really wanted was to step closer to her.

Elizabeth sipped her chocolate and then broke off a bite of toast. He had seen her in her nightclothes last night. She'd felt the heat of his gaze, hotter than the fire behind her, burning into her. While she'd tried her best to cover her erect nipples from his view, she doubted her success. His gaze appeared to settle on her breasts.

And she'd liked it.

For the first time in her entire life, she felt something odd and strangely appealing when a man looked at her. Not a man, a ruffian. He smelled foul, like a man who hadn't bathed in weeks. Of course, he probably hadn't the chance to clean much on the ship.

She was ill, that was surely the cause of this sudden departure from her normal manner. All this worrying over finding her mother's hidden diary had caused her to lose her senses. Most notably her sense of smell, if she found that barbarian attractive, she thought with disdain. Hopefully, he would have enough intelligence to bathe this morning.

Now with all the children in the house, she had no idea how to complete her search. Two of the last five rooms she had left to investigate were the children's rooms. She'd also wanted to check the ducal bedchamber once more. With William in there, she would never be able to search the room again. She had to find a way to get in that room. It made the most sense that the diary was in there. The only option was to wait until he left the house some time.

At least, he hadn't mentioned her leaving the house now that he was installed here. But she had to find out what William's intentions truly were, because even though she wasn't the duke's true daughter, the family name mattered to her.

She could never let him ruin the family name.

She pushed away the rest of her chocolate and toast, then strode from her room, determined to confront him. After searching various rooms, she found him in the study, huddled over the old desk.

He glanced up quickly and mumbled, "Good morning."

Elizabeth gripped the leather chair in front of her. He had bathed and shaved. At least now she didn't have to doubt her sanity. The man was beyond handsome. While his dark brown hair was still too long for the current style, his clean-shaven face showed a strong jaw and a chin with a slight dent in it. Even his nose was beautiful. Long and just a little crooked, as if it had been broken once.

"Can I help you with something?" he asked roughly.

Heat streaked across her cheeks. "I apologize. You look different this morning."

A slow smile moved his sensual lips upward. "As did you last night."

The heat on her cheeks burned her entire face. "I assume you found your bedchamber."

"Indeed. Is this what you came to discover? That I found my room?"

"No. I wanted to speak with you about what you said last night." She moved to take the seat in front of the desk when he remained quiet.

"You won't change my mind."

"But why?"

He let the quill drop from his hand, and it landed with a plop on the ledgers in front of him. "Why what?"

"Why would you wish to sell off what you can? Why would you leave the lands, the estates, the tenants, and the title?" The man had no idea of the history if he thought to leave without any consideration for the effects it might have on others.

"My reasons are not your concern." He sipped his coffee slowly and then stared at her again.

"I see. You do realize that you cannot sell off three of the estates."

His eyes narrowed. "So you informed me last night. I never understood this archaic idea that land can only go to the eldest male."

"It's actually quite simple," she said. "The reason is so the land always stays in the family. A person cannot sell off everything, and leave nothing to his heir."

"And yet, the only person of importance in this system is the eldest male. The rest are sent off with a small allowance." Will reached for his coffee again.

"That hasn't been a major concern as this family has

never been blessed with an overabundance of males. The College of Heralds had to search back five generations to find your father's connection to the family."

"So I am able to sell off any property not entailed?"

"Yes," she answered reluctantly.

"I see. This entailment was a method of protecting the family."

Elizabeth smiled. He finally understood why it was so important to keep the family lands. Perhaps getting him to comprehend the important history of this family wouldn't be so difficult after all. "Exactly," she commented.

"And as long as I'm alive, I remain the duke."

Elizabeth nodded. "Yes. And as long as your sons are born here or one of the English colonies, then the eldest living son would inherit upon your death."

"And if my sons were born in America?"

A flicker of doubt fluttered through her. "Your eldest son would be considered an American. Therefore it has been determined that our cousin, Richard, would stand to inherit. Or of course, one of his children."

"I see," he said, then stared down at the paper in front of him. Slowly, he looked up at her. "What about you?"

"I beg your pardon?"

"What happens to you?"

Elizabeth chewed her lower lip. "It is not my welfare that concerns me."

"Of course it is," he said with a smile. "It's only human nature to be worried about your personal welfare."

Rage infused her veins. "You think I am only concerned about myself?"

He leaned back against the leather desk chair in a

casual manner. "What other reason would you have for interfering with my business?"

She scraped back the chair, stood, and glared at him. "Not because it is my life you are turning upside down. Do you even know how many tenants the estates have? Or how many servants work for this family? Do you realize that every one of them might be turned out if you sell the lands?"

"That is not my concern."

Elizabeth did her best not to run from the room. She had to stand up to the man—make him grasp the lives he could be ruining.

"Indeed it is *your* concern. One of the duke's main responsibilities is the welfare of his tenants." She placed her hands on her hips, waiting his next rejoinder.

He leaned back further and crossed his arms over his chest. "We both know I am not suited to be the duke. Nor do I wish to play duke. My concerns are only for my family and their well-being. The rest of the world can go hang itself."

"You are a selfish man. You would turn out innocent women and children so you can have your way."

Will had taken enough of her waspish mouth for one morning. He rose to his full height, forcing her to look up at him.

"I am selfish? Because I put the interests of seven children first? Because I inherited a title that I had no desire for? Because I was forced to come to this detestable country and settle an estate I know and care nothing about?"

She cringed. "I'm sorry."

Slowly, she returned to her seat and stared at her hands. "I didn't think about how much all this must have upset your life."

"Not just my life. My entire family's life."

"True." She licked her lips. "But . . ."

"What?" he asked as he returned to his seat.

"This could make their lives so much better," she replied in a soft voice. "I can only assume you have more money as the duke than you did in Canada."

His fists instinctively tightened. "Perhaps," he bit out.

"Staying here would give all the children opportunities they would not have in York, or even in America. As the sister of a duke, the girls are inherently accepted into Society. The boys will be welcomed at Eton. They will all have the ability to make great matches."

"As you have?" The moment the words left his mouth, he regretted them. He knew nothing about her. She could be a widow, after all. But for some reason, he had to know more about her. He found her strangely intriguing.

She glanced down at her hands. "I could have made any number of matches," she mumbled.

"Of course," he said in a disbelieving voice.

She looked up at him with fire in her emerald eyes. "I most certainly could have. I haven't found a man who suited me yet."

"Ah, being selective."

"You don't believe me, do you?"

Will shrugged casually. "It really is none of my concern. However, as I understand these books," he said, looking down at the desk, "this house is not entailed, nor is it leased. I will be selling it as quickly as possible, so you might wish to decide where you will live. Perhaps with a relative?"

He watched the emotions play on her tight face and felt a stab of remorse. He didn't want to hurt the woman, but she had to understand that this country was not for him. He also knew that his brothers would never be welcomed at Eton, not as the sons of an American.

"I have four sisters, but I am not close to any of them. They are all much older than I." She clenched her jaw tightly as if attempting to control her emotions. "My aunt is normally here but departed for a visit. She will go live with her sisters."

"And you?"

"I suppose I could live with a friend of mine."

He was being completely insensitive to her plight. Her eyes blinked furiously as if she were attempting to hold her tears at bay.

"What about cousins?"

She looked away from him. "Apart from Richard, there is Nicholas, who is unmarried and lives with his young daughter. It might look improper if I moved in with him."

"I'm sorry," he whispered.

"You have nothing to be sorry for," she said, blinking away tears. "After all, you are the duke and you have the final say in all that matters in your house."

"Elizabeth," he started as she rose from her seat. "Please don't leave angry."

She looked at him, tears filling her eyes. "I am not mad at you, William. Only very disappointed. I thought that you or your father would make a much better duke than my cousin, Richard. I now see I was very wrong on that account. At least Richard would have had respect for the title and the lands."

She walked slowly toward the door and then turned. "I just need to know one thing."

"What is that?"

"Why is it so important that you return to America?"

"My future wife is there."

She frowned but nodded. "I see. And she can't travel to England?"

"Her father lost his son to the last war with the British, so the last thing he wants is for her to marry an Englishman. Not only an Englishman, but a lord of the realm."

She shook her head slightly as if confused. "You will always be the duke. If she loved you, it would not matter to her."

Will closed his eyes against the pain. "She would never disobey her father."

"If she truly loved you, her father's wishes would not matter," she whispered, then left the room.

Chapter 4

Will tried his best to put the frustrating woman out of his mind for the rest of the day. Unfortunately, it didn't seem to work. The fresh fragrance of her rosewater perfume remained in the room long after she'd departed. But her parting words ate at him.

If she truly loved you, her father's wishes would not matter.

Abigail loved him. She only hesitated to go against her father due to . . .

Will blew out a breath. She had to have a good reason. Was it money? Could Abigail be afraid he wouldn't be able to provide for her and their children? By staying in her father's good graces, she might be able to persuade him that Will was a good man. If her reasons truly stemmed from money, that issue would be out of the way now. Even if he couldn't sell off all that he'd wanted, according to Elizabeth, all of this was his. He could do as he pleased with the profits from the estates.

But his mind couldn't stop wondering if there was something else holding Abigail back. Had he been wrong about her feelings toward him? She was one and twenty now. If she had truly wanted to go with him, they could have married and left for England. Unless she despised England as much as he did. Her grandfather had fought the British for their freedom, and her brother died in the fight for Fort McHenry only three years ago. With a nod, he realized this reasoning made the most sense. She was most likely waiting for him to return so she could marry him.

Will stared down at the ledgers and papers in front of him and knew he was in over his head. He needed the professional assistance of a trusted solicitor to help him wade through the legalities of his inheritance. Except he didn't know a soul in London. He barely remembered any one of his acquaintances from when he was eight.

This, of course, meant he would be required to speak with the termagant again. Well, there was no time like the present. He pushed back his leather chair and walked to the front hall.

"Elizabeth!" he yelled from the banister.

"Your Grace, if I may . . ."

Will waved off the footman and shouted once more, "Elizabeth, get down here."

Soft footsteps sounded from the hall upstairs. She glared down at him. "Did you just shout for me to come down as if I were a servant?"

A quick rush of heat crossed his cheeks. He had forgotten that he wasn't in a small home without servants. "I suppose I did."

"Well, that is not how we speak to people in a civilized country." She turned on her heels and walked back toward her room.

"I don't think so," he muttered and then raced up the stairs. The door to her room shut just as he reached the hallway. He stormed to her room and rapped on the door. "Elizabeth, I need to speak with you."

"Then I suggest you use a nicer tone of voice."

Will clenched his fists and looked up at the high ceiling. "Elizabeth, may I have a word, if you please."

The door slowly opened and her smug face smiled back at him. "Do you need my assistance with something, Your Grace?"

"Can we talk in the study? I have a few questions only you can answer."

She nodded. "As you wish, Your Grace."

Every time she called him that, he fought against the annoyance he felt. "I believe I asked you to call me Will."

"Yes, you did, Your Grace." She opened the door to leave, and he noticed the valise on the bed.

"Are you leaving?" he asked softly.

"You did ask me to do so."

She couldn't leave yet. He had no idea how to survive in this country without her guidance. But he couldn't tell her that.

"You don't need to leave today."

"Thank you, Your Grace." A flash of relief passed over her face.

Will followed her into the study and shut the door behind them. Elizabeth sat in the seat in front of the large cherry desk as he sat in the leather chair.

"What do you need my help with?" she asked in a slightly harsh tone.

At least she'd stopped calling him your grace. "I believe the only way I can sort through all this mess is to find a trusted solicitor."

She smirked. "And why do you need my help with that?"

Will narrowed his eyes on her. "I don't know of any solicitors here. I thought you might be kind enough to assist me."

She shrugged and rose from her seat. "You might be wrong."

"Elizabeth, I'm sorry," he whispered.

"Do not be sorry. You are only doing what you think is right for your family. Personally, I believe you are very mistaken."

"I know how you feel," he tried again.

She walked to the threshold and turned back at him. "You have no idea how I feel. You're a man. You can do as you please. You don't have to worry about what people will think of you if they find out no one in your family wants you."

Her eyes widened and her mouth gaped. Quickly, she raced from the room.

Will stared at the empty doorway, unsure of what to do to help her. But he knew he had to do something.

Elizabeth grabbed her reticule and strode from her room. Bloody stupid man making her say something so appalling. Even if it was true. Her sisters didn't want her. They most likely either knew or suspected the truth. Her aunt would grudgingly take her in but then she would become nothing but a nursemaid to a group of old ladies.

"Are you going out?"

Elizabeth looked up from her fuming to see Ellie and Lucy walking up the stairs to their room. "Yes. I am off to pay a call on a friend."

"You're going visiting?" Lucy asked.

"Yes."

"May we join you?" Lucy asked, and then received a quick jab from Ellie's elbow.

"It's not polite to ask such a thing, Lucy," Ellie whispered.

"Your sister is right, Lucy."

Lucy's face fell with disappointment. "Of course. Ellie is always right."

Even though Elizabeth had four sisters, she'd only lived with Jane, and that was only for a few years. Elizabeth didn't understand how to handle the sisters.

"Lucy, you are not ready to face anyone yet," Elizabeth started softly.

Ellie bristled. "We're not good enough to meet a friend of yours?"

Oh dear, now both of the sisters were upset. "We need to prepare you for Society. Before you go out, you will need new gowns, shoes, bonnets, undergarments, everything. And you need to learn the rules of Society."

They both looked at each other and then at Elizabeth. Ellie's gaze moved toward the floor. "There is no point, then. My brother will only say it's a waste of money when we won't be staying."

"I shall talk to him when I return." The idea of speaking with that man made her blood boil. She had never met such an insensitive, arrogant, handsome man. Handsome! Dear God, no. She refused to be attracted to such a man.

"What are we to do all day?" Lucy asked. "At home we would be doing chores the majority of the day."

Elizabeth smiled. "Work on your music or your needlepoint while I'm gone. Monday I will have Madame Beaulieu here to fit you for your new clothes."

Both girls grinned.

"What about Will?" Ellie asked.

She shook her head. "I will take care of your brother. But now, I must go call on my friend."

Elizabeth walked outside and smiled. The deplorable rain of the past few days had finally stopped, and now the sun shone brightly and the air smelled clean. While she should have waited inside for the carriage to be brought around for her, she couldn't stand being in that house another moment.

When she finally arrived at Sophie's home, Elizabeth discovered all her friends were there. While they used to be known as the Spinster Club, even with Avis and Jennette now married, the women remained the closest of friends.

"Elizabeth!" Sophie announced, and then moved to give her friend a hug. "Is everything all right?"

Elizabeth sat in the floral chair by the window and shook her head. "As you predicted, he has arrived."

"Who?" Avis and Jennette asked at the same time.

"The duke." Elizabeth glanced outside at the carriage rumbling down the street. "Only it's not Edward. It's his son, William."

"What about all the children, Elizabeth?" Sophie asked. "Does the new duke have a few children?"

She glanced back at her friends and shook her head. "He is unmarried but he did bring his seven siblings with him."

"Seven?" Victoria said with a smile. "That should bring a little excitement into your home." Victoria ran a home for orphaned children, so she would know all about the noise children could bring into a home.

"Yes, and I have no idea what I'm doing with them all."

Victoria reached over and patted Elizabeth's hand. "I will call on you, and together we will get them organized and settled. You will have to hire a tutor for them. But I can assist with that as well."

A wave of relief slowly rolled over her. "Thank you, Victoria."

"Now," Sophie said, "what about the other issue?"

"What issue?" Avis asked, rubbing her extended belly. With only two more months until her first child was born, she looked more vibrant than Elizabeth had ever seen.

"Has he asked you to leave?" Sophie asked softly.

"Yes."

"I certainly hope you refused," Jennette said.

"Of course, I did no such thing, Jennette," Elizabeth replied. "It's his home now. I have no right to stay."

"But you *need* to stay," Sophie whispered.

Avis looked at them both and narrowed her eyes. "All right, what is going on between you two? There is no reason Elizabeth should *have* to stay in her father's home."

"But there's no reason she should have to leave either," Jennette pressed. She inhaled sharply and rubbed a spot on her belly. She and Avis would both be delivered of their children in about two months. Considering the infants would be first cousins, Elizabeth thought it sweet that they would be so close in age.

"Why do you need to stay, Elizabeth?" Victoria asked before taking a sip of tea.

Elizabeth sighed. She probably should have told her friends about her problem months ago. Maybe they might have helped her. "I need to find a diary I believe my mother hid in one of the houses. I have thoroughly checked the estates and found nothing. The town-home is my last chance."

"What is so important about this diary?" Avis asked.

Even knowing that her friends would never speak of the matter, Elizabeth hesitated. If word ever got out, she might be ruined.

"You can tell us, Elizabeth," Victoria said. "We won't speak of the matter outside of this room."

Elizabeth nodded. "I believe the diary will tell me who my real father was."

She watched the reactions of the women. Avis and Jennette both stared at her and nodded slowly as if confirming their suspicions. Victoria looked down at the Aubusson rug as if memorizing the patterns in it, while Sophie sent Elizabeth a sympathetic look. Of all the women, Sophie would understand the most. She was the daughter of an actress and an earl who wished to remain anonymous.

"Well, then," Jennette started, "you must do what you have to in order to stay in the house until you find the diary."

"But how? The man has seven siblings. I'm just an unwanted piece of baggage to them."

Sophie smiled. "Then you must prove to him that you are not an unwanted piece of baggage."

Jennette laughed. "Seduce the man."

Elizabeth rolled her eyes at Jennette and Avis, who both nodded at the suggestion. "I cannot do that."

"Not very handsome, is that it?" Avis asked before breaking into giggles.

Too handsome, Elizabeth thought. Far too handsome. And obviously in love with another woman. "He's practically engaged."

"Engaged, not married," Sophie added, stifling a chuckle.

Only Victoria didn't seem to find anything amusing

about her predicament. "You most certainly will do nothing of the sort."

"Of course I won't," Elizabeth replied. "But what am I to do?"

Sophie tilted her head and stared at Elizabeth. "You need to use your wiles to get your way. You wish to stay in the house. Make him understand that he needs you there. You can organize the children, you can assist him with the paperwork and invitations, and only you can completely understand his needs."

"Exactly what needs are we discussing?" Elizabeth asked as heat crossed her cheeks.

"He must learn how to go about in Society even if he only plans to stay here for a few months. If the children are old enough, they will also need your assistance," Sophie replied.

"The older girls desperately need my assistance. They actually wanted to come with me today, dressed in some distressingly worn-out cotton dresses." Elizabeth finally reached for the tea on the table next to her. She could do this.

How hard could it be to smile and be flirtatious to gain his acceptance?

Sophie tapped her foot against the rug with impatience. She glanced up at the clock on the mantel and fisted her hands. He was doing this deliberately. It had been over five hours since she sent that missive to him. He wanted to make her wait just as he had waited so long for his request.

Damn him!

She rose and crossed the carpet to the far side of the

salon and back again. What if he wouldn't help her this time? She needed him more than ever for this plan.

"You wanted me?"

Sophie sighed and turned toward the sound of Somerton's voice. He leaned in a nonchalant manner against the doorframe as if he had nothing better to do with his time.

"You kept me waiting," she replied before sitting back down on the sofa.

"It's a wretched feeling, isn't it?" Somerton moved from the doorway, and took the seat across from her.

"Very well, Anthony. The time has finally come to help Elizabeth."

"No," he replied with a shrug.

"What?"

"I've decided not to help you until you answer my question." The impertinent man crossed his arms over his chest in defiance of her wishes.

But Sophie knew the gambler was bluffing. "Very well, then. You may leave."

Somerton blinked and slowly his lips tilted upward in understanding. "Then I believe we are at an impasse."

"How so? I do not need your help—"

"Of course you do," he interrupted. "If not, why am I here?"

She hated it when he remained calm. He was so much more malleable when angry. "No one else can give you what you want, Anthony."

A dimple slowly creased his cheek. "I'm not so certain you can give me what I need, Sophie. If you could, why make me wait over a year for it?"

"I promised you the woman's name after we help Elizabeth."

"That was six months ago." Finally his voice rose, illustrating his true feelings.

"I never expected it would take this long for the duke to arrive." Sophie had started to doubt her own powers of prediction.

"Tell me something, Sophie," Somerton drawled. "Do you really know the woman's name?"

"Yes," she answered honestly.

"And you promise you will give me her name once we finish with Elizabeth?"

"Yes," she replied, looking down at the rug. He didn't need to know that it might take a bit longer for him to figure out her true identity.

"Before I agree, I want one answer." Somerton stood and walked toward the window. Drawing the curtain back, he glanced out.

"Very well," she whispered.

"What is the real reason you made me wait this long?"

"Because neither of you are ready."

"Ready for what?"

She stared at his hazel eyes, which appeared greener when he was angry. "For what is between you."

"You have no idea what is between us," he retorted.

Sophie continued to stare at him until he looked away. A touch of redness tinted his cheeks.

"I know exactly what is between you."

Chapter 5

Elizabeth waited until after dinner to approach William. She'd been so appalled by the children's manners during the meal, she almost left before finishing. These children needed more than just nice clothing. While Lucy and Ellie took control of the younger ones, Elizabeth followed Will to his study. She inhaled deeply before walking over to the table in the corner.

"Would you like a brandy, William?"

"Yes." He never even looked up from his papers.

How was she to use her wiles and flirt if the man ignored her? She poured a glass of brandy for him and a bit of sherry for herself. Perhaps the sherry would give her courage. Clearing her throat, she waited for him to look up and take the snifter.

He leaned back and appeared to notice her for the first time tonight. His fiery gaze burned her, making her mouth gape. Slowly, she reached out with the glass in her hand. His fingers grazed hers when he touched the glass and a spark of excitement skipped up her arm.

Why, after all these years, did the first man she felt

an attraction to have to be this mulish man? He grabbed the snifter quickly and stood to his full height.

"Let's sit by the fireplace tonight," he said, and then walked toward two velvet chairs close to the fire.

So much for having a desk between them. She'd assumed the gap would make her feel more comfortable. Now she would be able to see all of him. From his wide shoulders to his muscular chest to his . . .

Elizabeth shook her head to clear her thoughts away. After a brief moment of hesitation, she followed, and took the seat across from him.

"I believe you wished to speak to me about something?" he asked, then sipped his brandy.

She watched as he moved the glass to his full lips, and then her gaze moved to his throat. Never had she felt so mesmerized by a man before now. She had the oddest desire to touch his face, feel the heat of his body, and kiss his lips. Oh, dear!

"Elizabeth?"

"Yes," she said abruptly. Remembering Sophie's advice, she smiled at him in her most enticing manner. "I wished to speak with you about the children."

She glanced at the open door and frowned. Anyone might come upon them and overhear their conversation; she walked to the door and closed it.

"Is there a problem with the children? Did Ethan put a frog in your bed?"

"No," she exclaimed. "Would he do such a thing?"

William shrugged. "More likely to one of his sisters than you."

Now she needed to remember to check her bed every night. Sitting in the chair again, she said, "It is their manners. And their clothes. And their education. And—"

"There is nothing wrong with those children."

Oh, dear, she'd raised his anger. "Not entirely. But there is room for improvement. Children always need guidance, and to learn from adults."

He rose and paced by the fireplace. "It certainly isn't the boys' fault that their mother died when Sarah was three. Nor is it their fault that my father neglected them after their mother's death."

"Of course not," she whispered. Her heart went out to him and his siblings. "It must have been very hard on all of you when she died."

"My father's health declined shortly after my stepmother's death. Personally, I think after he lost my mother and then my stepmother, he wanted to be done with life. He'd loved them both so much."

"I am sorry," Elizabeth whispered.

"The last two years of his life were spent mostly in bed. I suggested we return to England to get better care for him, but he refused." He glanced away. "He wanted to die near his wives. After he died, I took over the care of the children, with Alicia's help."

"It must have been very difficult."

"I did my best," he muttered.

"I am certain you did," she replied gently.

She stood and placed her hand on his arm. Ignoring the sensation of touching him, she added, "But now you are in London and no matter how much you might not want to be, you are the duke. Even if you only stay a few months, Lucy and Ellie need proper clothing so they are not confined to the house all the time. They all need to learn better table manners, especially the boys. They were chewing with their mouths open at the dinner table."

"I suppose they could use some assistance." He stared down at her hand on his forearm.

Elizabeth knew she should remove her hand, but remembering Sophie's advice, she squeezed his arm instead. With what she hoped was a flirtatious smile, she said, "I can help you."

His brown eyes darkened. "Oh?"

"I can assist you so you are ready to face Society, too. You need a valet to cut your hair." Slowly, she reached up and touched the dark strands. His hair felt coarse to her fingertips but she loved the sensation. She'd never felt so bold in her life.

He reached for her wrist and held it tight. "Elizabeth, I am practically engaged."

Oh, God, he must think she was nothing but a strumpet. "I'm sorry," she said, pulling both her hands away. "I didn't mean anything by . . ."

He turned to face her fully, and gently clasped her shoulders. "Perhaps if I wasn't almost engaged . . ."

"No, I truly meant nothing," she said, disconcerted at being caught flirting with him, and more disturbed by the feelings of his hands on her shoulders. Her heart pounded in her chest as she fought for some semblance of sanity.

No matter how she tried, she couldn't look away from him. Why did she have to be attracted to him?

He shook his head slightly and removed his hands from her. "Elizabeth, what do you think I should do about the children?" he asked in a strangely hoarse voice.

Elizabeth moved back to her seat and sipped her sherry. "I can assist you so they get the proper clothing and education they need while here. But . . ."

"But what?"

She stared down at her hands and said, "I would need to stay here to show them a proper example."

Will sat down in his seat with a smile. Now he understood exactly what she had been up to with her contagious flirting. She wanted to stay in the house. An idea that made him cringe, and yet warmed him at the same time. The thought of her sleeping across the hall from him was a worry. The woman was pure temptation.

But she was right. The children needed a better example, and proper clothing and manners. He would resist her flirtations by thinking of Abigail.

Elizabeth pressed her pink lips together and looked down at her hands. "I guess I have my answer. I shall pack my things tomorrow."

"Elizabeth, you don't need to leave." But she did. Every move she made tempted him in a way he hadn't felt for a long time. He tried to imagine Abigail's face, but the only image in his mind was of Elizabeth lying naked in a bed.

"I believe you say that purely to ease your conscience. It is not necessary. I shall leave tomorrow."

"No," he said firmly. "You are right about the children. They need guidance in a way I can't give them."

"Lucy and Ellie really should make their bow before they enter Society. It's a rather large undertaking."

"Their bow?"

Elizabeth smiled at him. "They must be presented to the queen."

That was a terrible idea. A presentation to the queen would only make both girls want to stay here. They would see only the advantages of being wealthy and titled.

"William?" Elizabeth quizzed softly. "Should I make the arrangements?"

"Yes." That was not what he was supposed to tell her. He should tell her to leave right now and not to involve his sisters in anything to do with Society.

She rose gracefully from her seat and smiled down at him. "Thank you, William. Good night."

He watched the gentle sway of her hips in the pale green silk. What was it about her that made him say the exact opposite of what he should?

He loved Abigail. At least he thought he did. For the past five years, he'd waited for her to either disregard her father's objections or help him overcome those doubts. Still, Will's feelings had not changed for her. Had they?

During the past year, her letters had come less frequently, and there had been a distance to her writing. Why hadn't he fought harder for her hand in marriage? Why hadn't she done more for him after his father's death?

Dammit!

One full day in this damned country and already he felt confliction running through his veins. Abigail was the one for him. Even if he still felt some anger toward her for not marrying him. He couldn't want another woman. And yet, even as he had that thought, his erection pressed tightly against his trousers.

There was something about Elizabeth that stayed with him long after she'd left the room. Perhaps these lustful feelings were merely from denying himself for so long. When he'd first met Abigail, she'd only been sixteen. He'd promised himself that he would never dishonor her by asking her to give herself to him before marriage. They had only shared a few stolen kisses.

Will stood and moved to the small cherry table in the corner holding the spirits. Not much of a brandy drinker, he found a bottle of whisky. After pouring a small glass, he drained it in one gulp. He had to get out of this house . . . but he had nowhere to go. And according to Elizabeth, he would be ridiculed on the basis of his clothing.

A sense of incompetence filled him. The only other time he felt this inept was the first month after Father died. Only then, he had Alicia to help guide him with the younger children. Now, he had no one.

Except Elizabeth.

The next afternoon Will sat at his desk shuffling through his newly inherited huge stack of papers and ledgers. He'd barely slept last night with all his tossing and turning and dreaming of a woman he shouldn't even think of.

"Lord Somerton is here to see you, Your Grace."

Will shook his head and looked up at the footman. "Who?"

"Viscount Somerton, Your Grace."

Will frowned, thinking back to his short years in England. "Do I know him?" he muttered.

"I could not say, Your Grace."

He shrugged. "Show him in."

The footman nodded and then left. The loud sound of footsteps followed. A tall man with short light brown hair stood in the threshold.

"Will Atherton, as I live and breathe. You truly don't look any different."

Will stood and stared at the stranger. "Do I know you?"

The man rolled his head to the side. "Somerton. When you were six, you came to my father's home in Suffolk for a few weeks in the summer."

He did? Why did he have no memory of that summer? "Well then, welcome to my home, Somerton."

Somerton handed him a bottle of fine whisky.

"How did you know I drink whisky?"

"Just a feeling." Somerton sank into the deep leather chair by the fireplace. "How are you settling in?"

"Very well," he lied.

Somerton tilted his head with a slight smirk. Staring at the papers on Will's desk, he inquired, "Indeed?"

Will sat back down in his chair and blew out a breath. "No. I don't have a clue what to do with most of this stuff. The only thing I've figured out, thanks to Elizabeth, is that I'm not allowed to sell off most of my inheritance."

"Ah, yes. The joy of entitlement."

"You know something of this?" Will asked quietly.

"Of course, I do. But why do you want to sell off anything? The late duke was rumored to be as wealthy as—"

"He was, and apparently left the estates in perfect condition." Will stared at the bottle of whisky and wondered if two in the afternoon was too early an hour to open it.

"Then why . . . ?" Somerton halted as if he realized the question he asked was terribly improper.

"I need to sell things off and return to America." Why the hell was he telling this complete stranger about his life?

Somerton leaned back and smiled. "I understand."

"You do?"

"Someone is awaiting your return, and you want to show her what a success you are over here."

"Something like that."

Somerton rose and grabbed the bottle of whisky. "I believe this conversation needs a little nourishment."

He waited while Somerton poured two rather large glasses of whisky. Will reached out, took the glass from Somerton, and raised it to his lips. Before he could sip, Somerton stopped him.

"A toast," Somerton said with a genuine smile. "To friendships rekindled."

Will saluted him with his glass and took a long sip of the smoky liquid. "Damn, that is some fine whisky."

"Nothing but the best." Somerton returned to his seat. "Now, tell me more about this need to go to America."

Before he knew it, Will had explained everything from Abigail, to his sister, to Elizabeth. Although he did leave out a few details, especially with regards to Elizabeth.

"So Elizabeth has decided to stay and help you get your sisters ready for Society?" Somerton asked.

"Yes."

He smiled. "Excellent. Now how can I assist you with this?" He pointed toward the stack of papers on the desk.

"I need the advice of a good solicitor."

"I happen to know of an excellent man." Somerton paused for a moment as if struggling with his words. "But you will need more than that."

"Oh?" What else did he need? A solicitor would be able to help him sort through this mess and possibly find him a buyer for some of the land not entailed.

"Let me just say you don't look like a duke. And you don't act like one, either."

"I'm not a duke." Lord, the man was sounding like Elizabeth now. That stopped him short. Had Elizabeth asked Somerton to come here?

"Well, while you are in England, you are the Duke of Kendal. People will expect you to act a certain way."

"And if I don't?" he asked casually. Personally, he

didn't care if Society accepted him or not. He wouldn't be here long enough for it to matter.

"You said you wanted to sell off some of your estates and land."

"Yes," Will said impatiently.

"Then you must look and act the part. You will need to make acquaintances with these people, even if it's only a superficial friendship. The men you meet will be the ones most interested in what you are selling. You will need to join White's for this purpose."

At least Will didn't need to look like a complete incompetent—he did know about the gentlemen's club. Of course, he had no reason to tell Somerton that his own father was rejected because he wasn't deemed the right sort of man.

"And how do you suggest I go about making these changes?" Will asked as his eyebrows drew into a frown.

"I would suggest you speak with Elizabeth. She can help you hire a valet, and teach you some of the more proper protocols of Society."

Will tightened his muscles. The little minx was the reason Somerton was here. She must have decided to get some reinforcements to help keep her in this house. He gulped down the rest of his whisky and decided it was time for this conversation to end.

"Lord Somerton!"

Will turned at the sound of Elizabeth's voice. If he hadn't known better, he would have thought she looked shocked to see the viscount.

"Lady Elizabeth, it is a pleasure to see you again." Somerton rose and crossed the room to bow over her hand. "It's been months."

She smiled tightly. "Since Jennette's wedding, I believe." Somerton nodded. "November, then."

Will shook his head. Was he really supposed to believe this scene?

"Why are you here, my lord?" she asked softly.

"Renewing an old acquaintance," he replied.

"You know His Grace?"

"Only slightly. We met as children."

"How did you know he was here?"

Will watched the two interact and briefly wondered why Elizabeth seemed to be interrogating Somerton.

"Lady Elizabeth," Somerton said with a smug grin, "everyone knows he is here. Most have just been more polite than I and are giving him a few days to settle in. We both know in a few days, the invitations and calls shall be nonstop."

"Yes, I know."

"Then I should let you go, I can only imagine the work you have in front of you." After a nod to Elizabeth and a quick glance back to Will, Somerton left.

"Do you have any idea what kind of man you just let in this house?"

Chapter 6

Elizabeth fumed as she waited for his reply. The man had no sense of who in Society could help him—and who could damage his reputation beyond repair. Somerton definitely fell into the latter category.

"I take it you don't approve of Somerton?" William asked as he casually leaned back in his chair.

"The man is dreadful."

"Why? He didn't seem that terrible to me."

Elizabeth crossed her arms over her chest and breathed in deeply. She had to remember William knew nothing about Society. "Somerton runs with a bad crowd. There are rumors that he has killed several people—"

"Did they deserve to be killed?"

"What?" she asked incredulously.

"There are some people who are killed because they deserve to die. They have killed innocent people or done other heinous things." William reached for his glass of amber liquid and drank it down. He raised one eyebrow at her in question.

"I do not know the circumstances of the killings."

His lips drew upward into a smile. "Then you shouldn't be spreading rumors."

Elizabeth stomped her foot, then turned and walked away before she said something she regretted. As long as she could remain in the house, she would find time to search the remaining rooms. She strode back into the salon where Victoria sat waiting for her.

"Well? What did he think?" she asked in an eager tone.

Damnation. The man flustered her to the point that she forgot to ask him about the governess and tutor. "I forgot to ask him. We were discussing someone else."

Victoria shook her head with a small smile. "Who?"

Elizabeth rolled her eyes. "Viscount Somerton."

"I do not believe I have ever met him," she said with a shrug.

"It's just as well. He's not a man you would wish to know." Elizabeth rose from her chair, and said, "Let me try this again."

She walked back to his study wondering what to say to him. Peering around the corner, she saw him studying some papers on his desk. She gathered her courage and entered the room again.

He glanced up and smiled at her. "Did you finally remember what you wanted?"

She attempted to ignore the strange sensations his words caused. Or was it his smile? She shook her head slightly. "Might my friend Victoria and I have a word with you in the salon?"

"What is this about, Elizabeth?" His voice sounded deeper, with a hint of anger.

"Victoria had several wonderful ideas regarding the children, and I thought we should discuss them."

"Very well." He stood and she found herself looking

up to him. The man was far too tall. And far too handsome.

And almost engaged.

Although, Elizabeth had her doubts about the woman William said he wanted to marry. If Elizabeth loved someone like him, nothing would stop her from being with him. Nothing.

"Shall we?" he asked with a questioning look.

"Of course."

They walked down the long corridor together. Why did she have to be attracted to him? There were so many other eligible men. Well, he wasn't a possibility so she would stop thinking about this desire she felt.

He stopped as they reached the salon and glanced down at her. His dark eyes crinkled with humor as if she'd said something funny. Could he know? Did he realize the turmoil she was going through?

"I'm ready to face the lioness."

"None of my friends are really that dreadful. Maybe if it was the entire Spinster Club, I would tell you to be afraid," she said with a laugh.

"You have a club? Of spinsters?"

"No. It was a name one of my friend's husband called us before he married Avis," she tried to explain.

"So you're not all spinsters?" he asked.

"Not any longer. Both Avis and Jennette were married last year."

He tilted his head as if he were about to question her further but stopped.

"Let me introduce you to Victoria," Elizabeth said. They walked into the room and Elizabeth noticed Victoria's mouth gape. Seeing Victoria's reaction to the handsome man made Elizabeth realize the effect he would have on all the unmarried ladies of the *ton.* "William, this is one of my dearest friends, Miss Victoria Seaton."

Victoria stood quickly and bowed before him. "Your Grace."

William looked over at Elizabeth. "Does she have to call me that?"

"Yes. As will every one of your acquaintances. Now you take her hand and bow over it."

"Of course." He took Victoria's hand and kissed it softly. "It is a pleasure to meet a friend of Elizabeth's." He turned back to Elizabeth and said, "I did know what to do. I was just surprised by the 'Your Grace' again."

"You must become accustomed to it."

Elizabeth sat in her seat again and knew she'd better start talking because Victoria looked terribly nervous. "Victoria and I were discussing the children's education, Your Grace."

He narrowed his eyes at her. "And?"

"Since you don't believe you will be here for an extended period, she suggested we bring in a tutor for the boys and a governess for Sarah. I will work with Ellie and Lucy to get them ready to make their bow. And you, of course."

"Me?" William asked softly.

Victoria shifted in her seat as if ready to leave at any moment. Rarely exposed to the upper crust of Society, Elizabeth knew that speaking with the duke must make her friend feel uncomfortable.

"Your Grace, if I may?" Victoria paused, waiting for confirmation.

"Yes?"

"You and your sisters must be ready to face *them,*" Victoria whispered.

"Face who?"

Victoria looked beseechingly at Elizabeth.

"The *ton*, Your Grace," Elizabeth responded for her friend.

"Ah, Society. The English way of keeping people in their place," he sneered.

"Hardly," Elizabeth retorted. "Society is what makes us . . ." She stopped, realizing what she'd almost said was exactly what he had referenced. "Society is the social fabric of England. Our friends are in Society, our future husbands and wives must be in the same social tier."

"Or what?" he asked softly. "Does the world end if someone takes a wife beneath him?"

Before Elizabeth could reply, Kenneth appeared at the threshold with a frown on his face.

"Your Grace, Baron Humphrey and his wife are here to see you."

He glanced at Elizabeth and said, "Should I know them?"

Elizabeth felt the color from her face drain. "They are your cousins."

"I see. A courtesy call to welcome me."

Elizabeth couldn't keep her head from shaking. How could she have forgotten to warn him about Caroline and Richard? Thinking upon it, she wondered why it took them two days to get here. A little smile formed as she thought about their reaction to the news. They must be so put out by this development.

"Oh?" he asked.

"I must warn you that they were attempting to take over the estates before you came."

"Then I believe you should greet them with me." He rose from his seat and walked over to Victoria. After bowing over her hand, he added, "You are welcome in my home anytime, Miss Seaton."

"Thank you, Your Grace." Victoria paused and glanced over at Elizabeth.

"The children's tutor?" Elizabeth asked.

He looked at Elizabeth and said, "We will discuss that later."

Elizabeth nodded. Now she had to prepare for more manipulation, or rather, flirtation, to get what she wanted. She hated the idea that she was using her wiles in such a dreadful manner. But she had no other choice.

William waited for Miss Seaton to leave before questioning Elizabeth. "Is there anything else I should know about the baron?"

She looked away from him. "He feels he should have been named heir."

"Very well, then." He asked Kenneth to show the baron into the salon. After watching Elizabeth's ashen face, he realized there was something she wasn't telling him. And he was determined to find out what she was hiding.

An older man with graying hair walked into the room, followed by his very pregnant wife. They both stopped and stared at him before remembering their manners. The baroness curtsied deeply and murmured, "Your Grace."

The baron did the same, and then greeted Elizabeth.

Elizabeth only nodded at them both.

Will almost smiled as the tension in the room became palpable. "Cousin Richard, welcome to *my* home," he said deliberately to gauge their reaction.

Richard's face tightened visibly while Caroline's face paled in the afternoon light.

"Thank you, Your Grace," Richard said. "We wished to call and inquire on your trip. It was a safe and swift journey, I pray?"

"The trip went quite well. Though long. I had hoped to get here before Christmas but issues arose that required my attention."

"Of course," Richard replied as a slight blush reddened his face.

"So you intend to stay, then?" Caroline asked boldly.

That was their game. They only wanted to know if they should continue their attempts to take control of the estates. The last thing Will needed was someone waiting for him to leave to cause problems.

"I am the duke," he finally answered.

"Of course," she replied. "I only thought since you have lived in the colonies, I—we thought you might wish to continue living there."

Will leaned back casually. "True, but being a duke is quite an important position. Elizabeth has impressed upon me that fact very succinctly."

"I'm quite certain she did," Caroline mumbled, staring at Elizabeth. "Is she staying with you?"

"She is."

Caroline smirked at Elizabeth. "That is highly improper, Elizabeth."

"Oh?" Elizabeth replied. "We are chaperoned by his two adult sisters and, of course, the boys and Sarah."

Caroline frowned and pursed her lips. "Just exactly how many siblings does he have?"

"Eight, but Alicia is married and stayed in Canada. Did I get that right, William?"

"William, is it?" Caroline whispered to Elizabeth.

Will watched the interaction carefully. Caroline looked as if she wanted to throw something, preferably at him. Elizabeth appeared pale and unnerved by the conversation.

"I believe we must take our leave now," Richard said. "If you should need any assistance settling in, please let me know, Your Grace."

"I will at that," Will replied, stifling a smile. Richard was the last person he would go to for help. The undercurrent of tension in the room left a nasty taste in his mouth.

After the couple left, Will glanced over at Elizabeth, who looked relieved. "Are you well?"

"Yes. Richard and Caroline have been a thorn in my side for the past ten months. I should have warned you about them but it slipped my mind with all the upheaval in the house." She stared at the carpet for a minute. "I don't trust them, William."

"I don't, either. But there is nothing they can do."

"No, there is nothing they can do as long as you stay here," she commented. The dear woman was completely transparent.

"And yet, you know I have no plans to stay."

She took a step closer and smiled at him. He steeled himself against the aromatic scent of roses and spices that floated around her.

"Have you thought about the children?" she whispered.

The sound of her voice caressed his skin. He shook his head quickly to clear his mind. "The children?"

"Yes." She moved a step even closer. Her hand reached out to his hair. "They need a tutor, and Sarah a governess."

Dear God, she was mesmerizing him. And the worst part was, he was certain she knew the affect she had on him. "I don't think they really need a tutor for the few months we will be here."

Her green eyes clouded. Slowly, her full lips tipped upwards into a seductive smile, and all he could think about was tasting her.

He moved his head closer . . . closer, until he was a breath away. Would her lips taste as sweet as he anticipated? Her mouth parted slightly as if readying herself for his kiss. He stared into her emerald eyes. He suddenly wanted so much more than a kiss. He inclined his head to kiss her.

A loud crash from upstairs broke them apart. They stared at each other as if unable to fathom what had almost happened. The sound of shouting sent him toward the stairs. He stopped at the banister and looked back at her.

"Hire the damned tutor and governess. Obviously, I can't control them."

And once again, she managed to get her way. While he should feel angry with her attempts to flirt with him, he didn't. He understood her reasons far too clearly. Survival. Nothing more. Unfortunately for him, his body only wanted her closer.

He raced up the steps before one of his brothers killed the other.

She was a wicked woman. To use her wiles to get what she wanted had to be the worst thing she'd ever done. She had almost let him kiss her. The idea only stirred more sinful thoughts in her. Still, a little smile of satisfaction tugged at her lips.

Slowly, she walked up the stairs to his sisters' room.

After opening the door, she sat on the bed next to Sarah. "Did you get fitted yet?" Elizabeth asked.

"Yes! It was so much fun. Madame Beaulieu said she would make me dresses. Lots of dresses. I asked her if she would make one for my doll, but she said no." Sarah's legs kicked the side of the bed.

"I shall help you make a dress for your doll," Elizabeth replied.

Sarah smiled and leaned on Elizabeth. "Thank you, Lady Elizabeth."

The warmth of the little girl's appreciation went straight to Elizabeth's heart. She looked over at Ellie, who appeared overwhelmed with the choices she had to make. "I think I need to help your sister," Elizabeth said to Sarah.

"I don't know which fabrics to choose," Ellie whimpered.

"The white silk and pale blue muslin to start," Elizabeth said as she reached the table where Madame Beaulieu had laid out the fabrics. "The light fabrics will look wonderful on you."

Ellie clasped Elizabeth's hand. "Thank you. I could never pick all this fabric without your help."

Elizabeth smiled. "We will have you all set with clothing in no time." She turned to the dressmaker and added, "The white silk is for her bow. It must befit the sister of a duke."

"Yes, my lady," Madame Beaulieu replied. "I believe sapphires would be just the thing to set off the blue in her eyes."

"Sapphires?" Ellie murmured.

"That is a perfect choice, Madame. Nothing too ostentatious. I believe my mother had a beautiful sapphire pendant and earring set that should go perfectly with the gown."

Elizabeth prayed William wouldn't be too upset over the costs, but a court gown had to be the most beautiful gown a young woman would wear for some time. And it must conform to the queen's demands of what it should look like, no simple task.

Once they had all the fabrics chosen for Ellie, Lucy stood with a frown as Lady Beaulieu took her measurements. Madame Beaulieu and Elizabeth conferred for a few minutes on just the right fabrics for Lucy. With her darker coloring, the pastels that suited Ellie would look washed out on her.

"We cannot go too dark while she's so young," Madame Beaulieu said.

"I agree, but the pastels just aren't right on her." Elizabeth stared and wondered what Jennette did at this age and then remembered. "Ivory for her bow and light jewel tones for the rest."

"Are you certain?" the dressmaker asked.

"Yes. Lady Jennette did the same at Lucy's age."

Madame Beaulieu nodded. "I remember! I will do some of the same colors."

"Who is Lady Jennette?" Lucy asked impatiently.

"A dear friend of mine," Elizabeth replied. "And you can meet her soon. Once we are done with the fittings, we will have a few lessons on comportment. And I must hire a dancing instructor."

Lucy and Ellie looked at each other, then shrugged. "Comportment?"

"Manners," Elizabeth replied with a sigh. This might just be more difficult than she imagined.

Lucy snickered. "She sounds like Abigail with her fine manners and stiff posture."

"Abigail who?" Elizabeth asked, hoping this was the same Abigail who William regarded with affection.

Ellie shook her head. "Abigail Mason. Will actually thinks he's in love with her."

"And you don't?" Elizabeth prompted.

"No," Ellie and Lucy answered at the same time.

Elizabeth waited for the dressmaker to leave before she asked more questions. "So why don't you think your brother is in love with this Abigail Mason?"

Lucy flopped on the bed. "She is a horrible person. He can't possibly be in love with her. All she cares about is position and money."

"He has all that now. So why didn't she marry him before he came over to England?"

"Neither of us could figure that out, either," Ellie said. "I never understood what he saw in her. She seemed very . . . well, selfish. Maybe she's changed over the past five years, but I doubt a person can change that much."

Elizabeth frowned. None of this made any sense. "Do you think Will really loves her?"

Lucy laughed. "My brother is a fool when it comes to women. He thinks because she comes from a good American family that she must be the epitome of a wife."

"So it's her name and connections," Elizabeth whispered.

"Yes," Ellie said, nodding her head.

A name was more important to him than true love. A name.

Something she didn't even have.

Chapter 7

Richard followed his wife into their home on Cavendish Street. Caroline stormed into the hallway and threw her reticule on the floor. The ride from the duke's house had only served to increase her anger.

"There has to be something we can do!" she shouted.

Richard picked up the small purse and handed it to a maid. He followed his irate wife into the small salon. "I'm afraid there is nothing we can do."

"You saw the way he was looking at Elizabeth. And she called him by his Christian name! He probably has plans to marry her and have a passel of children like his father."

Richard took a seat and leaned his head back. Why did he think a younger woman would be a good thing? She was driving him mad, and further into debt.

"Caroline, he is the duke. As long as he is alive, I shall only be a baron. You must accept that."

"My—our children deserve better than that. Of course, you are now the heir presumptive. If something should happen to befall the new duke before he has children . . ."

Richard tilted his head back up and stared at his wife. "Do not even think it, Caroline."

His wife cackled. "I most certainly was not thinking of murdering him."

"Then what exactly are you thinking of?"

She crossed her arms over her extended belly. "As long as he does not have children, you or one of our children will become the next duke."

The woman had lost her mind. "And how do you presume to keep him from procreating? He is only eight and twenty. Hardly an old man."

"He must not ever marry," she answered simply.

"I'm afraid he doesn't need our permission, my dear. And there did seem to be something between the duke and Elizabeth."

"Agreed. So it is up to us to keep them apart."

Richard shook his head, exhausted from this conversation already. "And how do you propose we do that?"

"Rumors can be deadly to any relationship, dear husband. Especially amongst the *ton*."

"And what happens when he finds another woman?"

Caroline laughed. "I shall figure something out. If we keep his reputation in tatters, it might not matter."

Richard only shook his head. He knew better, and she should, too. Reputation be damned, when a lady can be a duchess, she will marry the devil.

Over the next few days, Elizabeth hired a tutor and governess. She brought in a valet for Will, made sure the boys had new clothing, and attempted to teach the boys their manners at the dinner table. For the most part, they had done quite well. Her only issue was the *boy* in front of her.

"Try it again," Elizabeth implored him.

William clenched his fists so tight she thought he might explode. For the past hour, she'd been attempting to teach him the complex rules of Society, starting with social rank. While she presumed he was an intelligent man, he could be as stubborn as a mule when he wished it.

"A duke is higher than all others in the social rank, except the king or queen," he repeated.

"And what about the prince regent?"

"Of course, how could I have forgotten about the man who has to pretend to be king because his father is insane."

He paced the confines of his study. With him striding closer to her and then retreating, her heart pounded erratically in her chest.

"But how does his rank compare to yours?"

He glared over at her until she felt forced to stare at the large Debrett's *The New Peerage* book on her lap.

"The prince is a higher rank but other princes are not."

She smiled at him. "That is correct. Princes can be raised to the rank of duke. Now, please list the ranks under yours."

William narrowed his eyes at her but quickly listed the titles. "This is the most trivial thing I have ever been taught," he said once he finished reciting the list.

"You cannot leave this house and interact with your peers until you understand and accept your position in Society."

"And why not?"

She pressed her lips together and closed her eyes, trying to gain a measure of patience. "You will be a laughingstock, if you do."

He sat in the chair directly across from her. "And if I am?"

"Then none of the gentlemen of your rank will have anything to do with you. They will refuse to speak with you regarding the sale of the estates. And you bring that disrespect upon your sisters . . . and me," she said softly.

He released a frustrated sigh.

She stared at him for a long moment. For the first time, she believed William realized exactly what was at stake if he didn't heed her lessons.

"When do you think I will be ready to face the world?"

"I would say another week or two." Perhaps by then she would be so immune to him that she would not feel this strange pull of attraction.

Will shook his head. "No, too long. Is there something we could do together with Ellie and Lucy before they take their bow? We're all going mad in this house."

"The opera would be an acceptable outing," she replied in a hesitant tone. "But I'm not certain you and the girls will be ready."

"We will all be ready," he said in a confident tone. "I shall make the arrangements."

"Now, back to our lessons." He leaned back and questioned her about the condition of the king.

She answered him quickly but continued to stare at his face. The valet she had hired for him had trimmed his hair, but it was still unfashionably long. Perhaps she should ask William about it. After all, if Mr. Stevenson wasn't doing his job properly then it was her duty to remove him.

A part of her hoped it was William's idea to keep his hair longer. It rather suited him. He would never be a conventional duke. The sun chose that moment to peek out from a cloud and brighten his hair such that strands of red could be seen.

As the late afternoon sun hit his face, she noticed the faint shadows of a beard. She wondered what it would feel like to touch his jaw. Or kiss his jaw. Was the hair bristly or soft? She had such a yearning to find out.

"Elizabeth?"

Elizabeth blinked and saw the confusion on his face. "Yes?"

A deep laugh escaped him. "What were you day-dreaming about?"

"Nothing important." Well, she wasn't about to tell him! She had a problem. Some people drank too much or used opium. Not her—she was obsessed with a man she barely knew.

"Are you certain?"

"Yes! Now where were we with our lessons?"

"I believe you were telling me about Princess Charlotte," he replied with a slight grin.

"Yes, Princess Charlotte," she said with a nod. "She is enceinte, and a late fall delivery is expected. Hopefully all will go well with this one . . ."

She continued to regale him with stories of the princess, but her mind wandered again. This time, she realized her major mistake of only moments ago. He'd wanted to know of things to do with the children and she'd only come up with the opera. There were still five rooms to recheck, and with all of them roaming the house at all hours of the day, she'd had no time to search those areas again.

"I believe we should be done for the day," she finally said, placing the book on the table.

William looked up at the clock and frowned. "It is only two in the afternoon."

"And a perfect time and day to take the children to Hyde Park for a ride. They must be dreadfully tired of staying in the house all day."

He tilted his head and nodded slightly. "I believe you are right about that. I thought those boys were about to kill each other yesterday."

"Perfect, then. I will tell them all to get ready." She stood ready to take her leave.

"You will be joining us, then?"

Elizabeth opened her mouth to speak and nothing came out. She needed a very good excuse. "I must decline. I need to call on a friend who is with child and cannot get out much."

"Of course."

Before he could say another word, she left the room. After telling the children to make themselves ready, she went to her room and stared out the window. Once they had departed, she would return to the boys' room and examine it again. Hopefully, she would find the diary and be done with this mess.

Of course, finding the journal might just lead to even more troubles. While she wanted and needed to discover the truth of her parentage, a part of her dreaded it. She would finally learn all about who she really was, and which man among the *ton* had had an affair with her mother.

Elizabeth hoped her mother's reasons for the affair would be justified in the diary. Many women had liaisons and dalliances, but perhaps her mother had fallen in love with the man. Elizabeth closed her eyes and shut out the pain. She wondered if her lustful thoughts about William had to do with her mother's influence. Was she just like her mother? Until she discovered the diary, Elizabeth would never know.

She glanced down and watched as the children and William crowded into two carriages. As the coaches drove down the street, she raced to the boys' room. She would check for any panels in the walls or by the fireplace, and if she had time, she would check for secret compartments in all the bureaus.

She would find that diary, and discover who she was.

Will breathed in deeply and tried to remember his stepmother's words about patience being the friend of wisdom, or something to that effect. "Boys, stay still or we will return to the house immediately," he barked.

So much for wisdom today, he thought.

Michael and Ethan gave each other one more slap to the thigh.

"Boys!"

Ethan's blue eyes widened in trepidation. "I'm sorry, Will. Michael keeps pestering me today."

"And what do you have to say for yourself, Michael?" Will asked, using his best father voice.

"I hate it here, Will. I want to go back home. I want to . . ."

"To what?"

Michael looked down at his legs. "I want to do chores, again. I want to go fishing and hunting with you."

James shook his head. "I love it here. No chores, only learning."

Will sighed. He should have realized it was boredom making the boys act out. While James, Lucy, and Ellie loved not having to do their chores, the work helped to tire the younger boys. He would have to find something for them to do that would keep them active.

"Look at the swans!"

Will glanced over at the other carriage where Sarah sat, pointing to the body of water with ducks and swans. He could feel her excitement even from this distance. A few riders passed them and nodded. He doubted any of them knew to whom they nodded and waved, but he reciprocated the gestures. He just had to play their games for a few months, and then he could return home.

And if he was lucky, Abigail would be waiting for him. *Abigail.*

He hadn't thought of her in days. Could he be forgetting about her? The thought was like a cold bucket of water over his head. Wasn't the heart supposed to grow fonder with distance?

His heart wasn't, and that terrified him.

She was supposed to be his wife. Forever. And yet the more time he spent away from her, the more he thought about her faults, and not all her good points.

"Will?"

Will looked over at Ellie and said, "Yes?"

"It's getting rather dark. I think we should return before it decides to rain on us."

He tilted back his head and realized his sister was correct. After ordering the carriage home, his thoughts returned to Abigail. Distance had to be the problem. Once he arrived in Virginia, he would call on her and court her until she agreed to marry him.

In fact, when he returned to the house, he would write her a long letter. While communicating would still be difficult with the distance, at least this would keep him in her heart.

Just as they arrived home, fat raindrops fell on their heads. The boys shouted and Sarah laughed, while Lucy and Ellie shrieked. They all raced to the door as the butler opened it for them.

A door slammed upstairs and Elizabeth raced to the stairway. "You are home already?"

Will chuckled as he glanced up to see Elizabeth's red tresses falling out of her stylish chignon. Even from here, he could see she could not have called upon her friend. "What happened to you?"

"What do you mean?"

"I thought you were going to call on a friend while we were at the park?"

"I . . . I . . . I tried but she wasn't at home."

Strange, he could have sworn she'd said her friend could not get out since she was with child. "When you have a moment, I would like to speak with you in my study."

She looked down at her clothing and gasped. "I really must change before dinner."

"Very well. But I would like to talk before dinner."

"I will be down presently," she answered, and then walked toward her room.

He turned to go to his study when his butler stopped him.

"Your Grace, I placed the post on your desk. There is quite an amount today. I believe word of your arrival has found its way through the *ton*."

"Thank you, Jeffers." At least reading the mail would give him something to do while he waited for Elizabeth.

He walked into the study and his mouth gaped. His previously empty desk was now littered with letters and invitations. Never in his twenty-eight years had he seen so much nonsense. He opened the first invitation and shrugged. The note was from the dowager Countess of Cantwell. He could only assume such a ball would be an important occasion, but he really didn't know if they would be ready to attend.

After dropping it into the "read" pile, he moved on to the next one. Another ball, this one held by the Earl of Hereshire and his wife. He tossed it into the same pile as the previous invitation. The next one contained vouchers for a place called Almack's.

Elizabeth walked into the room, then looked at the vouchers and laughed. "Well, that didn't take Lady Jersey long."

"Excuse me?"

"Almack's. You and your sisters need vouchers to attend on Wednesdays."

"So, it's like a club?" he asked, confused.

"Well, the ladies would never say such a thing, but truly, it's not that different. The patronesses decide who is acceptable based on social position and titles. However, even a duke can have his vouchers lost if one of the ladies deems you inappropriate."

Will just rolled his eyes. "Yet another example of why this country is crumbling."

She placed her hands on her hips and scowled at him. "There is nothing wrong with this country. I believe we proved ourselves quite nicely at Waterloo."

"Elizabeth, sit down," he said, pointing to the seat across the desk from him. "I didn't call you down here to argue about your country."

"Our country," she corrected.

Will barely restrained a growl. He refused to tell her this would never be *his* country.

"So why did you call me into your study?" she asked as she finally took her seat.

"I've been thinking about the boys. I know the tutor will start on Friday with them, but they are not getting enough physical activity."

"You can take them riding every morning," she suggested.

"Yes, but they still need more. I was thinking we should go to one of the estates for a while. That would give them space to wear themselves out every day, and the girls and I would have a quiet space for our daily etiquette lessons."

Her face drew pale. "You want to go to the estate?"

"Yes, I do believe it is a sound decision. Don't you agree?"

"Actually, I think it is far better to stay in town. I mean, here you can slowly immerse yourself into Society without attending every function. At the estate you would be sequestered, except for the local squires who would, no doubt, pester you tirelessly to come to their soirees and musicals, put on solely for your benefit."

How did she get that all out in what sounded like one sentence? Her eyes darted from him to the papers on his desk as if she were suddenly nervous around him.

"Elizabeth, what is the real reason you don't wish to go to the estate?"

She opened her mouth and then shut it quickly. She pressed her lips together and then shook her head slightly. "I have two dear friends who are both with child, and I don't wish to leave them when they might need me."

Again, it sounded like a feigned excuse. She obviously wasn't about to tell him the truth. "Very well, if you think of some activities the boys can do to get them out of this house to expel some energy, we will stay here."

"I will make certain they have plenty of outside activities." She leaned back into the chair looking very relieved.

"Would you like to help me with this?" he said, pointing to the piles on his desk. "I have no idea who any of these people are but they all seem to want me to attend a function of theirs."

She smiled softly, making his heart beat a little faster. Her full rosy lips seemed to beckon to him. He couldn't think of her in such manner. Abigail was the woman he wanted. Not Elizabeth.

And yet, Elizabeth was here and Abigail refused to consider coming with him. Elizabeth was the woman helping him sort through this mess. Even though doing so might make her lose her home.

"I would be happy to help you sort through the invitations. I should have mentioned that most men of your position do hire a secretary to assist them with all this." She grabbed a pile of invitations and quickly collated them into three piles.

"I will not be here long enough for a personal secretary," he said.

"Right," she said with a nod. "This stack is the definite refusals." She handed him the first mound of papers. "This is your personal mail."

Finally, she pointed to the third stack. "These are the invitations that we will need to determine if you wish to attend. Some are balls, a few musicales, and dinners."

Will looked at the third pile and sighed. There still had to be at least fifteen invitations to sort through. He quickly scanned his personal mail and paused at the familiar handwriting.

"All right, we'll start in a minute. I'd like to read this letter first."

A wave of guilt passed over him for his passionate thoughts about Elizabeth. It would never happen again. After breaking the seal, he skimmed the note and then slowly read it again.

"William, is everything all right at home?" Elizabeth asked.

Had she noticed the pained expression he knew was on his face? "It's a note from Abigail."

He crumpled the letter, stood, and then hurled it into the fireplace. After walking toward the window, he stared out at the courtyard but saw nothing. "Her father is pushing her to marry Josiah Harwood. She doesn't agree but cannot disobey her father."

"Why not?" Elizabeth whispered. She stood behind him even though he'd never heard her move.

"She could never defy him. He wants her to marry a wealthy, patriotic American." He felt her hand on his arm and shook off the flash of desire that raced up his forearm. "She believes it might be best if I stay in England."

"I don't understand, William. You are all those things her father wants in a husband for his daughter."

Pain scorched his head and heart. "No, I am not." He turned and stared at her. "I'm a bloody Englishman. A goddamned duke."

Her face crumpled almost as tightly as the letter from Abigail. "But once you sell everything and return, you shall be all that her father wants."

"You do not understand," he muttered. He closed his eyes as her soft hand cupped his face.

"Try making me understand," she whispered. "I only want to help you."

"I will never be good enough for them. To them I'm nothing but a poor farmer. And not even an American one at that. Nothing I do will ever convince her father that I am an American. Not even giving up this damned inheritance."

He opened his eyes and saw tears in her green eyes. This wonderful, sensitive woman was crying over his pain. And that wasn't right. He couldn't move his gaze away from her eyes, her lips, that pert little nose that he wanted to kiss.

And why couldn't he? Abigail didn't want him any longer, if she ever had wanted him. Right in front of him stood a beautiful woman who openly flirted with him, teased him, and seemed to desire him.

Slowly he lowered his head toward hers. He paused barely an inch away from her lips. If she moved, he would let her go. But she did not.

He curved his hand around her neck, bringing her closer, until their lips met. Shock and desire soared throughout his body as they kissed. All he'd wanted was a little comfort from her. Something to make him forget his pain. And now, all he wanted was to lay her down on the sofa and make love to her all afternoon. He wanted to leisurely explore her body and kiss every freckle, wherever they might be.

He let his tongue glide across her lips, hoping she would open for him. And she did. But he never expected the all-encompassing passion as her tongue touched his, met him, and caressed him. He moved his hands to cup her face.

She tasted sweeter than he ever imagined. A combination of honey and cinnamon, and it drove him mad. He trailed his hands down her back, pressing her closer to him, to his rising erection. Damn, how he wanted her.

She moaned softly as his lips moved to her nose and then back to her beautiful lips. He could stay here all night, kissing her, making love to her.

Slowly he realized she was drawing away from him. Cool air swept between them. She stared up at him with wonder and confusion in her eyes.

"I'm sorry," he whispered.

Chapter 8

Elizabeth blinked several times as the reality of what they had done dawned on her. He kissed her. And she'd kissed him back.

Passionately!

She had only been kissed like that one other time. Only it hadn't felt like William's kiss. His kiss made her feel as if she were drowning in desire. The intensity of his lips against hers all but burned her into a cinder. No man had ever done this to her.

Never in twenty-six years.

And instead of chastising him for his affront, she stood there staring at him, hoping he would kiss her again. Slowly the reality of their moment together made sense. He hadn't kissed her because she was a sensual woman. She just wasn't Abigail.

Any woman would have done for him.

"Elizabeth, I do apologize."

"I need some air," she muttered, racing toward the door. She didn't need air but she desperately needed her friends.

"Elizabeth!"

Before he could say any more or come after her, she walked out the front door. Luckily, the rain had stopped as quickly as it had started. But now what? Jennette's home was the closest, but she couldn't walk there without a maid. With a sigh, she reentered the house and called for Susan to accompany her.

She couldn't get her mind off what had happened between her and William. His lips touching hers was the most incredible thing she'd ever imagined. For the first time in her life, she understood why Avis had gone off with her husband, Banning, before they were married. And why Jennette was always telling Elizabeth that when she found the right man, marriage wouldn't matter.

But it did matter, didn't it?

Her mother had impressed upon her the importance of a good marriage. Then again, her mother had had an affair and Elizabeth was the result. Perhaps it had been guilt plaguing her mother, not some sense of moral righteousness.

Finally, she and Susan reached the door to Jennette's home with her husband, the Earl of Blackburn. Elizabeth knocked on the door, not surprised that their butler hadn't seen her coming. Jennette was still in the process of setting Blackburn's house and staff to rights.

"Lady Elizabeth, come inside before the rain starts again," Mr. Woods said as he opened the door.

"Thank you, Woods. Is Lady Blackburn at home?"

"Please wait in the small salon and I will check."

Elizabeth walked into the salon and noticed the changes Jennette had made in the past six months. Almost everything in the room was new. Not that Jennette was a spendthrift, but Blackburn's home had been in a dismal state of disrepair when she married him. Together, they were rebuilding their home and his fortune.

"Elizabeth, how wonderful to see you," Jennette said as she flowed into the room. Her extended belly looked even larger today.

Jennette sank into the rose-colored chair and sighed. "I am absolutely huge."

"No, you're not," Elizabeth said. She sat across from her friend and stared at her hands.

"What is wrong, Elizabeth?"

"Nothing." Now that she was here, the words wouldn't come out. "I had hoped maybe Avis and Sophie, or even Victoria, would be here."

Jennette smiled, then pulled herself out of her seat. "I will ring for tea."

Elizabeth watched as Jennette spoke in whispered tones to Woods, who nodded in reply.

"I shall be right back," Jennette said to her. "I need to let Matthew know that you need to talk."

"Am I disturbing you two?" Elizabeth stood.

"He will be relieved. I was reviewing what colors and fabrics we shall use in the nursery."

"Oh," Elizabeth said, and then returned to her seat.

She sat in the room as the clock ticked away the time. Woods brought in the tea on a silver tray, and still no Jennette. What in the world was keeping her? After close to ten minutes, a flushed Jennette raced back into the room.

"I'm so sorry it took me so long. Matthew had a few issues with some of the items I had chosen. He refused to let me leave until I heard all his complaints."

There was knocking at the front door, and then the sound of feminine voices in the hallway. "It sounds like you must have callers," Elizabeth said with more than a little disappointment.

"Of course we have," Jennette said with a smile. "Didn't you notice all the teacups?"

Elizabeth glanced over and saw the five teacups on the platter. She instantly knew who was joining them. Her lower lip trembled.

"Thank you," she whispered to Jennette as Avis, Sophie, and Victoria entered the room.

"You looked like you needed your friends," Jennette replied. "All of them."

Elizabeth could only nod as tears filled her eyes. "I'm so confused," she admitted.

"Tell us what's wrong," Sophie said with a gentle pat on Elizabeth's shoulder.

"My entire life turned completely upside down today." Elizabeth wiped away a tear.

"What happened?" Avis asked with a frown. "Did you find the diary?"

"No, I checked the boys' room today and there was nothing. No secret panels, no secret floorboards or cabinets. Nothing. I still have to recheck the study and the duke's bedroom."

"Then how did your life get turned around?" Victoria asked.

Elizabeth breathed in deeply to calm her frayed nerves. "He kissed me."

"Oh, my," Avis said.

"It's not just *that* he kissed me but *why* he kissed me," Elizabeth explained. "He didn't kiss me because he's attracted to me."

"Then why would he kiss you?" Sophie asked quietly.

"He was upset because the woman he wanted to marry had sent him a letter telling him she was marrying someone else." Elizabeth reached for her tea and gulped down the hot liquid.

Avis and Jennette looked at each other and shrugged. Sophie shook her head and Victoria said nothing.

"It makes no sense that he kissed you if he feels nothing toward you," Avis explained.

"And why is this bothering you so much?" Sophie pried.

Elizabeth should have known they wouldn't understand. "Because *I* felt something."

"Oh," was the collective response from the group.

"And?" Jennette asked.

"And?" Elizabeth fought to keep her voice from rising. "He kissed me and I felt something."

"Now, just to clarify," Avis started with a slight grin. "This thing you felt was good?"

Elizabeth shot her friend an evil look. "Yes, it was good." She sighed. "Too good."

"Well, that changes everything," Sophie said with a full smile as Avis and Jennette nodded their agreement.

"How does this change anything?" Elizabeth asked.

"Because now we know that you are both open to seduction, should it happen," Sophie replied.

Elizabeth pressed her fingers to her temples to keep her head from exploding. Her friends had lost their minds. How could they think William kissing her was good? Even if it felt better than anything she might have imagined.

"We are not both open to seduction, Sophie," Elizabeth commented. She was certainly not going to let him seduce her. Was she? Could she seduce him? The idea was too wicked to think about in front of her friends. "The last thing I want is a man who still believes he is in love with another woman."

Sophie walked over to her. "Is that really the reason, Elizabeth?"

"Of course!" Not that Sophie was likely to believe Elizabeth if her skills as a medium were as strong as Elizabeth had heard. She suddenly couldn't get the idea of seducing Will out of her head. Splaying her hands across his naked chest, feeling the warm muscles—oh, this fantasizing had to stop.

"Are you certain this has nothing to do with the diary and not knowing who your father was?" the inquisitive Sophie asked with a slight grin.

"Of course," Avis muttered. "That makes much more sense."

"Elizabeth would never want to get involved with a man until she knows her true background," Jennette said.

"That is why she never married, even though she had several offers," Victoria added.

Elizabeth walked away from Sophie and faced her friends. "Yes, you are all correct. I have no desire to look for a husband until I know who I am."

Sophie sat back down and shook her head. "It makes no difference who you are. To the world, you are the Duke of Kendal's daughter."

"It matters to me," Elizabeth sobbed. "You all know your fathers. Even you, Sophie. He might not want you to speak of him in public, but at least you know who he is. I don't."

Victoria stood and put her arms around Elizabeth. "I understand, Elizabeth. You won't feel complete until you know your background."

Elizabeth nodded on Victoria's shoulder. "I just want to understand who I am."

* * *

Will paced the confines of his study. He was an absolute idiot to kiss her. What was he thinking? And why wasn't he sitting in this room drowning his sorrows over Abigail in a bottle of whisky?

For years, he'd wanted to marry her. At first, he thought her to be too young, even though many ladies marry at sixteen. Perhaps he'd hoped she would see her father for the controlling bastard he was. Then he gave her time to convince her father that he was the right man for her. But over the past year, Will had begun to realize that she might not love him as much as she led him to believe.

Could that really be why her betrayal didn't hurt as much as he thought? Had he slowly been falling out of love with her? Strangely, he had never felt as free as he did at this moment. Kissing Elizabeth, while idiotic, also taught him that his desire for Abigail was finished.

He couldn't remember the last time he'd been with a woman. Between Abigail and his father's illness and subsequent death, a long time had passed since he'd enjoyed a woman's body. And Elizabeth's sensual body could satisfy any man. She had luscious curves and a slim waist. He could spend days getting to know her body.

Not that he would do such a thing.

She was a proper lady and no upstanding woman would let a man in her bed until the ring was on her finger. He really needed to stop thinking about her in such a base manner. But he couldn't get his mind off her. It was now two hours later and she still hadn't returned. She probably thought he was going to attack her. He would have to apologize to her again.

The front door opened and closed. Will raced out of the study and down the hall to make certain it was

Elizabeth. She spoke to the footman and started to walk up the steps, until she noticed him.

"Are you all right?" he asked softly.

"I am perfectly well, thank you," she replied stiffly.

"Can we talk in my study?"

She pressed her full lips together. "I am not sure that is a good idea."

"It will only take a moment." This time his voice brooked no denial.

Whether she walked toward him because she wanted to or because the duke commanded it, he didn't know. All that mattered was that she followed him into the study. He closed the door behind him.

"I think you should open the door, Your Grace."

Perhaps he did have his answer. The duke requested her presence and she knew her duty. Damn.

"I wanted to apologize," he said quietly. "What I did was inexcusable."

"You apologized earlier. Now if you will excuse me, I must get ready for dinner," she replied in a tight voice.

"One more thing, if you please," Will said firmly. "Tomorrow I plan to take the older children out for a drive. I would like you to attend with us."

"I have no need to see Hyde Park, Your Grace."

"I have no intention of going to Hyde Park, Elizabeth. We shall take a drive through some of the other sections of London. You will ride with us."

She tightened her jaw at his demand, but nodded. "As you wish." She stood to leave and then stopped as if to say more. Instead, she merely said, "Please excuse me now."

He let her go. At some point, she would have to get used to being in the same room with him again. They had too much to do, between getting Ellie and Lucy ready and helping him prepare for Society. He stared up at the portrait of the former duke and knew exactly how to get her alone again.

With a smile, he walked toward the salon to wait for everyone to assemble for dinner. He poured four glasses of sherry and handed one to Lucy and Ellie as they walked into the room.

"I really don't think I like this," Ellie complained as she took a sip. The pursed look on her face almost made him laugh.

"I like it," Lucy said before taking a rather large drink.

Looking around the room, Will was impressed with the progress Elizabeth had made with the children. They were all dressed for dinner, including the boys, and they had entered the room quietly.

Finally, Elizabeth walked into the room. He handed her a glass of sherry and smiled down at her. She wore a lavender gown with off-white lace that showed the beautiful swell of her lightly freckled breasts. He had such an urge to find and kiss every freckle on her body.

So much for getting himself under control.

"How did you enjoy your ride today?" She turned and asked the children.

"I saw two swans!" Sarah said as she bounced her bottom on the chair.

"You must have driven by the Serpentine," Elizabeth commented. "It is one of my favorite spots."

"Are there serpents in there?" Robert asked.

"No, just a lot of water fowl," Elizabeth replied with a laugh.

The footman announced dinner and the children walked toward the dining room. Will clasped Elizabeth's arm to stop her.

"William?"

He waited until the children left the room. "Thank you for what you have done with them. It's only been a little over a week, and yet, they are doing so much better."

She smiled and looked down where his hand touched her bare skin. "You are very welcome. The governess and tutor will make even more significant progress."

"I also hoped you would do me a favor."

"Oh?" She glanced back up at him, her green eyes shining with confusion.

"I think in order for me to learn more about my position here, I need to understand my background. My family history. Well, *our* family history. My father never really discussed how we were related to the late duke, or how my side of the family fit in."

She blinked and nodded slowly. "I think that is a lovely idea. I can teach you and the girls the family history after our daily etiquette lessons."

"I don't think the girls need this information just yet. But, I do. So after dinner we will start." He released her arm and held out his arm to escort her into the dining room.

"After dinner . . . tonight?"

"Yes. You noticed all the invitations. I need to start getting out into Society."

"I agree," she said in a hesitant tone.

"But . . . ?"

"I should have mentioned this before. As you know, the girls should not go to balls until they make their bow. Their first ball should be hosted by you . . . and held here."

Will stopped and looked down at her. "Here?"

Elizabeth nodded.

"Very well," he answered with a sigh. "Do what needs to be done."

Now that Abigail had deserted him, Will wasn't sure about his future. As much as he despised England, the country and his title could certainly benefit the children. But the idea of staying left a bitter taste in his mouth.

Perhaps returning to America was still the best option. There was nothing stopping him from heading out west into the territories. Yet, even as he had that thought, his gaze went back to Elizabeth.

Chapter 9

Elizabeth attempted to swallow another bite of ham but the meat was completely tasteless. She was supposed to teach him about their family history. But the lessons she would teach him would have nothing to do with her background. Only his.

She could do this. The key would be remaining detached. It was just a lesson in his family's history, nothing more. Elizabeth slid a glance over at him as he took a bite of his meal and her heart pounded. Remaining detached would be impossible.

She attempted another bite of food, then pushed her plate away. Food just wasn't about to taste right tonight. Instead, she sipped her wine.

Why would he want to start tonight? After what happened today, she thought he would ignore her for a few days. They would have to work alone with each other in his study!

"Are you all right, Elizabeth?" Ellie asked before taking a bite of her potatoes.

"I don't seem to have much appetite tonight," she replied with a shrug.

William's gaze burned her cheeks. "Would you like to postpone our lesson this evening?"

"No, I am really not hungry. There is nothing else." She'd be damned if she let him see her discomfiture. There was no reason she couldn't teach him about his family. He seemed completely unaffected by their kiss. This was obviously her problem.

He tilted his head and slowly his lips moved upwards. "Very well, then."

Dinner progressed at an excruciating pace. It had only taken the children a week to learn their proper manners at the dinner table. Now, instead of rushing through dinner, they took their time and made conversation.

Not that she usually understood any of it. Michael tended to steer the conversation back to something that happened when they lived in York. Elizabeth always noticed the way William's eyes lit up when speaking of either Canada or America. She wondered what he planned to do now that Abigail had refused him for good. ·

With Abigail no longer a concern, there was the one option Elizabeth had always rejected—seduction. Perhaps if Elizabeth seduced him, he would decide to stay.

What an absurd thought. She was not the type of woman to seduce a man. She glanced up the table at him briefly. After that kiss today, she could easily imagine him removing her gown, untying her stays, sliding her shift over her shoulders until it dropped to the floor. He would remove her garters and stockings slowly as she savored the feel of his rough fingers on her soft thighs.

She sighed.

"Are you certain you are all right, Elizabeth?" William's voice interrupted her erotic thoughts.

Elizabeth blinked and noticed every one of the children looking at her. Heat blistered her cheeks.

"You look quite flushed," Lucy added.

"I am well." She pushed back her chair and stood. "If you will excuse me, I need to finish something before we begin our lessons."

She left the room and strode to her bedchamber. Once there, she paced and paced until she was certain she had worn the old carpet to threads. One kiss and she was fantasizing about him. Utter madness. The kiss meant nothing to him and it should mean nothing to her, too. She was a fool to think otherwise.

But the truth was she'd been fantasizing about Will since she met him. That sizzling kiss only increased her fascination with him.

A light knock on the door sounded. "Elizabeth, may I come in?"

"Yes, Ellie."

Ellie entered and smiled at her. "I hope you don't mind if I disturb you."

"Of course not. Is something wrong?"

Ellie walked to the window and glanced outside into the square. "It's just that I saw that look on your face during dinner, and thought you might want to talk to someone."

She knew! "What do you mean?" Elizabeth squeaked.

"When Alicia and David first met, she was the same way. The daydreaming, followed by the flushed cheeks. You were thinking about a man, Elizabeth."

Elizabeth closed her eyes. As much as she would love to confide in someone, she just did not think his sister was the person. "You must be mistaken."

Ellie giggled. "I'm sure I am not. Alicia later told what had caused her to look so embarrassed. So I really do understand. Is it Will?"

"What?" Elizabeth clutched the bedpost for support. "What would make you think that?"

"I saw the look you gave him before you started woolgathering. It was almost indecent."

Elizabeth covered her mouth with her hand. "Oh, my God! Do you think he noticed?"

"He's a man. They are oblivious to most things. He can't even see that Abigail is playing games with him." Ellie sat on the end of the bed.

"But Abigail wrote him a letter stating her father wanted her to marry some other man, and that she agreed with him." Elizabeth finally plopped down next to Ellie.

"Indeed? That's odd," Ellie considered. "Lucy and I have always thought she was up to no-good with Will. It was as if she was making him believe she would eventually marry him when we all knew she would never do such a thing."

"Well, I don't think you have to worry about her any longer."

"Does that mean you have set your cap on Will?" Ellie asked quietly.

She could never fall in love with a man until she knew the truth about herself. "No, Ellie."

Ellie shrugged. "That is a shame. Of all the women interested in him, I like you the best."

Elizabeth had no idea how to reply. She couldn't tell Ellie that William was the only man she'd ever really desired. That would only encourage her. "Thank you, but I am not interested in your brother."

"Very well, I must get the children ready for bed."

Ellie stood and walked toward the door. She stopped and then looked back at Elizabeth. "If you do change your mind, I shall support you in any way I can."

"No, Ellie." Elizabeth shook her head as Ellie walked out the door.

She hoped she'd convinced his sister. Now she just had to convince herself.

Will watched Elizabeth enter the study. She looked calmer and more relaxed than at dinner. "Good evening, Elizabeth."

"Good evening to you, William."

Will just chuckled. "Do you think you could call me Will? The only time I was called William was when I was in trouble."

She nodded as she took her seat across the large expanse of his cherry desk. "As you wish, Will."

"I know we had talked about reviewing our family history, but I would rather try to make some headway on these invitations."

"Very well," Elizabeth said, looking relieved. She reached for the stack of invitations she had reviewed earlier. "The dowager Countess of Cantwell is a must. However, the ball is in three days so only you would be attending."

"You are not going?" he asked.

"I had originally declined because of the upheaval in the house. Now that everything is settling down, I suppose I could attend."

He had a strange suspicion that there was another reason she had declined. "I insist you go with me."

"As you wish." She glanced down at the next invitation before adding, "If you think you are ready to face them."

"Them?" he asked.

"Society. They can be a vicious bunch."

Will was certain her lack of enthusiasm had something to do with this. "Is that the voice of experience speaking?"

"Yes. Two of my dearest friends have had to deal with the gossipmongers of the *ton*. Avis made one small mistake and they cut her—"

"What exactly did she do?"

Elizabeth pressed her lips together but the movement of her shoulders proved she was trying to suppress a laugh. She covered her mouth with her hand and coughed delicately. "She had a bit of bad timing."

"Oh?" He had a feeling he knew exactly what had happened.

"She chose the wrong time to announce that she and her now husband, Banning, had gone away together to his summer cottage."

"She said this in front of others?"

"She was attempting to save Banning from being compromised by a foolish woman. Avis thought it was just the three of them on the terrace." Elizabeth did let a small giggle out.

"And I take it there were a few more people out on the terrace?"

Elizabeth nodded. "About twenty people, including Banning's mother and sister."

"Are they happily married now?" Now that he and Abigail were finished, he wondered if he would ever feel like marrying another woman again. His father loved both his wives deeply. Will wanted that same type of love from a wife.

"Yes. She is with child, and should give birth in a few months."

"And your other friend?" he asked, relaxing against the chair. This was one of the first true conversations they'd had without a lesson in protocol or rank being thrown in.

"Banning's sister, Jennette. But honestly, it was her husband who had to deal with the whims of Society. He accidentally killed Jennette's former betrothed. Society rejected him, even when he inherited his father's title. No one wanted a poor earl with the reputation of a murderer for their daughter."

"Yet, Jennette ended up married to him?"

"They fell in love when she was trying to help him find a wife," she said with a sigh.

"Elizabeth," he started softly, "why haven't you married?"

She blinked and stared at him. "What?"

"You don't seem like the type of woman who would want to remain a spinster. You're beautiful—"

"No, I am not."

"You are, and don't interrupt me when I'm complimenting you. You appear to be everything a man would want in a wife—beauty, family, money."

Her face paled.

Damn. He must have hit a sore spot. Perhaps she had been betrothed and something happened. "I'm sorry. That is rather personal."

Elizabeth looked away. "I just never found the right man. When I first came out, the men courted me because of my family connection and my inheritance."

Will frowned. He'd been through the books and her inheritance was a pittance. He had even considered raising her allowance to compensate for her lack of funds.

"As I became older, I realized that I wanted more

than just a man who wanted me for the duke's money," she added.

The duke's money. Not her father's money.

That was not the first time she'd referred to her father as the duke. He must have been a very difficult man if that was how she considered him. Will's father had told him a few things about the family and none of it was good.

Perhaps it was time to get them back to the subject. He forced out a laugh. "Well, I believe the original question was whether or not I'd be able to handle Society yet. And the answer is yes. So we both should accept Lady Cantwell's invitation."

"Very well, we shall put this in a pile of acceptances," Elizabeth said, handing the note to him.

They quickly sorted through the rest. Some invitations were accepted and some rejected. Before long, they had completed his correspondence.

"Shall we start on the family history?" he asked.

"I shall do my best. The family bible has most of the genealogy of the family, and that is at the estate in Kendal."

Will listened as she told him about the first Duke of Kendal being granted his lands and titles for service to King Edward III. While Will listened, he watched her face intently. Her green eyes sparkled like emeralds as she talked about their shared ancestry. She was a fascinating woman and seemed to love her family history.

Still, he had to focus his attentions on his life. Returning to America was the only thing that made sense to him. Perhaps when he arrived, he would discover Abigail hadn't married and wanted him again. Maybe he could convince her to move away from her father's overbearing influence. But the more he thought about her lately, the less he wanted her.

"Should we stop for the night?" Elizabeth's gentle voice asked.

He glanced over at the clock and noticed it was only ten. "Did you wish to retire?"

She smiled at him. "I thought since you had your eyes closed, I was putting you to sleep with my stories."

"Sorry, I was thinking of something else for a moment. I was not bored by your stories, but fascinated. Tell me exactly how we are related."

"As I told you, this family has not been blessed with very many male heirs. Most of the men were lucky if they had two sons who survived. The fifth duke seems to be the exception, and he had three sons who survived to adulthood. Robert, and the twins, William and Henry, were all born within five years of the duke's marriage, with Robert being the eldest. William and Henry were given a small fortune, and each went different paths."

"How does our dear cousin Richard fit into all this?" Will asked.

"He is a descendant of Henry, the third born, while you are descended from William, whom I believe is your namesake. That is why you were the rightful heir to the dukedom."

He wouldn't disillusion her by telling her that his mother named him after his maternal grandfather.

"So I am the 10th Duke of Kendal, is that correct?" he asked.

"Yes. It is an important history."

"I suppose it is," he said, unconvinced that being a duke was particularly important.

"You don't think so?" she asked with a frown.

"I'm sure a few hundred years ago, having a man

who gave his fealty to the king and managed large areas of land for him was important. It kept the land civilized. But today? I can see no reason for it."

Elizabeth stared at him, unable to say anything. After all she'd told him about the service to the king, the marriages brokered over lands, and how the tenants depended on the duke's favor, how could he believe this was not important? Anger at his apathy rose high within her.

"I cannot believe you don't care," she shouted as she stood. "People, your relatives, died for this country and your lands. Tenants starved under other lords, but not under the duke. The Duke of Kendal always cared for the people working for him."

"Elizabeth, sit down," Will said sternly.

"No, I will not. The English system of government has stood strong for centuries. The Duke of Kendal has always played an important part of that structure, and you sit there ridiculing your own history!"

Elizabeth leaned over the desk and stared into his brown eyes. There was only one thing she was concerned about now. "Are you staying here now that Abigail is marrying another or not?"

His eyes narrowed on her. "I do not believe that is any of your business."

"It is my business to ensure the families who have depended on the duke's grace until now are still cared for by someone."

"I am the duke, as you so like to remind me, Elizabeth. What I do or when I do it is none of your concern."

"While I am living in this house, it is my duty to protect this family name."

"Then perhaps it is time to leave the house."

Elizabeth watched in shock as Will strode from

the room. She could hear his heavy footsteps march all the way down the hall, and then the front door slammed behind him. She remained in the study, frozen in place.

She let her damned temper get the best of her again. To ask such a question the very day Abigail sent him that letter was dreadful. Of course, he would have a violent reaction. He asked her to leave all because of her anger.

Oh, God! What had she done?

Chapter 10

Will walked the dark London streets, wondering how to get out of the mess that was his life. He didn't want Elizabeth to leave the house. She had a stabilizing effect on all of them that he needed now more than ever. Which meant he would have to swallow his pride and apologize for getting angry.

He understood her reasons for becoming mad at him. She only wanted to protect her family's history. Her name. But she just didn't realize that it meant nothing to him. Having grown up in America and Canada, it didn't matter who he was; he could become anyone he wanted. And he wanted that for his siblings, as well.

Even if he decided to stay here, highly unlikely that it was, his stepbrothers would have to make their own way. While being the stepbrother of a duke might assist them, Will wasn't certain that was a good thing. He only wanted the best for them.

Would having too much money and position be a hindrance to them? He doubted it.

"So what brings you out tonight?"

Will blinked and looked over at Lord Somerton, who was leaning against a building. If Somerton hadn't spoken, Will would never have seen him lurking in the shadows.

"Don't tell me you've already decided to become a member?"

"A member? Of what?" Will asked, feeling terribly confused by the viscount's question.

"White's? You are directly in front of the building." Somerton casually walked closer to him.

"White's? Oh, no. I was just out for a walk."

Somerton chuckled. "A walk? At eleven in the evening? Even in Mayfair, you must take more care. You look like hell."

Will shrugged. "So I assume that means White's is out of the question."

"They will take you as long as you pay their fee. But I happen to know a much better place." Somerton inclined his head up the street. "My carriage is up this way."

"Very well," Will said, wondering exactly where they were headed.

Somerton remained quiet as they walked together toward the carriage.

"Why were you in the shadows?" Will asked, his curiosity finally getting the best of him.

"I was waiting for a friend who did not arrive."

That made no sense, Will thought. Why wait outside? Instead of questioning him further, he kept his mouth shut. Somerton was an interesting man in a strange way.

They reached the carriage and started off for another club. Will glanced out the window as silence filled the carriage. Should he even be here with this man? Elizabeth had tried to warn him about Somerton, and he had been lurking in the shadows like a criminal.

"Have you been out to any balls yet?" Somerton asked, breaking the strangling silence.

"Not yet. I have accepted the dowager Countess of Cantwell's invitation. Will you be there?"

"God, no. I hate those blasted balls. There really is only one reason to attend."

"Oh?" Will asked.

"Marriage, man. The mamas are there, proudly displaying their babies for you to fawn over. Their only goal is to get those daughters off their hands as quickly as possible."

Will considered this for a moment. Perhaps he should decline, since he had no desire to marry an English lady who could barely think for herself. Except Elizabeth. She certainly had a mind of her own.

"Ahh, we have arrived," Somerton drawled. He climbed down and waited for Will.

"So where exactly are we?"

"Lady Whitely's." Somerton walked up the steps. "Come along, Kendal."

Kendal. He would never get used to that name. The door opened and the sound of voices carried out. "Is Lady Whitely having a party?"

"Every night," Somerton replied before entering the house.

Will walked inside and stopped. The room blazed with candlelight and scantily clad women. While he had been in a brothel before, he'd never seen one this luxurious. Red velvet chairs and sofas created intimate nooks for conversation—and other things.

A few men glanced their way and inclined their heads toward Somerton. Several of the women looked at both of them and smiled. He could hear the whispered tones debating about which girl Somerton might pick tonight.

"Somerton, this really isn't my type of place," Will said.

"Come along to the back room. We're only here for a drink and to talk. If you choose to do something else when we are done, that's your business."

With a sigh, Will followed Somerton to the back room. The noise from the front room didn't carry this far, and the women in here lifted trays heavy with drinks for the gentlemen. Somerton and Will took a seat that overlooked the torch-lit gardens. Will looked around and realized that even this house of sin would have put his home in York to shame.

"Can I get you a drink, Lord Somerton?"

Will looked up to see a tall woman with flowing blond hair standing next to him. The dress she wore was nothing but red sheer fabric with embroidered flowers covering her most private parts. Not that the embroidery covered all that much.

"We shall have a bottle of your best whisky, Venus."

She nodded but glanced over at him with a wink. "Are you going to introduce me to your friend, Lord Somerton?"

"I'm not sure he would like his presence known yet, darling."

Her full painted lips pouted slightly. "All right, then," she replied and turned around to walk to the bar.

Will couldn't help but watch her all but bare hips swaying under the sheer gown. "Nice place, Somerton."

"I thought you might need somewhere you could relax for awhile."

Venus returned with a bottle of whisky and two glasses. She leaned over Will's shoulder to place the bottle and glass in front of him. Her full breasts rubbed against his back.

"If you need *anything*," she whispered in his ear, "just let me know." As Venus backed away, the overpowering bouquet of her perfume lingered.

Somerton reached over and grabbed the whisky bottle. After pouring them both a glass, he leaned back and said, "To titled gentlemen who can get anything they want."

Will wasn't sure that was a good thing or not. His parents had taught him that hard work brought success to people. And he had believed them . . . until he returned to England. Regardless, he lifted his glass in agreement and then swallowed a large amount.

The sound of heels clicking on wood drew his attention to the door. An older woman who looked to be in her mid-forties walked straight toward them, ignoring all the other men who greeted her. While the girls were dressed in sheer fabrics, this woman wore an elegant blue-striped silk dress. She looked far more like a woman he would meet at a ball than a strumpet.

Somerton looked back, shook his head, and muttered a curse under his breath.

"Good evening, Anthony." The "lady" put her hand on the back of Somerton's chair. "So now you come to my establishment and don't greet me before entertaining yourself?"

"Good evening, Lady Whitely," he said, taking her hand to his lips.

"Much better. Now tell me who this handsome devil is."

"Will, this is Lady Whitely. She owns the house. Lady Whitely, this is my friend Will Atherton."

"Good evening, Lady Whitely." Will stood and kissed

the back of her hand. He had to admit this was a first—treating a common whore like a true lady.

"Good evening to you, Your Grace." Lady Whitely smiled up at him. "Do you think I wouldn't have heard of you?"

"I would not know."

"Everyone knows you are in town, Your Grace." She turned back to Somerton. "I would like to speak with you soon."

"Tomorrow."

"Very well," she said with a quick nod, and then departed.

Will drank another glass of whisky and then leaned back in his chair and laughed. "I guess this is one of the reasons Elizabeth warned me about you."

"She did? I barely know the chit. Why would she not like me?"

"Something about your reputation," Will commented. The whisky was finally helping him relax. So he sipped down some more.

Somerton shrugged. "So I have been known to frequent a brothel. I'm no different than most men."

"True enough. But she mentioned something about killing a few men."

"All lies to make me look nefarious in the eyes of the *ton*." Somerton leaned in a little closer and asked, "So how is the fair Lady Elizabeth?"

"Angry."

Somerton grimaced. "At you?"

"Of course at me. She gets along fine with the children, and she and Ellie seem to have forged a friendship."

"What exactly were you two arguing about tonight?"

Will sipped his drink to gather his thoughts. "Family."

"Yours or hers?"

"Ours. It's very important to her that I learn all about the exalted history of the Duke of Kendal. Not that I give a damn about it." Will gulped the rest of his whisky and poured another glass.

"Ahh," Somerton replied. "But by not giving a damn, as you so eloquently said, you have insulted her."

"I never insulted her."

"The woman is a spinster. All she has is her family, and by dismissing her relatives, you are rejecting her."

Damn the man for being so intuitive. "I think I asked her to leave tonight," Will muttered before drinking another glass of whisky.

"You did what?" Somerton slammed his glass on the table, and everyone in the room stared at them both. "Go on about your business," he barked to the room.

Will related the high points of the argument. "I told her that it might be time for her to leave my house."

"You ass." Somerton stood and pulled out Will's chair, too. "Let's go."

"Where are we going?"

"You are returning to your home with your tail between your arse and apologizing to the lady." Somerton pulled Will's arm and dragged him down the hall. "She has nowhere to go if she leaves your house. Not only that, but you need her right now."

"I don't need her," Will lied. He needed Elizabeth in more ways than he could count.

"Indeed?" Somerton stopped only when he reached the front step. "Could you really manage all those children alone? Could you get your older sisters ready to make their bow to the queen? Would you have managed hiring servants, tutors, and a governess?"

"No," Will admitted.

"Exactly."

* * *

Elizabeth knelt down and felt the underside of the desk in Will's bedroom. No matter how she tried, she couldn't get enough leverage without getting all the way down on the floor. Lying down on the rug, she scooted her bottom until she was completely under the desk.

"Please," she begged the desk to give up its secrets. She pressed her hands against the underside of the desk. At least this desk had ornate legs and only one large drawer. She vaguely remembered her mother using this desk to respond to her correspondence. It only made sense that there was a secret compartment in it.

She pulled at the back and sides of the drawer but nothing budged. After skimming her hands all along the underside, she realized there were no secrets from the desk for her now. Tears welled in her eyes. She would never know who she was.

By tomorrow, she would be packing her things and living with Sophie. Elizabeth rubbed her palms against her eyes. She was such an idiot to let him draw her into an argument.

"Why didn't I keep my mouth shut?"

"I'm really not certain. But then again, I have no idea why you are in my bedroom and under my desk."

Elizabeth sat up so quickly, she banged her head against the desk. "Ouch!"

She inelegantly crawled out from under the desk, only to find Will staring down at her. His brown eyes were almost black with anger. So much for thinking his rage might have dissipated with time. He actually looked more irate now than when he left.

Realizing she stood in front of him in nothing more

than her night rail with a dressing gown over it, she pulled the dressing gown tighter.

"Would you like to explain what the hell you're doing in my bedroom?"

"Umm, I was looking for something," she said.

"Under the desk?"

Elizabeth cringed at the harsh tone of his voice. "Shhh, the children are asleep."

"They are upstairs and cannot hear a·thing." He folded his arms over his chest. "What are you looking for, Elizabeth?"

"Something that belonged to my mother." She prayed he would stop his interrogation at that.

"And?"

"And what?"

Will blew out a breath as if he were having trouble containing his anger. "Why would it be under the desk?"

She sidestepped him and started for the door. "It is nothing that concerns you."

Before she could reach the door, he pulled her back toward him. "Try again."

Her heart pounded in her chest. "I already told you it has nothing to do with you. Now if you will excuse me I must go pack."

His lips tilted up into a smug smile. "You're not going anywhere until I hear the truth."

He pulled her a step closer until she could smell the stench on him.

"Oh, my God, you smell like whisky and cheap women," she said, pushing away from him.

"I don't think any of those women come cheap."

Elizabeth's mouth gaped. "You . . . you . . ." Nothing more would come out of her mouth. She had no idea what to say to a man who had just returned from a brothel.

"You might be right about Somerton being a poor influence, though," Will said with a chuckle.

"I might have known you were with him."

"Now, where were we?" he asked. "Oh, yes, back to why you are in my bedroom at night." He pulled her closer again. "Not that I mind, but you should have given me some warning."

He drew her against his chest. "I believe I must have misjudged you, Elizabeth."

"H-How so?" She was so close to him, if she wanted to kiss him, his lips were only inches away. And blast it, she did want to kiss him again.

"I didn't realize that you were the type of woman to enter a man's bedchamber," he said, then brought his lips down on hers.

This evening's kiss was far more sensual than the afternoon version. His lips pressed to hers until she opened slightly to taste him. She savored the fine smoky whisky on his breath, and his tongue ignited a fire that burned to her loins. His hands reached for the ties on her dressing gown and released the tight knot. He spread the gown open, revealing her light cotton night rail.

He broke away for a moment to glance down. Her nipples were hardened into tight peaks that ached for his touch. With a groan, he kissed her harder this time. He brought his hand up to cup her breast and stroked his thumb across her nipple. Molten moisture rushed to her womb. Her hips rocked against his in an age-old ritual.

She moaned softly against his lips as his thumb

continued its exquisite torture. He skimmed his hands down her back, flattening her to his chest.

She knew she should break away from his intoxicating body. Instead, she brought her arms around his neck tighter and rubbed her aching breasts against him. She wanted him to touch her there again. Worse, she wanted him to touch other places on her body.

How could something she knew was wrong feel so wonderful? This man was completely wrong for her. So, if that was true, why did she want to feel his naked skin on top of her? Oh, God, she was becoming a wanton. Her friends' influence had finally rubbed off on her.

She broke away from him and ran from the room. Once she reached her own bedroom, she locked the door behind her. If he walked in here, she would have no self-control. She sat on the bed and waited, her heart pounding. Twice in one day, he had kissed her. And not just a cousinly peck on the cheek, but a passionate kiss meant to heighten her desire.

He never did find out what she was looking for in his room. Now she had the rest of the night to come up with an excuse. Was that possible? What would a lady attach to the bottom of her desk?

Jewelry?

Perhaps that was the answer, or excuse, as it were. She could tell him that her mother had hidden some of her jewels so her father would not sell them.

Elizabeth lay back on the bed. That made no sense. Her father wouldn't need to sell any of her mother's pendants.

A letter? That made the most sense. Her mother had hidden a letter from her father because . . . she was having an affair. No! Because her mother had stashed some money in a safe place, and left the note somewhere in the house. Elizabeth thought she could find the note, and therefore retrieve the money to use for her own security.

Perfect!

At least it would be perfect if Will believed her.

Chapter 11

Will paced the salon, waiting for everyone to finish their preparations. He needed to show the children the darker side of London. They had to realize that not everyone lived as they did now.

"Please rethink this idea," Elizabeth begged him.

Those were the first words she'd spoken to him since entering the room. She'd made no mention of their encounter in his bedroom, and right now, he had no desire to speak of it. When they returned, he would ask her for a better reason why she'd been in his room last evening.

"I agreed not to take Sarah, Robert, and Ethan, but the others should see how England treats its downtrodden. Today we will take Ellie and Lucy, and tomorrow I will take the boys."

"And I suppose America has no poor?"

"Of course they do. Just nothing like the severity of London's poor."

"I do not believe you. All large cities have issues with poverty," Elizabeth commented. "And many people are flocking to America now. Their poverty will only grow."

"True enough," Will said, as he strode past her chair again. He suddenly stopped and turned back to her. "Have you ever even seen what I'm talking about?"

"I have lived in London most of my life."

"Yes, but have you ever really seen the areas I am speaking of?"

"I have been to Covent Gardens."

"But Whitechapel, St. Giles—have you been there?"

She glanced away from him. "Of course not! It is not right to take them there. The entire area is nothing but crime and poverty."

"And that is exactly what they need to see," Will said.

She stepped forward and smiled at him. "Please, rethink this, Will," she said in a wholly seductive voice. "You would not wish to put your sisters in danger."

As cute as her overt attempts at flirtation were, he was in no mood for them today. "No, Elizabeth."

She lifted her hand as if to caress his cheek. He caught her wrist in his grip and she started.

"I said, no," he said in a quiet tone. Releasing her hand, he stepped back.

Finally, Ellie and Lucy entered the room.

"Will, I really do not think I should go," Ellie said softly. "I have a touch of a headache—"

"Then the fresh air will do you good," Will replied.

"The air is far from fresh down there," Elizabeth added. "It is quite putrid with the coal smoke and fumes."

"Enough!" Will clenched his fists in frustration. Every one of them was against him.

"I can't wait to go," said Lucy in an excited tone.

"We might see some pickpockets, or maybe even a murderer!"

"Oh, I think I am going to be sick," Ellie whispered.

"You are not going to be sick," Will commanded. "The carriage is waiting. We need to depart."

Will walked out to the landau first and waited as his sisters clamored into it. Elizabeth took his hand but shook her head as she climbed inside. She would never understand the importance of this trip. His life had been nothing like this in either America or Canada. While his father had been on a diplomatic mission, the salary had barely covered the expenses.

Will had farmed to keep the food coming in, but moving to Canada had reduced his planting season. The winters were far harsher than when they'd lived in Virginia before the war. They had never starved, but he knew what it meant to be hungry.

The coach rumbled down the street toward the east end of London. Familiar sites turned to strange buildings and poorly dressed people. Will glanced out the window, noticing the air turning thicker with smoke as the fumes permeated the coach.

"Will, I really think I am going to be sick," Ellie tried again.

He knew his sister well enough to know that she was never sick. Still, glancing over at Elizabeth's ashen face, he had second thoughts about this trip. She stared out the window as they slowly rolled past an elderly woman sitting on the walk. People passed by her without even looking down at the poor soul.

Could Elizabeth think this would happen to her? They never had discussed their argument from last night. She might think he still wanted her to leave. And that was the last thing he wanted. Somerton was right.

Will needed her.

The scenery turned worse as they headed into the area of Whitechapel. As instructed, the groomsman turned down some of the smaller streets, and the poverty was far greater than he had expected. Children no older than his ten-year-old stepbrother Robert roamed the streets in threadbare clothing. Will watched as one child who looked to be about ten picked the pocket of an elderly man.

"Will, what is a pawn shop?" Lucy asked when they paused for a moment in front of one.

Will glanced out quickly and then turned his head back to the window. A woman who looked very much like Elizabeth's friend, Miss Seaton, walked out of the pawnbroker's shop with a slight smile upon her face. He slid a glance to Elizabeth, who also stared out the window toward the woman.

"Will?" Lucy prompted again.

"It's when you give something to the man inside, who will then give you money for it." Will again stole a look at Elizabeth. Her face was completely white now.

"Will," Ellie started, "you are a duke now. Why can't you do something about all this?" She pointed out the window. "Surely, you must have some influence so changes could be made."

"Those changes could only be made in Parliament," Elizabeth said. "Besides, you all won't be here long enough for Will to make any real changes. Those things take time."

"We're not really leaving, are we, Will?" Lucy spoke up.

Will understood that Lucy and probably Ellie, too, seemed to like England better than America or Canada. Of course, for them it might have something to do with the lack of chores here and the beautiful gowns.

"I thought we had been through this already," Will said. Why did they think something had changed? Couldn't they look around and see how horribly this country treated its citizens? Soon they would return to their huge home in Mayfair, with more food for dinner than most of these people had in a week.

He felt Elizabeth's eyes burning into him, waiting for an answer to Lucy's question. "I don't know yet," he finally answered.

As they finished their drive and headed back to the relative safety of Mayfair, Will thought about Ellie's questions. Was there anything he could do about the plight of the poor? He had no idea how to move about in political circles. But for the first time, he wanted to find out.

Will waited in his study for Elizabeth to enter the room. He'd summoned her over an hour ago. Hearing a commotion at the front door, he strode to the hallway to find out which boy was in trouble now.

"Have the carriage brought around once the rest of my trunks are packed and carried down," Elizabeth commanded the footman.

"Going somewhere?" he asked, leaning against the wall.

"I believe last evening you asked me to leave," she retorted without even glancing back at him. "Where are the children? I need to say good-bye."

"The children are out for a walk and some fresh air. I asked you to join me in the study an hour ago." Will moved away from the wall and stepped closer to the footmen. "Return Lady Elizabeth's bags to her room. She is going nowhere."

Elizabeth turned her fiery gaze on him. "How dare you! I shall do as I please." She looked back at the footmen. "Do not move these trunks."

The two footmen looked at each other and then back at Will. "As you wish, Your Grace." They picked up the first trunk and carted it back up the stairs.

"Now," Will said, clasping Elizabeth's arm. "I believe we are scheduled to talk."

Elizabeth pulled her arm out of his grip but walked silently down the hall toward the study. Her stiff posture spoke volumes about how she felt today. Once in the room, she sat in the chair across from the desk and folded her arms over her chest.

Will stifled a chuckle. "How are you this afternoon?" he asked politely.

"Perfectly well, thank you," she muttered.

"Excellent." He leaned back in the leather chair across from her. "I believe we were having a discussion last night about why you were under the desk in my bedroom. Shall we continue?"

"No, thank you."

He smiled. "I think we shall."

Elizabeth let out a frustrated sigh. "Very well. I was looking for a note that my mother had secreted somewhere in the house. She and the duke were having some marital problems, so she hid a bit of money in case she needed it. She wrote a note to remind herself where she put the money."

Will almost laughed at the absurdity of her explanation. "She thought she wouldn't remember where she hid the money, so she hid a note to tell herself?"

Elizabeth's face reddened. "Yes."

"And she hid this note under that desk?"

She licked her lips. "I believe so."

"Where anyone might come across it, such as a maid?"

"I . . . That is what she told me," her voice squeaked.

Will wondered exactly what it was Elizabeth was searching for last night. Obviously, she wasn't about to tell him. "Very well, then. I believe we should get back to our family history lesson."

"We should?" Elizabeth bit down on her lower lip. "I thought you wanted me to leave."

"Elizabeth, even though you had several sisters, you told me they were all much older than you, correct?"

She nodded in reply.

"So I'm guessing you never had many arguments with people, did you?"

She shook her head.

"I told you to leave in the heat of anger. I did not mean those words," he said softly, hoping she believed him. As much as she tempted him, he didn't want to see her leave. He needed her. And he knew she needed him, too.

Elizabeth looked down at her sage gown. "I must apologize, too. I know this has been difficult for you and your family."

"And I realize how important this family's name is to you."

Her face paled. "It is," she whispered, still staring at her gown.

Will wondered at her quiet answer. Perhaps she's just feeling a little out of sorts today because of his anger.

"Tell me about your father."

"My father?"

"Yes, the previous duke. What type of man was he?"

"I cannot talk about this right now," she mumbled. She rose quickly and started for the door.

Will beat her to the door and stood before it like a

sentry on duty. "You said you would tell me about my history and the history of this family. I would like to know about your father."

Her eyes filled with tears. "You know, don't you?" She spun away from him and faced the fireplace. "You found it and now you know the truth."

He approached her slowly as if he were trying to get close to a wounded animal. He gently placed his hands on her shoulders. "Elizabeth, I don't have any clue what you are speaking of."

"Of course you do." She moved away from his grip and turned to face him. Tears rained down her cheeks. "How could you not know? Everyone knows, or at least suspects."

He shook his head. "Suspects what?"

Her misery turned to anger. She grabbed his hand and pulled him with her out the room and down the hall toward the music room. Slamming the door behind them, she pointed to the portraits on the walls.

"Look at them," she demanded.

Will did as she said and stared at the paintings on the wall. There were portraits of four women with blond hair and blue eyes, who all looked to be about sixteen when they had been painted. And then there was a portrait of Elizabeth at the same age. He smiled at the painting of her.

"What exactly am I supposed to see other than you and your sisters?"

She pointed to a large portrait over the fireplace and said, "That is my mother."

Trying to maintain some patience, since this was apparently important to her, he nodded. "She was a very lovely woman."

"And I look nothing like them," she whispered. "Nothing."

"Just because you have red hair and freckles doesn't mean anything. You probably have another relative you look like."

"No, I don't. There is not one painting of anyone in any of the estates who has red hair. Just me! I am the only one." She dropped to the sofa and placed her hands over her face.

He sat next to her and attempted to pull her into his arm. She pulled away and stood.

"Elizabeth, you cannot assume just because you have red hair that you're not the duke's daughter."

"I don't have to assume," she mumbled. "I know I'm not his daughter."

Will rose and drew her into his arms. "What do you mean, you know?"

Her lower lip quivered. "He told me I wasn't his daughter. After my mother died, he told me. Perhaps he wanted to punish me for her death, I don't know. But he told me that my mother had an affair, and I was the result. I don't know who my father is."

The anguish in her eyes struck straight to his heart. He pulled her close and held her tight against his chest. Her tears dampened his shirt and the edges of his cravat. He forced himself to ignore the sensual feel of her warm body touching his. Comfort her, he told himself.

Gently, he caressed her hair and several pins fell to the floor. Her tears slowed to a stop but still she clung to him. Warm lips kissed his jaw and he knew he was in deep trouble. He wanted to take away her pain, make her forget for a moment the torment in her heart. But the minute her lips touched his skin, he was lost.

This was wrong.

She needed comfort, not passion. As he tried to draw away, she tightened her arms around his neck and pulled his lips to hers. He tasted the salty tears on her lips until she opened for him. Deepening their kiss, he realized he was done for. She didn't want his comfort any longer.

Drowning in the flaring passion, he removed her hairpins. Her glorious red tresses curled down her back and he threaded his fingers through them. God, he wanted to see her naked with all that hair flowing down her back. He wanted to see her rosy nipples, erect and ready for his mouth.

He walked them both to the sofa and brought her down on top of him. He moved her leg so that she now straddled his hips. Her warmth pressed down on his hard cock and he wondered just how much control he had left.

Grabbing her hips, he rubbed her against his trouser-covered shaft. The sound of her low moan dropped his control lower. He had to stop this madness.

"Elizabeth," he mumbled against her lips. "We need to stop."

Elizabeth moved away slightly. While she knew he was right, she needed him. And she did not want to stop. Not now. She wanted to feel his body in hers. She wanted the intimacy of being with him.

"Elizabeth—"

She cut off his words with a kiss. She didn't care if he tried to stop her. She wanted more than just a kiss. The need to feel something other than misery was driving her to the edge. She wanted him, and she was going to have him. To hell with the consequences. For once in her life, she was going after what she wanted without fear.

She wrenched at the neatly tied cravat and loosened it until she could pull it away from his strong neck. Warmth emanated from him, and she moved her lips to his strong jaw. His head tilted back against the sofa, giving her access to his neck. As she kissed down his neck, she worked at the buttons on his linen shirt, but with his jacket still on, she had no way of removing it. Moving her hand to the bare skin revealed, she heard his hiss.

"Elizabeth, this is—"

She kissed him again before he could deny her. Finally, she drew back and placed her finger on his lips. "Don't," she pleaded.

For a long moment, he stared at her as if trying to make up his mind. Then he slowly drew her finger into the hot recesses of his mouth and swirled his tongue up the length. She shivered as he gave her a wicked smile. He removed her finger and moved his lips to the palm of her hand. Tiny shivers raced down her skin. She'd never realized what a sensitive spot that was until now.

He trailed his lips up her arm until blocked by the green silk sleeves of her gown. Undaunted, he progressed to the buttons on the back of her dress. As each button popped out, her dress slipped down a little more until he reached her shoulders and drew it down over her arms.

Elizabeth shivered again as he stared at her with an intensity that made her tremble with hot need.

"If we continue much further, there will be no going back," he whispered as he kissed her neck. "I won't stand for regrets, so if you want me to stop, say so now."

"No," she whispered hoarsely.

"Oh, God," he muttered against her neck. "You have no idea how much I want you."

"I think I do," she replied.

He loosened her stays and then pulled her breasts out of their cotton prison. As he drew his thumb across her pebbled nipple, she shivered and moaned. Moist heat flowed to her womanly folds and without thinking, she rubbed herself against his hardness.

Hearing his groan of pleasure, she smiled. She needed more than this teasing. And suddenly, his mouth was on her breast, laving her, suckling her, driving her completely mad.

"Will," she moaned.

"Yes," he replied, and then moved to her other breast.

"Please," she begged, though not sure for what. An end to this exquisite torture? "Please . . ."

He skimmed a hand under her skirts until he found her folds. Elizabeth almost jumped as his finger crossed over her sensitive spot. But he didn't stop. He rubbed her nub until she shook with passion. Need spiraled within her, stronger with each caress until she didn't think she could go higher. Suddenly she couldn't keep her eyes open as a million stars burst behind her lids.

He kissed her as she moaned into his mouth, her body shaking with desire and spent passion. She felt him fumble with his trousers and then felt a thickness between her folds. This time it wasn't his finger rubbing against her.

Will fought his urge to slam himself into her. Bringing the top of his penis along her slick folds, he finally found the opening he sought. Lifting her hips, he slowly brought her down on him, enveloping him with her moist heat.

He barely sensed the thin barrier give way as he filled her. Her small "oh" was the only reaction. At this point, he didn't care. He needed her. He wanted her, and nothing would stop him from loving her.

"Elizabeth," he moaned and then kissed her. He prayed he hadn't hurt her. She'd been hurt too much already.

"Will?"

"Hmm?"

"Should it feel this good to have you inside me?" she whispered.

He stared down at her green eyes and smiled. He almost lost his control right then. "It's only going to feel better."

He kissed her deeply and lifted her hips slightly to test her soreness. A long moan was his answer. Her hips moved again, only this time, it was all Elizabeth's doing. She placed her hands on his shoulders and slid up his hard length.

Closing his eyes, he leaned his head back against the sofa. He couldn't remember the last time he'd been with a woman, and never had he been with one like Elizabeth. A lady. Not a servant or strumpet. She felt right. This shouldn't feel so damned good. It was wrong.

Feeling her tighten against his cock, he clasped her hips and moved with her. As she shivered her release, he let go to the sensations of being deeply inside Elizabeth. Never had it felt like this before. She collapsed against him, breathing hard.

What had he done?

Chapter 12

Elizabeth noticed his muscles tense and wondered if he regretted their actions. She should feel terrible about it. But she didn't. Languid with spent desire, she rested her head against his shoulder. His heartbeat echoed in her ear, strong and virile, just like Will.

"Elizabeth," Will started slowly, "we need to talk."

"No," she said, and then kissed a spot of skin on his chest.

"Elizabeth." This time his voice brooked no denial. She sat up, still feeling him inside of her. "Yes?"

"Not like this." He slid her off his penis and pulled his handkerchief out of his jacket. After gently wiping her folds, he glanced at the bloodstains on the handkerchief. "Why didn't you tell me?"

"It wasn't important," she lied. Saving herself had been important until he arrived. Now she understood Avis and Jennette so much more. They could not wait for marriage, and neither could she.

Not that she was waiting for a proposal from him. She couldn't marry him. She didn't even know who her father was.

"I don't believe you," he said, pulling up his trousers. "A woman doesn't wait until she's twenty-six to give herself to a man unless it's important."

"Will, I said it wasn't important. I was a virgin and now I am not." Elizabeth tried to shrug casually while hiding her tears. Why did she suddenly want to cry?

She watched him button his shirt and retie his cravat. Her fingers itched to touch him again. This was bad. Very, very bad. She turned her back to him and asked, "Would you mind?"

His fingers tightened her stays and then moved to the small pearl buttons on her gown. "Elizabeth, I find it difficult to believe that you are so flippant about your virginity."

"I am perfectly well, Will."

Once he had finished, she glanced around the room to make sure things were in their correct places. Everything appeared normal to her. But she would never be able to look at that sofa again without remembering what they had done there.

"Elizabeth."

She finally turned around and faced him. Her lover. Her heart skipped a beat. How could he look more handsome now than ever before? Was it just the concern for her etched upon his face?

"The item you were looking for last night"—he paused before continuing—"did it concern your father?"

While she hadn't expected a return to this conversation, at least it had moved him away from the subject of her virginity. "Yes, Will."

"Would you tell me what you were looking for? I might be able to help."

There was no point in denying him. He knew the

truth now anyway. And finding herself unable to resist the sincerity in his voice, she nodded.

"I found several of my mother's journals. There was nothing in them about my father, but she made reference to a hidden diary. I've searched all the estates and just needed to recheck a few rooms here."

"So you thought to inspect your parents' bedroom while I was gone last night," Will added.

"Yes," she admitted. "It makes the most sense that the journal would be there. But sometimes I wonder if perhaps the duke found it and destroyed the evidence." Elizabeth moved to the chair closest to the pianoforte. Somehow, the sofa just didn't seem like the correct place for such a conversation.

"When your father, excuse me, the duke told you that he wasn't your father, did he mention anything about evidence?" Will asked before moving to the pianoforte bench.

"No. That's when I started to review my mother's diaries. I thought she might have mentioned something in one of them." Instead, all her mother left was this mess. Elizabeth had no idea which gentleman was her father. Every ball she attended, her gaze searched out some similarity between the older men and herself.

"You said you searched in all the rooms in this house, then?" Will ran his fingers up the keys of the pianoforte. The sound resonated in the room.

"As I reread the diaries, one entry made me think she might have hidden it in a secret compartment. So I checked the boys' room a few days ago when you took the children to Hyde Park."

Will smiled over at her and her heart jumped. "So that explains your disheveled appearance at the time."

Elizabeth smiled back at him. "Yes. You came home earlier than I'd expected."

"I would like to help you, Elizabeth," Will offered.

"How could you help me?"

"I was thinking that maybe tonight instead of a history lesson, you and I could check my study. Perhaps your mother thought if she hid it under the duke's nose, he would never find it."

"I think it would be very helpful to have some assistance."

And didn't that sound like a witless thing to say.

This whole situation seemed entirely like an odd dream. They had made love, or was that sexual congress if you weren't in love with the man? And she was not in love with Will. Period. Which meant what they just did was a simple case of lust.

Not love.

She had only known the man for a little over a week. That was hardly enough time to fall in love with a person. Desire was one thing, but love another thing completely.

So if she wasn't in love with him, why was she sitting here staring at him like an adolescent girl? Why did she think his offer to help her find the diary one of the sweetest things anyone had ever done for her?

Why did she want to take his hand and lead him back to his bedroom, lock the door, and stay in bed with him for the rest of the day?

Lust, not love.

She didn't believe in love at first sight. And a week was first sight in her opinion.

"I believe the children have returned," Will said, interrupting her musing. He rose from his seat and held his hand out to her. "Shall we see how the outing went?"

"Yes. I'll be there in a moment. I need to put my hair back up."

"Of course." Will walked to the door and opened it before looking back at her. "Is two weeks enough time to plan our wedding?"

Will watched Elizabeth's bemused expression and smiled inwardly. As much as she'd tried to be calm and emotionless about making love with him, he was certain it had upset her. It was only natural after a woman's first time.

"I beg your pardon?" she finally managed to say.

"Our wedding? We need to set a date."

"There is no date," she said, striding toward him as she pinned her hair. "There is no wedding."

"Indeed?"

"If you think I plan to marry a man who is still in love with another woman, you are mad!"

"So you have no issue having a child out of wedlock?" he asked.

She blinked as the reality of the situation finally seemed to hit her. "A child?" she whispered.

"Yes. That is how they are made."

"I know that," she cried. "But we most certainly did not make a child just then."

Will understood her denial. "We won't know for sure until—"

"A few days," she cut him off. "We will know in a few days. I'm never late."

"Very well, then. You will give me your answer within the week."

"All right. But I will not marry you unless there is a

child." Elizabeth pushed past him and walked down the hallway. She must have made some excuse to the children because she didn't even slow her pace as she passed them in the front hall.

"Will!"

The excited sound of the children made him smile. After spending the last two years taking care of them, he would have thought the idea of his own child less appealing. And yet, it warmed his heart to think about holding his little son or daughter. He had always thought it would be he and Abigail in a small farmhouse in Virginia.

But if Elizabeth agreed to marry him or truly was pregnant, all his dreams of leaving England would be for naught. She would never leave here, and he could not ask her to go with him.

"Will, were you and Elizabeth arguing?" Ellie walked up to him with a scowl on her face.

"No," he answered.

"She certainly didn't seem happy when she just ran up to her room."

"We just finished our lesson on family history. That is all. Perhaps something upset her. If so, she didn't tell me about it." Will walked toward his study. "Now, I have work to do."

He had nothing to do but wanted to be finished talking to his sister about Elizabeth. Sitting behind the desk, he looked at the picture of the former duke. Imposing seemed the best word to describe him. He must have been furious to discover his wife had been with someone else.

Will knew he would never stand for a wife like that. Although, if the late duchess had been anything like

Elizabeth, she must have been in love with the man. He was certain Elizabeth was in love with him. He'd seen it in her eyes. And no matter what she said, she wasn't the type of woman to be with a man without love being involved.

At the same time, he understood her reason for rejecting his proposal. Did he still love Abigail? The more he pondered the question, the firmer his resolve. Five years ago, he had loved her. Even two years ago. But after she rebuffed his last proposal, his love for her started to die.

The passage over to England had given him plenty of time to think about their relationship. Against his father's wishes, Will had offered to become an American for her after the war ended. Doing so would have relinquished his ties to England and the title. She had told him she couldn't be responsible for him giving up something so noble.

Another excuse, he thought. She had been full of excuses for the past five years. And while maybe he didn't love Elizabeth, he might come to love her.

A fact that Elizabeth might not accept. She struck him as the type of woman who would never marry a man who didn't love her.

"What the hell am I supposed to do?"

"Not quite sure. Maybe if I knew the problem I could assist you."

Will turned his head toward the door where Somerton stood leaning against the frame. "Afternoon, Somerton. Did the footman forget to announce you?"

"He was busy cleaning up a mess the puppy left in the hall."

Will's mouth gaped. "What puppy?"

Somerton smirked. "The one I brought for the boys."

"What the hell is wrong with you? A dog is the last thing I need."

Somerton entered the room and sank into a chair. "I just assumed the children might need something to take their mind off Lady Elizabeth's departure."

"Elizabeth is not leaving."

"Indeed," Somerton said with his smirk turning into a grin. "You figured out a way to make her stay, then?"

"I apologized." And then possibly got her with child, he thought.

"And yet, you don't look pleased." Somerton walked over to the bottle of whisky and poured two glasses. He handed one to Will and sat back down.

"Why are you here again?"

"The puppy." Somerton seemed to be enjoying this far too much.

"And you can take it with you when you leave," Will replied.

"Lord Somerton."

Will turned and looked at Elizabeth. His breath left him, seeing her with the children surrounding her and Michael holding a small black-and-white puppy.

"Good afternoon, Lady Elizabeth." Somerton rose and bowed to them.

"The children have something they would like to say." She nudged Ethan, who nudged Michael and Robert.

"Thank you," they chorused.

"You are welcome, children." Somerton returned to his seat.

The children ran out of the room and the puppy started to bark. Elizabeth stayed behind.

"That was a generous gesture, my lord," she said softly.

He watched as Somerton eyed Elizabeth carefully. A sensation akin to jealousy streaked through Will. From everything he had heard and seen, Somerton was a disreputable rake. Not that Will was any better making love to her on a sofa.

"Lady Elizabeth, is that a new gown?" Somerton asked.

"No, my lord."

Somerton rubbed his chin. "Are you certain? You look different today." He quickly added, "In a very good way."

Elizabeth's eyes widened and moved to Will. "Thank you, my lord. I shall leave you both in peace."

Somerton grinned. "Never understood why she remains a spinster."

This time, Will had no doubt about the emotion swirling through him. "Perhaps she never found the right man."

Somerton tilted his head. "Any decent man can make a woman fall in love with him. It just takes a little courting." He drained his whisky glass and stood. "Good day, Kendal. Enjoy the puppy."

Will rolled his eyes. "Good day, Somerton."

"And I have decided to attend the countess's party tomorrow night. It's been a while since I danced with a lovely woman."

Did he mean Elizabeth? The sneaky bastard left so quickly Will didn't have time to question him.

Elizabeth waited patiently as her maid put the final touches on her coiffure. Susan had placed small violets throughout her hair to match the tones of Elizabeth's silk dress. As she sat in front of the mirror, her thoughts returned to Will. She had been avoiding him since yesterday's colossal mistake.

But she reasoned every woman was allowed one rather large error in her life. Will was hers.

What was wrong with her? Letting him make love to her in the music room in broad daylight!

She could have stopped him but she hadn't. Nor had she wanted to stop him. In her heart, she knew she had been the aggressor, not him. She had kissed him, untied his cravat, and rubbed herself against him like a common trollop.

Yet, all day she'd wondered if the only reason she acquiesced was to make him stay in England. Could she really have been manipulating him? She clenched her hands into tight fists. That would make her a terrible person.

No other reason came to mind. She didn't love him. His company was pleasant enough but what she felt wasn't love. While he did seem to make her heart beat faster, lust was the answer. Her mother had warned her about that emotion.

Sometimes she wondered if lust was what had led her mother to her affair. Elizabeth hoped that it was love. She didn't want to believe her mother would do such a thing just for passion.

Although, that was exactly what Elizabeth had done. Unless she really had thought making love with him would make him stay in England. She did not know which was worse, lust or manipulation.

"The violets are perfect!" Susan said as she stepped away.

Elizabeth looked in the mirror and agreed. "You do

know how to make me look my best." She turned to her maid and smiled. "Thank you."

Susan bobbed a quick curtsy. "Enjoy your night, Lady Elizabeth."

And Elizabeth decided she would enjoy tonight. Since the duke's death, she had only attended a few balls. She missed the excitement of a party, the sense that something wonderful might happen.

She walked to the stairs and stopped. Looking down, she saw Will and her breath caught. He wore the dark brown jacket she'd secretly told his valet to suggest. The color looked magnificent on him and highlighted his hair.

As she walked down the steps, she gripped the rail tightly, hoping she could manage the stairs while staring at him. At the sound of her footfalls, he turned.

His full lips slowly lifted upward into an appreciative smile. He held out his hand to her as she reached the bottom tread.

"Good evening, Elizabeth."

"Good evening, Will," her voice sounded breathy to her ears.

Without a doubt, the most talked about man at the ball would be Will. As he held his arm for her, she realized she hadn't completed certain aspects of his lessons. They must discuss this now.

"Will," she started as she entered the carriage.

"Yes, darling."

"Do not call me that again," she snapped. "We must talk about a few things before we arrive."

Will sat back against the squab and sighed. "Now what?"

"First, I, along with everyone else at the ball, will

call you Kendal or Your Grace. Do not for any reason allow someone to call you Will. I am to be referred to as Lady Elizabeth."

"Yes, dear."

She could just make out the humor in his voice. The dratted man was taunting her. "On to the dances," she said and paused. "You must dance."

"Of course, sweetheart."

"Stop that!" She breathed in the scent of his tangy soap and sighed. "You must not dance more than twice with any lady."

"Why not?"

"It shows you favor that lady. She will get ideas, and so will her mother. You are a young unmarried duke. Everyone will want you to dance with their daughters."

He folded his arms across his chest. "And if I don't wish to dance with them?"

"You really should with a few. But don't leave the ballroom with any of them." Dreadful thoughts of young ladies attempting to compromise themselves with him crossed her mind. "Some of the ladies will try to get you into a position where you both will be seen in an unsavory light."

"Why exactly would I want to be alone with any of these women?"

Her mouth opened then shut. She looked over at him and saw the slight grin on his face. "You might have urges," she said.

"I might at that." His smile widened and he leaned forward. "Then again, I would much prefer another *talk* in the music room."

Elizabeth stiffened. "That will not happen again."

"Oh, I don't believe that."

They rolled to a stop, effectively halting their conversation before she could give him a good set-down. He jumped down and held out his hand to her. She took his hand and walked toward the door with him.

She hoped she hadn't forgotten to warn him about anything. Mentally she ticked off the items: titles, determined mamas, determined young ladies, number of dances, and . . . ? There was something else.

The widows! They were the worst of the lot. She paused in her step, making him stop.

"Yes?"

"The widows," she said.

"Excuse me?" Will asked, looking down at her as if she'd lost her mind.

"They will proposition you just so they can say they slept with you," she whispered.

"Indeed?" he replied with a slow grin lifting his lips. "I might enjoy this ball after all." He gave her a little tug and led her into the countess's home.

The liveried footmen held open the doors to them as they entered the hallway. A thrill of excitement shot through her as they walked toward the ballroom at the back of the house. The last ball she'd attended, she had ended up taking Jennette home due to an incident.

They skirted the dance floor, still arm in arm, and made their way to Lady Cantwell. The eccentric old woman sat in a purple velvet chair surrounded by her ancient friends.

"My dear friends, the new guard is approaching," Lady Cantwell announced with a cackle.

"'Bout time," replied Lady Shipley. "I'm getting tired of the social scene. Let the younger crowd have it."

"Hush, Roberta," Lady Cantwell reprimanded, and then glanced up at Will. "William Atherton, the Duke of Kendal."

Only the cantankerous Lady Cantwell could get away with calling the newest duke by his Christian name. Elizabeth watched the interplay between them with interest.

"Yes, my lady." Will took her outstretched hand and bowed over it.

Using her cane, she heaved herself out of the chair. With her petite stature, she craned her neck to look up at him. "I hear you spent time in the colonies."

Elizabeth cringed.

"I spent ten years in America when my father was there on a diplomatic mission, and then in Canada once the war started."

"Very good," she replied. "I would like to know more about the old colonies, so you will call on me in a week."

"As you wish, my lady," Will said with a quick bow.

"Now, Elizabeth, dear child." Lady Cantwell turned her attention. "I do hope you won't lose this one."

Elizabeth frowned. "I beg your pardon?"

"This one," Lady Cantwell said, tilting her head toward Will. "I expect to hear of an announcement soon."

Elizabeth's mouth gaped. "Lady Cantwell, His Grace is my cousin. There is nothing more than that."

Lady Cantwell laughed again. Taking Elizabeth's arm, she walked her away from the crowd. "My dear child, we all know that the duke is not your cousin."

"Wh-what do you mean?"

The woman's bony hand tightened on Elizabeth's

arm. "You know exactly what I mean. A father does not leave his youngest unmarried daughter with nothing."

"I have a dowry," she said defensively. Not much of a dowry, but it was something.

"When you want to speak truthfully about this, please call on me." Lady Cantwell left Elizabeth standing by a potted palm.

Elizabeth glanced up to see Will walking toward her. Oh, God, not now. She couldn't speak to him with her emotions in a knot. The last time she had tried, she ended up on a sofa in the music room with him.

She turned and stepped onto the dance floor in an attempt to lose herself in the crowd. Hopefully, she would find someone she knew to talk with before Will found her. If only Avis and Jennette had attended. Or better yet, Sophie.

Elizabeth could really use Sophie's advice. Not paying attention, she walked into the man in front of her.

"I am dreadfully sorry," she started as the man stopped and turned.

"I most certainly am not," Lord Somerton said. "And since you are so dreadfully sorry, I believe you must repay me with a dance."

"A dance?" she squeaked.

The crowd on the dance floor parted as the dancers took their position. She wanted to refuse his request. But glancing behind her she noticed Will coming upon them quickly.

Somerton held out his arm as his hazel eyes stared at her. "You don't seem like the type of woman who would refuse me due to my past transgressions. Are you?"

She had no time to make this decision. "Of course not, my lord. I would love to dance with you."

They moved together on the dance floor. Elizabeth felt as if everyone was staring at them, mostly her. Perhaps she should make conversation with him.

"I have not seen you at many balls, my lord."

"I normally detest them. But I am finding this one quite entertaining."

"Perhaps you are ready to turn over a new leaf. Put away your rakish ways."

Somerton smiled down at her in such a way, Elizabeth felt as if she were about to be devoured.

"I don't think so," he replied.

Chapter 13

Will halted his stride as he watched Elizabeth take Somerton's arm and start a waltz. He clenched his fists as Somerton held her close and looked down at her as if she were a treat. Will would have to kill him. Jealousy raged in him as the couple danced.

A man near him chuckled softly. "Good God, Somerton, what are you up to now?"

Will turned to the man. "You know Lord Somerton?"

"Indeed I do."

"How well?"

"Only as well as Somerton will let anyone know him." The man finally turned to face him. "Do I know you?"

"William Atherton."

The man's blue eyes shone with surprise. "Your Grace," he said with a quick bow. "Banning Talbot, the Earl of Selby."

Did everyone have to bow down to him like he was a god? "Selby, then. What can you tell me about Somerton?"

"He is devious, a little mischievous, and quite a rake."

"Illegal activities?" Will asked as his gaze went back to the dancing couple.

"Rumored but highly unlikely. Although, he is a man who gets what he wants." Selby paused and smiled. "I am curious why he is dancing with Lady Elizabeth. I'm actually more curious why she is dancing with him."

"You know Lady Elizabeth?" Will asked.

"I married one of her dearest friends," Selby replied with a smile.

That was right. Will remembered Elizabeth speaking of her spinster friends. "One of the spinsters, then?"

"Ah, yes. The Spinster Club. There are only three left now. Elizabeth, Sophie, and Victoria. I rather doubt any of those ladies will end up married."

"Why is that?" Will couldn't contain his curiosity.

"Sophie is the bastard daughter of an earl, or so everyone says. Yet, no one seems to know who the man is. Not exactly what most men prefer. Victoria is too busy running her home for the orphans." Selby's gaze then locked onto Elizabeth and Somerton again.

"And Elizabeth?"

"You are the new duke—don't you know?" Selby asked softly without glancing away from the couple.

"Only a rumor, Selby."

"And one that has gained momentum with your arrival. It has been noticed by many that none of your sisters have red hair, either."

"I see," Will muttered. He could never let Elizabeth know that the rumors were increasing. "Tell me, Selby. Should I be concerned about Somerton dancing with her?"

"If he were dancing with *my* wife or sister, I would be more than a little worried," Selby said.

"Is your wife with you tonight?"

"No, Avis is with child and didn't feel she could manage a ball."

Finally, the dance ended and Somerton brought Elizabeth back to him.

"Thank you for the dance, Lady Elizabeth," Somerton said with a wink to Elizabeth. "Selby, good to see you."

"And you, Somerton."

"Lord Selby, did Avis decide to accompany you?" Elizabeth asked in a hopeful tone.

"No, she and Jennette stayed home but I needed to speak with someone here tonight." Selby looked over at Will and then back to Elizabeth. "Did Nicholas arrive home yet?"

"No. You know how he is about coming to town when his father is here," Elizabeth replied.

Will's eyebrows furrowed. Who the hell was Nicholas? The name sounded vaguely familiar but he couldn't remember why. "Nicholas?"

"My cousin. The Marquess of Ancroft."

Of course. He had to get his jealousy under control.

"Selby, now that you are here, you may have the honor of introducing the duke to all the acceptable people," Somerton said. "We all know that is not my forte."

Selby and Elizabeth both laughed.

"No, we all know your specialty," Selby commented. "I'm surprised Lady Cantwell allowed you in. Then again, she does love to stir the pot."

Will felt as if they were speaking another language. What was Somerton's specialty? Will had never felt so out of place as much as he did here. He knew no one. And yet, everyone else seemed to know each other.

"Come along, Kendal," Selby said, inclining his head toward the refreshments. "It is time for you to be part of the *ton*."

Selby moved them through the crowd with a nod to several people along the way. They passed the refreshment table but Will managed to grab a glass of wine from a footman before they entered the next room. Several tables had been set up for cards and other games.

As they walked in, most men stopped talking and leveled curious stares at them. Selby made the introduction to some of the most powerful men in England. It suddenly dawned on Will that many would consider him a powerful man in this country.

"I haven't seen you at Parliament yet," the Earl of Wexford commented. "I do hope you make it soon. We have many issues that could use a new voice."

Parliament? He could attend? He'd become so used to America where only the elected officials had anything to do with government.

"I am settled in now so I shall be taking my place in Parliament soon," Will said to the earl.

"Excellent," Wexford replied before continuing with his game of cards.

Selby led him back out to the ballroom. "You don't have any idea what is involved in being a duke, do you?"

"No," Will admitted.

Selby reached into his jacket pocket and then handed him a card. "Call on me tomorrow and I will help you out."

"Thank you, Selby."

Selby nodded. "Unfortunately, we are now onto the moment you shall hate."

"Oh?"

"It is time to meet the women."

"And I will hate this?" Will asked.

"Trust me. You will despise them. They all have one thing on their mind: marriage."

"I see."

As Selby introduced him to several of the ladies, Will slyly scanned the room for Elizabeth. He finally found her on the dance floor again. Only this time, it was with a tall dark-haired man Will didn't know. Elizabeth's face lit with excitement as they danced across the floor.

Who the hell was she dancing with now?

Selby continued to walk with him and introduce him to more ladies. Will made a few requests for dances but his concentration remained on Elizabeth. When the dance finished, she and her partner headed for the terrace doors.

His heart sank to his stomach. But anger quickly swept over him. After making his excuses, he strode toward the terrace. The cool night air did nothing to diminish his fury.

Elizabeth stood near a rosebush whose buds were about to burst open. The man remained next to her, standing too close, and they appeared far too intimate.

With jealousy eating at him, he walked up to Elizabeth and said, "I believe this is our dance."

He clasped her arm and tugged her toward him.

"Elizabeth?" the man questioned.

"It is all right," she replied with a shake of her red hair.

As they advanced on the ballroom, she withdrew from his grip. "How dare you?"

"Excuse me?" Will grabbed her arm and led her onto the floor. "I find you out on a darkly lit terrace with a man and you are asking me how I dare?"

"The man happens to be my cousin Nicholas. He decided to surprise me by attending. I was telling him about you." She yanked her arm out of his hold and headed for the terrace again.

"Elizabeth, wait," he called out to her but she had disappeared. Several people openly stared at him.

Will blew out a strangled breath and walked to the door. When he opened the door, Nicholas stood there waiting for him.

"Who the bloody hell are you to make a fool out of my cousin?" Nicholas demanded.

"Also, her cousin," Will replied. Although, if Elizabeth was correct, only Nicholas was truly her cousin.

"The prodigal duke has returned," he sneered.

"Yes, I have. And now I must apologize to Elizabeth. I had no idea you were her cousin."

"She is walking along the path," Nicholas said.

"Thank you."

Nicholas narrowed his eyes. "Do not hurt her again."

Will accepted the warning without another word and walked away. The gravel crunched under his feet, alerting anyone who might be outside to his presence. The path twisted and turned but Elizabeth seemed to have disappeared. He stopped to listen.

A small sniffle sounded from around the next bend. The noise from his shoes warned her of his approach.

"Go away, Nicholas. I don't want to talk."

He turned the corner and halted. The dappled moonlight highlighted her position on a bench. He'd never seen anyone look so forlorn and yet so absolutely beautiful in all his life. The violet silk dress shimmered in the soft light.

"It's not Nicholas."

Elizabeth turned her head at the sound of Will's raspy voice. She wiped away a tear.

"Do you honestly think I want to talk to you?"

He stepped closer. "I would think not."

"Exactly. So please leave me alone."

"I cannot," he whispered so softly she was not certain she heard him.

"Will, you embarrassed me in front of Nicholas and half the *ton*. Why?"

"I have no idea," he admitted, taking another step closer. "I was furious watching you go outside alone with him."

"He is my cousin. I love him dearly, but he is like a brother to me." Elizabeth stared down at the violets embroidered on her dress.

"I am sorry."

Elizabeth looked up to find him directly in front of her. His masculine presence made her feel dainty and insignificant. And she didn't want to be that any more. She stood and faced him. She was tired of not knowing where he stood on a certain issue. While confronting him could cause even more problems for her, she knew she had no choice.

"If you knew I wasn't carrying your child and Abigail arrived in England, would you marry her?"

Will's eyes narrowed. "What kind of question is that?"

"A fair one, I think," she retorted, placing her hands on her hips. "And one that deserves an answer."

"This has nothing to do with Abigail."

"Oh? We would never have made love if Abigail hadn't sent you that note," she whispered harshly.

"How can you be so certain?" He pulled her against him as if to prove a point.

"Because you are not a rake. And you would never hurt the woman you love." Elizabeth blinked to keep her tears from overflowing. She wished he had given her an immediate rejection of the idea that Abigail's presence would make a difference. But he hadn't.

She wondered at the pain hammering her heart. Was it just self-pity?

"Elizabeth," he whispered.

Don't look in his eyes, she told herself. Instead, she kept her vision strictly on his snowy cravat. "You know it's true, Will. What we did was a . . . a . . ."

"Don't say mistake. Because it was not that." He tipped up her chin, forcing her to meet his soulful brown eyes.

"It was an accident. Neither of us was ready for the passion."

"I think you're wrong," he whispered.

Elizabeth frowned as her stomach pitched. "I cannot do this, Will. You still love her and I have my answer. You would go with her."

She pushed away from him and started to walk the path to the house.

"You might be wrong, Elizabeth."

She paused in her stride but refused to look back at him. "But I might be right."

* * *

Will sat on the bench and stared down at the small stones. Why didn't he just give her the answer she wanted to hear? He picked up a rock and pitched it toward the stone fence. If Abigail showed up tomorrow, what would he do?

He laughed at the idea of little Abigail doing such a thing. But seriously, would he marry her? If Elizabeth wasn't with child, could he still marry Abigail?

"No," he whispered.

He'd had enough of Abigail's games and manipulations. She had toyed with him for years. First telling him she had to wait until she was eighteen, then the war was the problem. After the war, she had told him that her father would never agree. But as far as Will knew, she never broached the subject with her father. And she'd never let Will talk to him about it, either.

Why did he let this go on for so long? He had wasted five years of his life waiting for something that would never happen.

Now he had the chance to turn his life around. He could be a member of Parliament and maybe make a difference in this country. That was something he might have only dreamed about in America. Here he was an important man. While maybe his importance was due to circumstantial reasons, he could still use the opportunity as a means to make a difference for people who didn't have a voice.

Slowly, he stood and made his way back to the ballroom. As he stood on the edge of the dance floor, he once again searched for Elizabeth. This time, he found her speaking with Lady Cantwell.

Elizabeth looked flustered by the older woman's conversation. He decided she definitely needed saving.

"Elizabeth, have you forgotten about our dance?"
he asked as he reached their position.

"Yes, Your Grace." Elizabeth turned to him with a
look of gratitude in her green eyes. "I must apologize
again for stranding you on the dance floor earlier. I
felt faint."

The other ladies surrounding them all murmured
about the stale air.

When Elizabeth put her gloved hand in his, a familiar yearning crept up his arm to his chest. It felt exciting and comforting at the same time. They reached
the dance floor just before the next waltz started.

"I'm sorry," he whispered. "I would never hurt you."

"I know that." She looked away from him. "Have
you danced with any other women?"

He shook his head.

"You must do that immediately after our dance.
Otherwise people will talk."

"What if I don't care if they do talk?" He tightened
his grip on her hand. "What if I want to dance with
you all night?" he whispered near her ear. He felt her
tremble slightly and smiled.

"I will not allow it," she said and pulled away.

"I wasn't asking for permission."

She blinked and visibly swallowed. He knew she felt
the attraction between them.

"You will not ruin my reputation or that of any
other women at this party," she replied stiffly.

"But I only want to ruin you . . . again," he whispered.

"I already told you that would never happen again,
so please stop referring to the day in the music room."

"If only I could."

Her eyes flashed a warning at him. "You had best not even think of it."

"But I cannot stop thinking about it." He pulled her closer again just to feel her quiver. "Can you?"

Chapter 14

Two days after Lady Cantwell's ball, Elizabeth had the answer she'd been waiting for. While she should rush and tell Will that she wasn't with child, she decided to avoid him for one more day. After his lewd banter at the ball, she had no desire to see him again.

If only that were true.

She did want to see him. And she wanted to see him naked and lying in bed. There was something dreadfully wrong with her. Never in her life had she felt this way about a man. Now it was all she could think of, and at all times of the day and night.

Unfortunately, avoiding him the past two days had only made the yearning worse. At least for the next few days, she wouldn't be able to act upon those lustful feelings. But she supposed she should stop ignoring him.

A light knock sounded on her bedroom door. "Yes?"

"Miss Seaton is here to see you, miss. Shall I tell her you are not at home?" her maid asked, peeking through the doorway.

"I shall be down presently."

"I will show her to the small salon, then."

"Thank you, Susan."

Elizabeth wondered what might bring Victoria around this afternoon. Having not seen her friend since their outing to Whitechapel, this would give her the opportunity to question Victoria. Elizabeth doubted it could have been her friend in such a crime-ridden section of town.

After a quick check in the mirror, Elizabeth walked down the stairs, still looking to avoid Will. Thankfully, he didn't seem to be about today.

As she reached the front hall, she stopped and asked Kenneth, "Where is His Grace?"

"Out, my lady."

"Out? With whom?" she asked.

"Lord Selby," Kenneth replied.

Well, at least Avis's husband was a huge step up from that wastrel Somerton. Elizabeth continued into the small salon where Victoria sat staring at a painting Jennette had done a few years ago.

"Victoria," Elizabeth said before sitting down on the brocade sofa. "What brings you here today?"

Victoria smiled and pushed a strand of blond hair out of her face. "I wanted to make sure Mrs. Weston was working out for little Sarah."

"Mrs. Weston is wonderful. She has been working with Sarah to teach her to read. Sarah loves her."

"Oh, thank God," Victoria mumbled and quickly covered her mouth.

"Why do you say that?"

Victoria slowly removed her hand from her mouth. "I have never made a recommendation for a friend. I was worried that Mrs. Weston would not work out with Sarah."

"She is perfect." Elizabeth wondered why Victoria

seemed so relieved. It was just a governess. Elizabeth remembered having three different ones when she was a child.

"Victoria, you will not believe this but the duke insisted on an outing to Whitechapel with the older girls the other day."

Victoria's brows furrowed. "Why would he insist on taking them there?"

"To show them the poverty of London, and how dreadfully we treat our poor. But as we drove past a pawnbroker's shop, a woman walked out of the store. She looked exactly like you."

Victoria's face paled slightly, but then she said, "How odd. You must have been mistaken since I never go to that section of town."

"I figured as much. I just thought it fascinating that there is another woman who looks so much like you."

"Perhaps she is my long-lost twin," Victoria said with a laugh.

If her laugh hadn't sounded so forced, Elizabeth might have believed her. It could not possibly have been Victoria. But Elizabeth hadn't convinced herself of that yet.

"How are the plans for the ball?" Victoria asked, effectively changing the subject.

"Good, but I'm getting nervous." Elizabeth waited while a footman brought in tea for them. She poured a cup for them and handed one to Victoria.

"The ball?" Victoria reminded her.

"Yes, of course." Elizabeth added some cream to her tea. "I have never planned a ball by myself."

"You will do wonderfully."

"Will you come? Please?" Elizabeth already knew

the answer but hoped that for once her friend would disregard Society.

"You know I cannot. I am not one of you," Victoria answered with a nonchalant shrug.

"You are the daughter of a vicar. Surely, there must be a lord in your background somewhere? That is all these people care about."

Victoria smiled and shook her head. "No lords that I am aware of."

"Come anyway?"

"I cannot. But I want you to tell me all about it next week."

Elizabeth closed her eyes. "Please do not remind me that it's only six days away."

"If you need my help, please, just let me know."

"Thank you, dear friend." Elizabeth wanted desperately to tell someone what she'd done with Will. The secret was driving her mad. But of all her friends, Victoria was the last one she could mention an indiscretion to without getting a long lecture on the sin of sexual congress before marriage.

This was one secret she had to keep to herself.

Will opened the door before the butler could reach it. He hadn't felt this invigorated in months, maybe even years. For the first time, his life had direction. He knew what he was going to do now.

After taking the steps two at a time, he opened the door to his room. His valet walked in behind him.

"Good evening, Your Grace."

"Good evening, Stevenson." Will removed his own jacket while his valet opened the linen press. "Is there an engagement tonight?"

"The opera, Your Grace."

"Of course. We are to dine here, though, correct?"

"Yes, Your Grace."

"Very well, then. I leave my attire in your fine hands."
Will washed up at the basin while Stevenson picked out
the perfect jacket for dinner and then the opera.

Twenty minutes later, he was dressed and ready to
eat. He entered the salon to find Elizabeth and his
siblings waiting for him. Stopping at the threshold,
he was once again amazed by the transformation of
the children. The boys, while fidgeting, were well
dressed and relatively quiet. Sarah, dressed in a pretty
pink dress, sat on the wingback chair with a smile on
her face.

"Where have you been?" Elizabeth asked, approaching him with a glass of sherry.

"I attended Parliament with Lord Selby." Will took
the outstretched glass and sipped it. The fruity essence
of the liquor teased his tongue.

Before he could take another sip, the footman
announced dinner.

"Are we still to attend the opera tonight?" he asked
Elizabeth as she walked past him.

"Yes, I think Ellie and Lucy will enjoy it."

"And tomorrow we work in my study."

She paused and then agreed. "Very well."

They rushed through dinner to get to the opera.
Ellie and Lucy could barely contain their excitement
during the carriage drive.

"Are you certain we look all right, Elizabeth?" Ellie
asked, looking down at her saffron dress. "I've never
worn anything as exquisite as this gown."

"You both look beautiful. I expect many gentlemen
will stop by our box during intermission."

Will didn't like the sound of that. His sisters were too young for suitors.

As if she'd read his mind, Elizabeth said, "Don't worry, Will. They have not made their bow yet. Most of the gentlemen will respect that and only call after."

"Then perhaps we should postpone their bow," Will muttered.

"No, Will!" Ellie and Lucy said in unison.

Elizabeth laughed. "He will not cancel on the queen."

"I might," Will replied with a smile.

"No, you will not."

"If you say so," he said with a chuckle. The carriage stopped and they all clamored out. As they walked inside and to their box, Will heard the whispered murmurings of their arrival.

They took their seats and he couldn't help but notice the people covertly pointing to their box. He sensed the eyes of several women both young and old on him as he shifted uncomfortably in his seat. Never in his life had he felt this out of place.

"Do sit still, Your Grace," Elizabeth said sharply. "Everyone is staring."

"At me."

"Of course. You are the duke. Your position demands respect and admiration." Elizabeth smiled at him. "And there is that fact that you are an unmarried duke."

"Maybe I should alter that state quickly," he replied with a meaningful glance at her.

"Perhaps you should decide if you are staying in this country or leaving," Elizabeth retorted.

"Leaving?" Lucy looked over at them. "You are not still thinking of leaving England, Will. What more could you want than this?"

He had no chance to reply as the musicians started

playing. Athough, it gave him more time to think. What else could he want? Until a week ago, he would have said America has everything he could ever want. But America didn't have Elizabeth, and she would never leave England.

Should that matter? He had known her for just over a fortnight. That wasn't enough time to know her or to love her. If he left, she would stay behind. And while that should not bother him, for some reason it did. He liked her companionship, even when she became waspish when he did something wrong.

He slid a glance over at her. She stared down at the stage, entranced by the performance. The opera did nothing for him. He found the music too shrill, and his mind continued to wander.

The emerald dress she'd worn tonight complemented her eyes. The lower cut bodice allowed him a perfect view of her rounded breasts, and he steeled himself against the sudden rush of desire. He wanted her again. Only this time, he wanted to strip off each piece of clothing and lay her nude body on his soft bed.

Far too quickly, intermission started and the door to their box opened as the footman announced their first guest.

"Lord Hampton, Your Grace."

A young man with jet-black hair and blue eyes bowed to them all. "Your Grace, it is an honor to finally meet you."

"Hampton, good to meet you." Will watched as the man blatantly stared at Lucy. "This is my cousin, Lady Elizabeth," he said, looking over at Elizabeth. "And my sisters, Ellie—"

"Eleanor and Lucia," Elizabeth finished for him with a glare.

"You may call me Lucy," Lucy said.

Elizabeth groaned softly. Her frustration at his sister's manners was clear.

"Lady Lucia, it is a pleasure," Hampton said, bowing over Lucy's hand. "And yours also, Lady Eleanor."

Ellie appeared rather put out by Hampton's obvious favoritism of Lucy. Within five minutes, Ellie had nothing to be envious of, as the entire box filled with young men vying for her attention, as well.

Will noticed Elizabeth's color and wondered why she looked so uncomfortable. He leaned over and asked her, "Are you well?"

"Yes, I am perfectly fine," she snapped.

Oh, yes, any woman who answered like that was fine, he thought sarcastically. "Why are you uncomfortable?"

"I am not!" She stood and made her way through the crowd to the door.

Unable to leave his sisters alone with all the young bucks, he was forced to sit through another excruciating ten minutes without Elizabeth's company.

Elizabeth stood against the wall trying to catch her breath. Inside that box she'd felt as if she were suffocating. She was a fraud. Ever since her father's declaration that she wasn't his daughter, she considered herself a sham. Tonight, watching all the men pour into the box to visit with Ellie and Lucy, all those painful sensations had returned.

She wanted to be Lady Elizabeth in truth.

The only way for that to happen was to marry Will and become the duchess. She couldn't do that. If she had only wanted a title, there had been plenty of men during her first two Seasons who would have married her just to be associated with the duke's name. She wanted more than just a title. She wanted love.

She had watched Jennette's parents and had seen how much they loved each other, even with their huge difference in ages. That was Elizabeth's aspiration. She wanted love, and to forge a union that would last, with no infidelity.

She was certain a love like that existed. Perhaps just not for her. Her stomach roiled. Why not for her? Her friends seemed to have such a love. What was wrong with her that she could not have that too?

"Are you unwell, Elizabeth?"

Elizabeth looked up to see her cousin, Richard, staring down at her with concern on his face. "I am all right. The box filled with young men looking for an introduction to the duke's sisters. I needed a little air."

"Queasy, then?" Richard asked, looking even more worried.

"Only slightly. I am perfectly all right now and will return to the box."

Richard held out his arm for her. "Let me escort you back."

"Thank you, Richard." Perhaps now that Will was here, Richard had given up on his idea of being duke.

"You must take better care of yourself, Elizabeth. Have you thought about taking a husband?"

"A husband? You know I have a very small dowry, Richard. Who would want me?" Elizabeth hated how pathetic she sounded.

"There must be someone you might have an interest in," Richard continued.

Elizabeth felt heat scorch her cheeks. "No, there is no one."

* * *

Richard returned to his seat next to Caroline. He had a terrible feeling about Elizabeth.

"Well?" Caroline asked.

"We cannot discuss it here."

"Then we shall depart now," Caroline commanded.

"Of course."

They slipped out of their seats and waited impatiently for their carriage to be brought around. As soon as he sat down across from her, the interrogation began.

"What happened?"

"Elizabeth was standing outside the box against the wall with her hands on her stomach."

"Why?" Caroline asked.

"She said she needed air because of all the young men in the booth seeking an introduction to the duke's sisters."

Caroline tilted her head and then nodded. "Well, that makes sense. Those boxes are a bit confining."

"Yes," Richard drawled.

"But you don't believe her?" Caroline's brows drew downward forming a crease in her forehead.

"I cannot say why, but I think there is more going on here than she is admitting."

"You can't mean . . ."

Richard nodded. "She looked pale and had her hand on her stomach."

"It's impossible. He's only been here a fortnight." Caroline paused and bit her lip. "She wouldn't even know for certain by now."

"Maybe she doesn't know. Maybe she doesn't even suspect yet."

"We can't let this happen," Caroline said. "I think there is only one option."

Richard shook his head. He hated this idea more than any other idea she'd ever fabricated. "I think we should wait."

"Oh? Until she is fat with child and a ring already on her finger?" Caroline glared at him. "This has to end now."

"Caroline, this isn't right."

Caroline laughed in a shrill tone. "This isn't right? But allowing that upstart colonial to become duke is?"

"We both know that is out of our control."

"Out of our control?" she almost shrieked. "You and the duke's relatives were twins. For all we know, your relative could have been mistaken for the younger son and you could be the rightful heir."

Richard shook his head. She would never give up until she became duchess, or one of her children became duke. He doubted that she cared one bit for how he felt about any of this.

"Caroline, the twins were marked so there could be no mistake."

"Marked?"

"Scarred on their bottom. There could be no switching of their identities."

"It matters not. You still deserve to be duke," Caroline insisted.

Richard wanted to reach over and strangle his wife. But he couldn't. He knew he'd lost because no matter what he said, Caroline would do as she pleased. It had been that way for the past five years.

"Very well, Caroline. Do as you wish."

Chapter 15

The next morning Elizabeth pulled another book off the shelf in Will's study. She flipped through the pages, looking for anything that might lead her to a clue about her mother's diary. Will had yet to join her so she relished the peace. The children were attending to their studies, and it was the first time since Will had arrived that she had been in the study alone. Already, the room was starting to feel like his.

After placing the first book back, she reached for another. This was a volume of poetry by Byron. Remembering her mother's love of poetry, she turned each page carefully, expecting something to be there. Other than a small violet pressed into the center, the book contained nothing but poetry.

"How is the hunt going?"

Elizabeth turned at the sight of Will and sighed. The morning sun illuminated his brown hair with reddish highlights. The black jacket he wore spread across his broad shoulders. He looked too handsome. Oh, drat. She had to get herself under control.

"No luck so far," she replied in a voice lighter than she felt.

"Well, let me start over here." Will started at the other end of the cherry bookshelves. "What exactly are we looking for?"

"A diary. Or a piece of paper that might refer to where something is hidden. Or maybe some reference to a secret drawer or panel."

Will chuckled. "So we are looking for something but we don't know exactly what."

Hearing him say that made her realize just how unlikely it was that she would ever discover the truth of her heritage. She stared down at the book in her hands and wanted to throw the damned thing across the room.

Warm hands closed over her shoulders as Will's breath caressed her neck. "I am sorry. I know how much this means to you, and my remark was thoughtless."

"But true," she murmured. "There is a very good chance that I will never find out who I am."

"Who you are?"

"Yes."

"Elizabeth, you already know who you are."

Elizabeth gave into temptation and let her head rest on his strong shoulder. "I don't know what you mean."

He turned her and stared down at her with those dark brown eyes. She sighed. She could get lost in his eyes.

"Are you being coy, Elizabeth?"

"No. I have no idea who I am."

"You are a beautiful, headstrong woman. You hate your freckles and your hair only because you don't know where they came from. You love to pick and arrange flowers. You know your mathematics because the estates' books are in excellent condition."

"How do you know so much?" she asked. Her heart thumped loudly in her chest. How had he come to know her so well so fast?

"Because I've been watching you." He gently caressed her cheek. "You enjoy having the children around. You might possibly be about the best organizer I have ever met. Within a week my brothers were dressed and ready for dinner with better table manners than my stepmother could give them."

She closed her eyes. Everything he said was true but it didn't ease the ache in her heart. "Thank you, Will."

"But it didn't help, did it?"

"A little," she whispered with a shrug.

"Then I suggest we search through this bookshelf with all due haste."

Elizabeth shook off the pain she felt, opened her eyes, and found him still staring down at her. "I shall keep searching on this side."

"And I will take this side," he said, pointing to the far wall.

Will walked over to the shelf and removed another book. "Why didn't you tell me about Parliament?"

Elizabeth looked over at him, confused by his question. "What do you mean?"

"You never told me that as a duke I had the right to sit in the House of Lords."

"It never really crossed my mind. Besides, you were so intent on leaving England I didn't think you would have an interest."

"I find the political process fascinating. Even in England." He replaced the book and reached for the next one.

"Have you decided to stay?" she whispered.

"Is there a pressing reason I should?"

"I am not sure." The words popped out of her mouth before she realized what she'd said. She should have just told him that she was certain there was no baby. But she could not. At least if he didn't know then he might stay long enough to understand what a wonderful country England truly was.

"I see," he finally answered.

She glanced over and saw the frustration on his face. All she wanted to do was change the subject as quickly as she could. "I believe Lucy and Ellie are ready for their bow, don't you?"

"As you have been the one working with them, I defer to you on that."

Hearing his stiff tone, she went silent, hoping the floor would swallow her. She wanted him to stay so much it hurt. She knew she should tell him the truth. Once he learned she wasn't with child, he would be free to leave.

For the next few days, Elizabeth and Will scoured the study and the children's rooms. The only room left was Will's bedroom, but that would have to wait until after the ball. Elizabeth knocked on the door to Lucy and Ellie's room, eager to see if they were ready for their presentation at court.

"Come in," Ellie said.

Elizabeth opened the door and put her hand over her mouth.

"Oh, no!" Lucy exclaimed. "Please don't tell me we look dreadful."

"No," Elizabeth replied. "You both look beautiful."

"Are you certain, Elizabeth?" Ellie's blue eyes

shimmered with fearful tears. "These dresses are so old-fashioned."

"It is what the queen prefers. You both will be wonderful." Elizabeth clasped Ellie's hands.

"I am terrified," Ellie admitted.

"You will do fine." Elizabeth turned and looked at Lucy. The younger woman seemed far more confident than her older sister. "Are you all right, Lucy?"

"Yes. I am quite excited to get this over with, though. I want to dance at the ball with a handsome man."

"Very well, then." Elizabeth moved toward the door. "It is time to meet the queen."

"Oh, God, I think I'm going to be sick," Ellie whispered.

"No, you will not," Lucy retorted. "You are not going to ruin this."

"Ladies, drape your trains over your left arm like this." Elizabeth showed them with her own gown.

"Elizabeth, these hoops are horrendous. How do you sit in them?" Lucy whined.

"You only sit during the carriage ride. Once we enter the queen's drawing room, you will not sit until we are finished. When we return you should immediately change into your ball gowns." Elizabeth opened the door and walked to the steps. She glanced down to see Will pacing in the hallway. "Are you ready to see your sisters?"

"Yes," he answered, staring up at her. A slow smile crossed his face. "You look . . ."

"Thank you."

Elizabeth waited at the top of the steps while Ellie and then Lucy walked down the stairs. The entire time, Elizabeth prayed neither woman would trip and fall down the steps. As Lucy reached the bottom riser, Elizabeth started her descent.

She hated court dress but she would never tell Ellie or Lucy that. A nervous energy filled Elizabeth as Will held out his arm for her. She was not certain if it was his touch or just the presentation creating this disturbance.

They arrived at St. James Palace a few minutes later after a quiet carriage ride. After walking into the long Gallery, they waited. Elizabeth attempted to ignore the pain in her back by watching Will. He barely moved during the two-hour wait.

Finally, Ellie was called for and Elizabeth's stomach knotted. "Don't forget," she whispered to Ellie as she straightened the feathers in her hair, "you must walk out backwards. Never turn your back to the queen."

Ellie's eyes watered as she walked into the Presence Chamber. Just after Ellie left, it was time for Lucy to go.

"I know, Elizabeth. Don't turn my back on the queen," she said with a smile.

Elizabeth had no idea how Lucy could be so calm about this. At her own presentation, Elizabeth had felt much more like Ellie. But Elizabeth had had her mother to depend on for advice.

"They will do perfectly," Will said.

Within a matter of moments, it was over. Ellie returned to the Gallery with a look of shock upon her face.

"She kissed my forehead," Ellie said.

"You are the sister of a duke. As such, you are nearly royalty." Elizabeth watched as Lucy returned with almost the same expression on her face as Ellie had shown.

"I just met the Queen of England," Lucy whispered. "The queen."

Elizabeth smiled at Will, who appeared quite proud of his sisters.

"Thank you," he said as Ellie and Lucy clamored into the carriage. "They could never have managed this without you."

"You are welcome. But you might not want to thank me," Elizabeth said. "By giving them their come out and the ball, they may never wish to leave England."

Will stood at the threshold to the ballroom as the crowd grew larger. Elizabeth had informed him that most of the *ton* had accepted his invitation, but he hadn't realized just how many people that entailed.

He couldn't even remember half the names of the people he'd been introduced to this evening. There were dukes, earls, viscounts, and a rumor that the Prince Regent himself might make an appearance.

"Everything is perfect," Elizabeth said as she reached his position. "Ellie and Lucy did so well today."

"All thanks to you," he replied.

He could never have managed this without her. And tonight, she looked radiant in her pale green silk with an embroidered peacock at the hem. The neckline of her gown plunged dangerously low, displaying the fine curves of her breasts. While a part of him wanted to cover her so no one else could see, the lecherous part of him wanted to slide the sleeves down and let that dress fall to the floor.

"Do you think Ellie and Lucy are enjoying themselves?" she asked softly.

Will blinked and attempted to focus on the conversation, and not think about how he'd like to enjoy her tonight.

"Yes," he said absently.

"Your Grace, I believe you are woolgathering." Elizabeth glanced around the room. "It is time for you to dance."

"Is that an invitation?" The idea of her body being closer to his sent desire straight to his loins.

"Absolutely not. The first dance belongs to Ellie, and the second to Lucy."

Damn. "Then I expect you to save me a dance later."

"Perhaps," she answered coyly before walking away toward the small refreshment table in the corner.

He stood there for a moment watching the gentle sway of her hips, trying to get his desire under control. He had to stop thinking of her in such a manner.

Seeing Ellie surrounded by a group of young men, Will strode toward her. "I believe we should dance."

"Of course," Ellie said, but her gaze remained on one man in particular.

Will had no idea who the man was but would ask Elizabeth later. "Are you enjoying yourself?" he asked his sister.

"Yes. Now that my presentation is finished, I can relax and enjoy the party."

They lined up for a quadrille. The dance gave them very little time to talk so they both just enjoyed the moment. Will wondered if Elizabeth was correct that the girls might not wish to leave England. On the voyage here, he would have scoffed at the idea, but now, it was indeed a possibility.

As he made the intricate dance steps, his gaze went to the doorway. Richard and Caroline stood there silently scanning the room. Will had the oddest sensation of foreboding come over him. They were up to something, but what?

When Ellie's dance finished, he found Lucy and danced with her. With her darker looks, Lucy seemed to be attracting more attention than her sister.

"Lucy, please remember Ellie's sensitive nature when you speak of the men who danced with you tonight."

Lucy frowned at him. "I would never do anything to hurt Ellie. I know the men are flocking to me. But that is only because I am more outgoing than she is. Ellie has always been shy."

"Thank you for thinking of her."

As the dance ended, Will looked around for Elizabeth. He finally spied her in the corner by the entrance speaking with two women who were obviously with child. Selby and another man walked up to the group. And Will decided he would, too.

"Selby, good to see you here," he said once he arrived at the group's position.

"Your Grace, lovely party," Selby replied.

Both ladies bowed and mumbled, "Your Grace."

"Well, one of you must be Lady Selby," he said with a smile to put them at ease.

"Lord Kendal, this is my wife, Avis," Selby said.

The shorter woman with tawny brown hair smiled back at him. "It is a pleasure to meet you, Your Grace."

"I don't believe you have met Lord Blackburn," Selby said, looking toward the tall man next to him.

"Your Grace," Lord Blackburn said with a nod.

"Blackburn."

"May I introduce my wife, Jennette," Blackburn said, moving slightly so Will could bow over her hand.

"Lady Blackburn, it is a pleasure to meet another friend of Elizabeth's."

"Thank you, Your Grace." The woman had similar

coloring to her brother, Selby. The black hair and blue eyes looked even more striking on her.

"Perhaps we should leave the ladies to catch up on their gossip," Selby suggested.

Will agreed but looked back at Elizabeth with a yearning in his heart. He had wanted to dance with her. Now that would have to wait until later.

They walked to the gaming room where various tables had been set up for cards and other games of chance. He noticed Richard sitting at one of the tables—and losing from the looks of things. Richard nodded slightly at him.

"Selby," Will asked softly. "What do you know of my cousin Richard?"

Selby shrugged. "Not much. If you are looking for information on a person, Somerton is your best bet. He can find out things on anyone."

Blackburn muttered his agreement.

Will considered this for a moment. "I think I shall find him right now."

"If he is in attendance, he is most likely in this room," Blackburn stated.

"He's a gambler?" Will asked.

"A damned good one," Blackburn replied.

Will glanced around the room and found Somerton in a darkly lit corner playing cards. Unlike Richard, Somerton seemed to be winning a large amount of money. He looked up as Will came closer.

"Might I have a word?" Will asked.

"Of course, Your Grace."

Somerton tossed his cards into the pile in the middle of the table, collected his winnings, and stood. "Is there a problem?"

"Let's talk outside."

They walked to the doors that led to the small garden. Will found a private corner to talk.

"What do you know about my cousin Richard?"

"The Baron Humphrey?"

Will nodded.

"I have never had the need to learn anything about him," Somerton replied.

"I was told you are a man who can find out anything about another person."

Somerton laughed. "Who told you that? Selby?"

"Exactly." Will waited to see if Somerton would say more, but as usual, he did not. "Can you find out what the man is about?"

"What do you want to know?"

"Everything. His finances, his love life, anything of importance."

"Very well, Your Grace. I will see what I can find out about him."

"Quickly."

Somerton frowned. "Do you think there is a reason he would hurt you?"

The thought had briefly crossed his mind. Though he suspected Caroline pulled the strings. She might be the one to want him dead.

"I doubt it. But he was upset that I became duke over him."

"That is the way these things are done."

"Still, I don't trust him."

Chapter 16

Elizabeth looked around the ballroom and suddenly wished everyone would just leave. The pressures of the last few days had finally caught up with her, and all she wanted to do was retire to her room. Or better yet, Will's room. What was she thinking?

Ever since she spied him in his formal attire, she wanted nothing else but to strip each article of clothing off him one piece at a time. She closed her eyes and tried to remove the images of him standing naked in front of her.

"Elizabeth, are you all right?"

Please don't let that be Will, she pleaded to herself. Without opening her eyes, she knew it was him. Please don't let him be naked!

She slowly opened her eyes to find Will staring at her with his head cocked slightly.

"Elizabeth?"

"I am well, Will. Just a little tired." And suddenly, she wasn't tired any longer. His presence seemed to invigorate her.

"Shall we dance, or are you too weary?"

"I am not too tired for a dance." *With you,* she added silently.

She took his arm and tried to ignore the shock of desire that raced up her limb. This yearning was so wrong. She had tempted fate when she made love with him the first time. It was pure luck she was not with child. A second time would be asking for trouble.

As the waltz started, she told herself to pay attention to the music, not the man next to her. While she tried, her attempt failed miserably. She couldn't help but notice the aroma of his soap that had a hint of vanilla and cloves. His gloved hand burned through her own glove.

"You are very quiet tonight," Will said softly. "Is something on your mind?"

She couldn't tell him. "No, I am hoping everyone is having an enjoyable night."

"I'm quiet certain they are." Will stared down at her with a small smile. "Though I am slightly concerned about Ellie."

"Why?"

"I cannot discuss it here. Meet me in the study after the dance. We can talk in private there."

A private conversation with him. In his study. Alone. This was such a bad idea. "Very well," she answered.

For the rest of the dance, she tried to think about the music and not the fact that they were going to be alone in the study where she could kiss him, caress him, strip him of his clothes. When the waltz ended, she looked up at him and said, "We cannot go to the study together."

"Why ever not?"

"People will talk."

Will sighed. "Very well, you go ahead. I shall meet you there in a few minutes."

Elizabeth nodded and as she walked away, she made her excuses to her friends, telling them she was going to the ladies' retiring room. Once she reached the study, she poured herself a glass of sherry to calm her frayed nerves. As she drank it down, she realized what a mistake that was, since she'd eaten very little this evening. But as she finished her first glass, she poured another. A little dizziness couldn't be a bad thing.

After ten minutes, Will finally entered the room.

"Lock the door," Elizabeth said.

He raised one eyebrow at her and then did as she requested. "Exactly why am I locking the door, Elizabeth?"

"Not for what you think." *Or I want.* "Sometimes during parties, people will search out a place to be alone with another person. If anyone were to come upon us alone in the study, they might think the worst."

"And the worst would be . . . ?"

Elizabeth narrowed her eyes at him. "I think you know exactly what I am speaking of."

His smile turned positively lecherous. "I believe I do."

"Tell me why you are concerned about Ellie," she said to get them off the subject that had been on her mind all evening.

"She's only danced with three men. And one of them twice." Will sat in the chair nearest the fireplace. "I'm worried about her, Elizabeth."

"Ellie is not like Lucy. She's shy and quiet and prefers a smaller group of friends. Lucy will always have friends and men around her."

Will frowned. "I'm not sure I like the sound of that."

Elizabeth laughed and took the seat across from him. "Lucy is a very smart girl. She knows she's pretty but doesn't use her looks to gain attention. She lets her personality do that."

"And Ellie?"

"I think Ellie will be all right. As the Season continues, she will find some friends with whom she has a lot in common. They will help her through the next . . ."

She trailed, realizing that Ellie might not be here next year.

"Next what?"

"They will help her through for as long as Ellie is here." Elizabeth looked away from him to the empty fireplace. She didn't want to think about how lonely it would be here without him and his siblings.

"We should get back," she whispered.

Will nodded and stood at the same time Elizabeth did. With only a step between them, Elizabeth couldn't move. One step and she would be back in his arms where she yearned to be. One step and she could kiss him. One step and she might make the same mis—

Suddenly, he moved and brought her into his arms, kissing all thoughts of mistakes out of her head. She wrapped her arms around his neck, desperate to get closer to him. His tongue lashed across her lips, forcing her to open for him.

The velvety roughness of his tongue scraped across hers, sending warmth to her belly. She moved her hips against his, eager to feel his rising manhood. As she moved her hands to his cravat, he clasped her wrists to stop her.

Pulling back, she felt heat scorch her cheeks. How could she have thought he wanted her like this again? She was a foolish woman.

He brought his forehead against her. "You have no idea how much I want to continue this right now. But we cannot."

Oh, God, he was being the logical one. That was

supposed to be her responsibility . . . and one she had been quite remiss at lately.

"Of course not," she whispered.

"Elizabeth, if we didn't have a house full of people"—he paused and looked down at her—"you would be flat out on that sofa right now."

Her mouth gaped. She swallowed down the lump in her throat.

"We must get back to the ball."

Elizabeth blinked and understood. People might realize they were missing. "Yes. You go first. I'll wait here for a few more minutes. Go to the gaming room. Then people in the ballroom will see you leaving there and assume you were in there all along."

Will gave her a half smile. "You are quite decent at coming up with believable excuses for misbehavior."

"Just go," she said, pointing to the door.

After Will left, Elizabeth sat back down in the leather chair. The sound of a throat clearing forced her to look back at the door. Caroline stood in the threshold with a haughty smile on her face.

"You really should be more careful with your reputation, Elizabeth. It is the only thing you have to offer a husband," Caroline remarked and then turned to leave.

"Caroline, wait!"

Caroline stopped and turned back. "Yes?"

Elizabeth rushed to the door, pulled Caroline fully into the room, and closed the door. "Nothing happened, Caroline. You must believe me."

Caroline rolled her eyes. "Indeed, Elizabeth. You were alone with a man in a locked study for several minutes. Anything might have happened."

"Please. Do not tell a soul." Now she was pleading with the devil.

"I won't this time. But you must never let this happen again." Caroline turned on her heels and walked away.

Will closed the door to his bedroom and untied his cravat. Finally, as the first pink rays of dawn stretched forth, the party was officially over. While he should be exhausted and want for nothing more than his bed, he had other things on his mind. He couldn't forget the image of Elizabeth's face as he forced himself to push her away this evening.

After kicking off his shoes, he removed his jacket and tossed it on the chair. His valet had retired hours ago at Will's request. He stopped his movements and glanced at the door. Did he hear a soft footfall outside his room? Or was his mind playing tricks on him?

He strode to the door and flung it open only to find an empty hallway. Damn. The door across from his slowly opened, revealing Elizabeth in her ivory nightgown.

"Is everything all right?" she asked softly.

"I thought I heard something out here." Will watched as a pink flush tinged her cheeks. Either she had been outside his room or she was just embarrassed at being seen in her nightclothes. He didn't care. Seeing her standing with the dim candlelight behind her, he wanted her.

And he wanted her now.

Determined to be done with pretending they felt nothing toward each other, he shut his door and walked toward her. Her green eyes widened with each step he took.

"Will?"

"Step back into your room, Elizabeth."

She blinked and then moved into her room without a word.

Will walked inside, shut, and then locked the door. He turned toward her, praying she wouldn't turn him away. Unable to move, he stood with his back to the door, transfixed by her beauty.

She raced toward him and then kissed him soundly. "I didn't have the courage to come to your room," she said breathlessly. "I wanted to. I walked into the hall but I just couldn't—"

He cut her off with a searing kiss. Denying his feelings for her for the past week had been hell. As he kissed her, he moved them back toward the bed. He had to get some control before he tossed her on the bed and plunged right into her.

She slowly drew away from his kiss. Staring into his eyes, she whispered, "I want to remove your clothes. I want to see you."

So much for self-control tonight. "Yes," he answered, and then stood still waiting for her sensual fingers to touch him.

She started with the buttons on his shirt. As each one popped through the hole, his heart beat a little faster. She reached down to pull his shirt from his breeches. He clenched his fists as her hand innocently brushed the bulge in his trousers.

Closing his eyes, he lifted his arms for her to tug the shirt over his head. She gasped slightly. He opened his eyes to find her staring at his chest. Tentatively, she skimmed her soft hand down his shoulders, down his chest and his stomach, until she reached the first button on his breeches. She stilled her hand for a moment as if uncertain she should continue.

He gave her a smile for encouragement. She pressed

her lips together and released the first button. Quickly, all the buttons were undone and he tensed as she slipped his breeches down his legs.

"Oh, my," she mumbled.

He shook his breeches and undergarments off his ankles and took a step back. "Well?"

Her gaze burned through him, igniting a fire that needed dousing immediately. "I want to touch you," she whispered.

He grabbed her hand and placed it on his chest. "Then touch."

As he stood there praying for control, her hand slowly brushed across his nipples. He released a small groan. Encouraged, she slid her hand down until she reached his erection.

"May I?"

"God, yes," he answered, putting his hand over hers to show her how to touch him.

Her hand slowly stroked him until he knew he had to stop her.

"Elizabeth," he said softly against her ear. "You need to stop what you're doing."

She pulled back. "Am I doing something wrong?"

"No, darling, far too right." He placed his hands on her shoulders and pushed her night rail off until it landed at her feet.

Her rosy nipples were waiting for his mouth. He lifted her up and carefully placed her on the bed. She moaned as he brushed his tongue across one of her nipples. Feeling her hips move under his, he knew she wanted this as much as he did. He brought her nipple into his mouth and suckled until she squirmed under him.

"Will," she moaned.

He wanted to hear her moans, feel her writhe, and

taste every bit of her. Trailing hot kisses down her belly, he slid between her legs. She stiffened slightly before letting her legs fall apart to him.

Elizabeth almost jumped out of her skin as his mouth stroked her folds. When his tongue slid across her nub, she moaned. How could this man she barely knew touch her in such an intimate manner? And she didn't mean physically. Only a week ago, she told herself that she could not possibly love him. But now, she wasn't so certain.

His tongue continued its assault on her, sending her passion soaring. Gradually, the pressure built, the need increased, and she wanted him now.

"Will," she pleaded. "Please."

He chuckled softly against her told, "No, Elizabeth. I want to feel you come against my mouth."

And as he stroked her again, she did just that. She shook with pleasure, moaned his name, and still wanted more. He shifted his position and gave her exactly what she desired—him. Plunging into her, she gasped with the fullness of him.

"Are you still sore?" he asked.

"No," she groaned as he slid back out again.

"Elizabeth," he moaned.

She lifted her legs higher on his hips sending him deeper in to her recesses. Never had she felt something as incredible as being with Will. She wanted this to go on forever. But now she recognized the feeling of pressure building inside her. She closed her eyes and let passion take over.

Digging her fingernails into his back, she was overcome with the sensations. She let go and felt him tremble as his release washed over him. Slowly, he lowered his body down on hers. She felt his erratic breathing on her shoulder.

She knew then that she loved him, and the thought scared her to death. He wasn't staying here. How could she leave her country? Her friends? The life she had known forever? The words she had said to him replayed in her mind.

If she truly loved you, her father's wishes would not matter.

And if that were the truth, if Elizabeth loved Will, she should be willing to go wherever he needed to be. No matter how much she wanted to be, she wasn't a strong woman. Having been raised with servants to tend to her needs all her life, she had no idea how to perform tasks some would consider simple. She couldn't cook her own meals. Oh, God, she didn't even know how to light a fire.

She had given herself to a man who needed a woman that she could never be.

He slowly rolled off her and then brought her up against his chest. "You are very quiet," he murmured.

She only nodded, unable to tell him of her fears. She didn't even know how he felt about her. She might just be a mistress to him.

A throwaway woman.

"Elizabeth?"

"I'm all right," she lied. "Just a little tired." And completely overwhelmed.

She didn't want to give him up, but what options did she have?

Chapter 17

Will crawled back into his bed before the servants awoke. The last thing he needed was to be caught sleeping in the same bed as Elizabeth. And yet, the idea of always sleeping with her warmed his heart. He lay in bed staring at the coffered ceiling, wondering about his reaction to her.

He had never really been intimate with a lady of quality before because he knew the expectations. While he'd offered Elizabeth marriage after their first tryst, she'd rejected him. Of course, that was due to her believing he still loved Abigail, which he did not.

But he wondered if there could be another reason why she snubbed his offer.

Maybe she had feelings for another man. Somerton came to mind. She never seemed to mind his dances, even if she did call him a scoundrel. Perhaps that was the type of man she preferred, the rake, the scoundrel, the man who would never do the right thing. Some women craved the excitement of that kind of man.

He honestly didn't believe that of her. She was the one who had warned him about Somerton.

Elizabeth seemed like a softhearted woman who wanted to be around people who loved her. He wondered if he proposed properly what her answer would be this time. Perhaps that was just the thing to do.

The more time he spent with her, the more she was coming to mean to him. He loved her. And the idea seemed slightly mad to him. Only a few months ago, he would have been happy to marry Abigail. Now he was certain she would never have made him as content as Elizabeth.

Now, after only knowing her for a few weeks, he had never felt so sure of anything in his life. He loved her. He wanted to spend the rest of his life with her.

She was a complex woman and he would never get bored with her. There would always be something new to learn about her. And he wanted to be the one to uncover her secrets.

Knowing he would never get back to sleep, he decided on a morning ride to clear his head. When he returned he would sit down and speak with Elizabeth honestly. He would stay in England if that was what it took to get her to marry him.

Marriage.

He had always thought it would be with Abigail. But now, he had no desire for her. The only woman he wanted was Elizabeth. Together, they would make a formidable couple. He would advocate for the rights of the poor within the House of Lords, and she could assist him. She would teach him about the estates and help him understand the importance of being a duke.

This was right.

With his day planned in his head, he rose from his bed ready to face the day. By this evening, he would be betrothed to a wonderful woman whom he would spend the rest of his life loving.

By the time Elizabeth rolled out of bed, it was nearly one in the afternoon. The stiffness between her legs reminded her of why she was so tired. She knew he had left before the servants woke, but she had missed his warmth. She missed the sensation of sleeping with her head on his chest. Moving her head to the other pillow, she inhaled the masculine scent of his soap that remained.

She called her maid for a bath and then sat back down on the bed waiting as the tub filled. Her head tilted to the large bedpost. The footmen trudged into her room weighed down with large buckets of steaming water. She wondered again if she had the courage to do what Will might request. To move away required learning to carry buckets of water, learning how to cook a meal. Learning so much.

Exactly the same issue he had with coming to England. He'd had no idea how to be a duke. But she had expected him to learn everything and fit in just because he'd been born in this country. She had wronged him.

Growing up in America and Canada had taught him valuable lessons. He and his sisters had learned how to be independent, how to do things for themselves. And she had belittled the importance of that education.

She had a lot to apologize for today.

"The water is ready, my lady," Susan said, waiting for Elizabeth to stand up so she could undress her.

"Thank you, Susan. I would prefer to be alone."

Susan tilted her head and said, "You don't wish for me to assist you?"

"Not today."

"How will you dress?"

How would she? She didn't even own front lacing stays. Most of her gowns had tiny buttons down the back that she would never be able to reach. With a sigh, she replied, "Come back in thirty minutes and I shall be ready to dress."

"Yes, my lady."

Once Susan had departed, Elizabeth removed her gown and slipped into the water. The steaming liquid eased her sore muscles and the tension melted away. If he loved her, they could make this work.

If he loved her!

What if he didn't?

He had to, she thought. She loved every thing about him. The way his smile brightened his face and caused his eyes to crinkle. Or the fact that he wanted to do the best thing possible for his siblings, including his stepbrothers. She loved that he cared so deeply for the plight of the poor.

What would Sophie tell her to do? Perhaps she should find out. A quick call on her friend would help her make the right decision. Being a medium, perhaps Sophie would already know if he loved her.

After a quick bath, she dressed and left for Sophie's house. The short carriage ride was over too quickly. Now she had to figure out what to say to her.

The door opened and her butler smiled down at her. "Good afternoon, Lady Elizabeth."

"Good afternoon, Hendricks. Is she at home?"

He leaned in closer and said, "She is with Lady Cantwell presently but should be done in about five minutes. Would you prefer to wait?"

"Yes, please."

She followed Hendricks to the small salon and sat in the wingback chair. A footman brought in tea and Elizabeth poured herself a cup. She grabbed a biscuit, too, and ate her first meal of the day. Hearing voices, she brushed the crumbs off her skirts.

"Good afternoon, Lady Elizabeth."

Elizabeth rose and bowed to Lady Cantwell.

"That was an exceptional ball last evening. You would have made your mother proud."

"Thank you, ma'am."

Lady Cantwell departed and Sophie entered the room. "What brings you here today . . . luncheon?"

Sophie looked down at the plate, which had originally held three biscuits, but only one remained.

"I missed breakfast," Elizabeth admitted with a laugh.

"How was the ball?"

Elizabeth told her all about the party, anything to avoid talking about what she'd come for this afternoon. Finally, there was nothing left to say. "Sophie, I need to ask you a question."

"Of course." Sophie sat back against the cushions and stared at her as if she already knew what the question would be. Knowing Sophie's skills, she most likely did.

"It is about the duke."

"And?"

"And me," Elizabeth whispered. "I think I love him but I'm not certain of his feelings for me."

"I cannot determine his feelings, Elizabeth."

"Can you help me figure out what to do?"

Sophie nodded. "What is the absolute worst that can happen if you tell him you love him?"

Elizabeth thought on that for a moment. "That he didn't love me, and wanted to leave England forever."

"Can you live with that?" Sophie asked softly.

"Live with it how?"

"What if he loved you but could not stay here, would you go with him?" Sophie asked.

"I think I would," she replied slowly.

"Could you marry him if he didn't love you?" Sophie picked up her teacup and slowly sipped it.

"No," she answered with all certainty.

"Even if you're with child?"

Elizabeth should have known Sophie would guess that they had been intimate. "That is highly unlikely."

"Ah, but not impossible." Sophie smiled at her.

"No, not impossible."

"I knew you two would succumb."

"Succumb?"

"To desire," Sophie insisted. "It was apparent how you felt about him almost from the beginning."

"Do you think he knows?" Elizabeth bit down on her lower lip, worrying about the answer.

"Most likely not."

"What should I do, Sophie? If I tell him how I feel and he doesn't return the feelings, he may leave."

"Or he might tell you how much he loves you." Sophie picked up the remaining biscuit. "Either way, you won't know if you don't tell him."

"Thank you, Sophie."

"Anything for my friends."

Elizabeth left soon so she could return home and tell him exactly how she felt. Then he would tell her how he felt about her and Abigail. Because no matter what, Elizabeth could never be with a man who loved another woman. It was wrong for both people.

As she entered the house, the silence made the hairs on her neck stick up. Where was everyone? She could hear the servants moving about, still cleaning up after the ball. But where was Will? Where were the children?

She stopped in the hallway. "Kenneth, where is His Grace?"

"His Grace went riding late this morning and has been gone since."

"And the children?"

"They all went for a walk, save Lady Eleanor and Lady Lucia. They are still abed."

"Thank you, Kenneth." She headed for the morning room hoping to get something to take her hunger away. The two biscuits had not filled her.

The house seemed foreign today. She'd become so used to the sounds of the children playing and squabbling with each other. Or Will's deep voice echoing through the house. The silence reminded her of how empty her life had been before Will arrived. She never wanted to go back to that old life again.

She found a small repast in the morning room and enjoyed a scone and some tea. She had nothing planned today but excitement filled her. The idea of telling Will how she felt both frightened and thrilled her, but she knew she could do it.

"Lady Elizabeth, the Baron and Baroness Humphrey are here to see you," Kenneth said from the doorway. "Shall I seat them in the receiving salon?"

What did they want today? "Yes, have some tea and cakes brought in, too."

Slowly, she scraped back her chair and walked toward the salon. Before she arrived at the room, she could hear Caroline's waspish voice.

"Keep your mouth shut, Richard. I will do the talking."

"Talking about what?" Elizabeth asked as she reached the threshold.

"Elizabeth," Richard said with a slight bow. "Is His Grace not at home?"

"No, he went riding." Elizabeth walked over to the yellow brocade chair, which just happened to be as far away as she could get from them.

Caroline shook her head. "The daft fool doesn't even know when to ride."

"Where I'm from, any time is a good time to ride."

Elizabeth had never been so happy to see Will. He leaned against the doorframe. His broad shoulders almost filled the doorway.

"Excuse me, Your Grace," Caroline murmured.

"Your Grace, we actually came to speak with both of you," Richard said diplomatically.

"And what would you need to speak to us about?" Will walked across the room and took the seat next to Elizabeth.

She glanced over at him and smiled again. A part of her wanted to tell him that he really should change out of his riding clothes, but watching his muscular thighs in his tight, buff breeches was quite enjoyable.

"Your Grace, if I may?" Caroline started hesitantly.

"Yes?"

"I noticed last night at the ball a certain closeness between Your Grace and Lady Elizabeth." Caroline fidgeted in her seat.

"Oh?" Will asked, raising an eyebrow at her.

"It must stop, Your Grace," she whispered.

"What Lady Elizabeth and I do is none of your concern," Will replied in a harsh tone.

"The gossips, Your Grace," Caroline tried again. "With her aunt gone, it is slightly improper for her to even be here."

"Hang the gossips," Will said.

"There is something else," Caroline mentioned and then looked away from them.

"And what would that be?" Will asked with sarcasm lining his voice.

Elizabeth was so thankful that Will had arrived when he had. As they talked, her fingers clenched and unclenched the muslin of her dress. She could never face them with as much ease as Will did.

Caroline leaned in closer. "Your Grace, surely you must know about her father?"

"What about her father, Caroline?"

"The former duke was not her father," Caroline whispered so the servants could not hear.

"She was born in a legally bound marriage. The duke never publicly denied her," Will commented. "To the world, she will always be the duke's daughter."

"I understand that, but it is not what I meant."

"Then tell us what you mean, Caroline." Will crossed his arms over his chest.

Caroline shook her head. "Your father was the duchess's lover. He fathered Elizabeth."

Elizabeth gripped the arms of her chair as the world around her spun. "No," she finally whispered. "That is not true."

"We didn't come to make trouble, only to warn you both that you mustn't get too close," Caroline said.

"No," Elizabeth said again. It couldn't be true. Will could not be her brother. Her stomach started to roil with nausea. She raced from the room before she embarrassed herself.

Will watched Caroline's eyes for any sign of untruth from her. "If you are lying about this, Caroline. I will—"

"I swear."

"How would you know about this?" Will asked.

Caroline took a deep breath. "My father was a very good friend of the late duke's. One night when the duke was good and foxed, he admitted the affair to my father. When I married into the family, my father wanted me to know. He thought I shouldn't treat Elizabeth kindly because of it. But I always told him, it wasn't her fault."

"So why now? You have had this knowledge for several years. Why did you think it was so important to tell her now?"

She glanced over at her husband who nodded at her. "I was in the hall last night when I heard the door to your study unlock. I saw you leave and then went in to extinguish the candle and found Elizabeth."

"Nothing happened in there last night," Will said. Only later, when it was nearly dawn.

"Elizabeth told me the same thing, and I believe you both. But just in case you two were getting . . . close, I thought it best that you should know."

Will did not believe her. His father had loved his mother and been devastated by her death. Only his stepmother's love had brought him back from the loss. He never would have cheated on Will's mother.

"I believe you should take your leave now," Will stated firmly.

"Of course, Your Grace." Richard stood and assisted his wife out of her seat. "We are both very sorry for any pain this might have caused you."

Will refused to acknowledge Richard's remark. He sat frozen in his chair, unable to do anything but think about what he and Elizabeth had done this morning. And over a week ago. She had yet to let him know if she thought she might be pregnant. There was a strong possibility that she was already with child.

After they left, he brought his hands to his temples. Rubbing his head, he thought more about the situation. To him, it just didn't seem feasible. But Elizabeth never knew his father and had no idea what an honorable man he was. Will knew it was up to him to tell her.

He stood and slowly walked up the steps to her room. He knocked on the door but received no reply. Quietly, he opened the door and saw her facedown on the bed weeping. He closed the door and approached her.

"Go away, Will."

He sat on the bed next to her and rubbed her back. Every muscle tensed under his hand. "Elizabeth, we need to discuss this."

"What is there to talk about? Apparently, I am your sister," she choked out. "Which means what we did just this morning was . . ."

Her tears broke his heart. "It was not incest, Elizabeth."

She rolled over on her back. "How can you be certain? We have no proof of who I am!"

"I know my father. He would never have done such a thing."

"You don't know that. Until my father told me, I would have said the same thing about my mother."

Will clasped her hand in his. "My father loved my mother with all his heart. When she died, I think he wished he had died, too. The only thing that kept him going was the children and his career."

Elizabeth shook her head. "Any marriage can hit a rough patch that later makes it stronger. You would have only been a year old. Anything might have happened to pull them apart and you wouldn't remember."

"No, you are wrong."

"Will, I went through the same thing when I found out about my mother. I denied the possibility and didn't wish to believe the story. But my father had nothing to gain by telling me." Elizabeth tried to reach for his hand.

Will pulled it away. "This is not the same. You heard the story directly from your father. We have no idea if Caroline is speaking the truth. The little I know of her, I would not believe her."

She sighed. "You are right about Caroline, but we can't possibly know the truth until we find my mother's diary."

Will stood up and paced by the bed. "Even then, there is nothing to say the information we need is in the journal. She might have taken her secret to the grave."

"It has to be there, Will. I cannot bear it any longer. I must find out who my father was." Elizabeth stood and wiped away her tears.

"It wasn't my father." Will stopped and stared at the beautiful woman in front of him. He wanted to drag her into his arms and kiss away her fears.

But he couldn't do that any longer. While there was any doubt about his father, he had to stay away from her. But he had to do something.

"Let's find that diary."

Chapter 18

Elizabeth searched in the dining room, desperate to find a secret panel that might hide a journal. At least this time she had everyone's assistance. Will had even questioned the servants to see if anyone knew of any hidden doors or panels. When the children arrived home, Will told their tutor they were done for the day. He then told them what he and Elizabeth were looking for so they could help. The children decided to search their rooms again for her.

By nightfall, they were no closer to finding the diary than when Richard and Caroline had left this afternoon. Elizabeth was starting to wonder if she had scoured the estates as carefully as she thought. Had she missed something there? She hadn't spent a large amount of time on two of the estates because her mother rarely went to them. They were too far from London and not in the best condition. It made no sense that she would have hidden her journal at either home.

She had focused her energy on the manor home in Kendal and the estate in Hampshire. After spending a month in each house, she had thoroughly searched the homes and found nothing. She banged her fist against the wall of the dining room in frustration.

"Are you all right?"

Elizabeth turned to see Will standing in the room, staring at her as if she had gone mad. "No, I am not all right," she admitted.

He drew her into his arms and held her. It was as though he knew no words would comfort her now. But being in his arms helped her immensely. If only she could stay here forever.

Slowly, she pulled away so no servant would see them. "Thank you," she whispered.

"I searched the music room, but to no avail," Will said.

Elizabeth nodded. "Why don't you try the salon? Maybe there is a panel I missed."

"Very well." Will turned and left her alone to her searching again.

At nine, Will told the children to go to bed. She sat in his study staring at the cold fireplace. A lone tear fell down her cheek.

"We will find it, Elizabeth." Will sat across from her but reached over to hold her hand.

"I'm not certain it is even here," she said with a shrug. "Maybe I missed something at the estates. Maybe there never was another diary. She probably burned it so my father would not discover it."

"Is there anyone who might have been your mother's confidante?"

"She was friends with most of the ladies of the *ton*. But I do not remember any special friend. I suppose I could try the dowager Lady Selby. They were close in age so maybe she will know more."

Elizabeth tried not to let the tentacles of defeat wrap around her, but she failed. She highly doubted Lady Selby was her mother's closest friend. The only time she remembered Lady Selby visiting was when Elizabeth and Jennette were playing together.

Will squeezed her hand. "We will find it."

"What if we don't? I know you are trying to remain positive but there is a very good chance we will never find the diary."

"I don't know what we will do then," he said with a frustrated sigh. "Pretend this never happened and pray you are not with child?"

She knew from his angry tone he didn't mean what he'd said, still the words stung. How could she pretend she wasn't in love with him? It was an impossible situation.

"Perhaps we should ask Somerton for help," he said.

"Absolutely not." Elizabeth drew her hand away. "I will not allow him to know our personal business."

"Selby told me he is the best."

"Will, I could never bear the embarrassment. He would assume we've been intimate. He might tell others. What if that did happen and Caroline's words are true? Everyone would discover that we had an incestuous relationship."

"Very well," he said. "We shall continue this your way. But if we don't uncover something soon, I will speak with Somerton."

Elizabeth nodded, fighting back the tears that seemed to be constantly near since this afternoon. Will rose and stood before her, holding out his hands to her. She took his hands and he drew her into a tight embrace.

"We will find out the truth. There has to be someone who knows what happened."

She desperately wanted to believe that. As she stood in the warmth of his arms, she thought of one person who might be able to help. Sophie would never reveal Elizabeth's secrets and her friend just might be able to use her powers to help her. Before she ever spoke to Lady Selby, she would call on Sophie again.

Feeling his breath on her forehead, she wanted to tell him how she felt about him. But now was not the time. There might not ever be a right time to tell him if Caroline's scandalous lies were in fact truth. If they did not find some proof soon, she would leave with her small allowance and try to forge a new life.

And attempt to pretend this never happened. As if that were possible.

The next morning Elizabeth left to visit Sophie while Will continued to search for the diary. He decided to investigate his room thoroughly, including taking apart his small desk. It made the most sense that her mother would have hidden a diary in their bedroom rather than another room in the house. After removing every drawer in the desk, he found nothing.

He sat in the chair and rubbed his temples. What was he missing? There had to be some clue they had overlooked. Perhaps Elizabeth had missed something in the other journals she had found.

Will lifted his head up and looked around the room. He couldn't give up. There had to be something here. Walking to the fireplace, he put his hands on the wood moldings above the mantel. The first panel didn't budge so he moved to the one on the right side. The panel moved and groaned slightly.

Examining the panel, Will realized that it lifted up. As it opened, he breathed a sigh of relief. He'd found it! He reached inside and pulled out a small leather-bound journal. After wiping off the dust on his trousers, he sat down in the chair by the fireplace.

He traced the gold initials JMK with his finger. He should wait and give the book to Elizabeth, but curiosity overcame his good intentions. Slowly, he opened the book. As he read the first page, a wave of disappointment crashed over him. This was not her mother's diary. It belonged to the late duke.

Will paged through the journal, hoping to find some mention of the duchess's infidelity. Instead, all he found was the infidelities of the duke. Apparently, the man had a voracious sexual appetite that his wife couldn't satisfy. Then again, neither could half the female servants in the house, and several ladies of the *ton*.

No wonder his wife had had an affair. The poor woman was probably out for revenge. Will tilted back his head and stared at the white ceiling. He couldn't show this to Elizabeth. It would break her heart to discover what her mother had gone through.

Will glanced back down at the open page on his lap and shook his head. The entry for the day simply read:

Camille and I have created the most intriguing wager. Whoever gets the first servant into bed with them at the country party this month wins one hundred pounds. I have no doubt it will be me.

Knowing Elizabeth's mother was named Mary, Will briefly wondered who Camille was, but assumed it was most likely his mistress at the time. He turned a few pages and read more.

> *Camille bested me after all. Of course, she did not realize that I also had the pleasure of watching her fuck that footman. Or maybe she did. She continued to turn with a smile toward the small peephole Langford has in every bedroom. The woman was glorious with her big tits bouncing as she rode that man. I had to stop myself from joining them. Not that Camille would have minded.*

Good God, the man was a pig. Feeling rather dirty, he scanned the rest of the journal for some entry regarding the duke's wife. After finding nothing, Will decided to return the diary to its hiding place.

Elizabeth waited for Sophie in the small salon while her friend finished with a client. Finally, she entered the room her blue silk swishing at her feet.

"I am sorry." Sophie sat down on the sofa next to Elizabeth. "I'm having difficulties with Lady Cantwell today. She overexerted herself and needs to rest before returning home."

"Oh," Elizabeth said with disappointment. "Would you like me to come back later?"

"No," Sophie said, waving her hand at her in dismissal. "Lady Cantwell will be fine. She just needs a few moments to catch her breath. I left a servant to attend to her needs. I could sense you needed me more."

"It's awful, Sophie." Elizabeth blurted out the story that Caroline had told them. She stared at the ornate rug on the floor. A fire burned across her cheeks heating them with shame. How did she get into this mess?

"This is a dreadful situation." Sophie frowned and glanced away for a moment.

"Is there anything you can do?" Elizabeth asked.

"Me?"

"Is there any way you can tell with your powers if what Caroline said is the truth?"

Sophie fell silent and stared at the empty fireplace. Finally, she answered, "I am sorry, Elizabeth. If your mother had intense feelings for the man, I might be able to read that from an object. Perhaps even getting a mental image like a portrait."

Before Elizabeth could ask her next question, Sophie continued, "But it would need to be a very important object. Something that he gave her or something that she poured her feelings into."

"Like the diary," Elizabeth said, deflated.

"Exactly." Sophie stopped and looked away from Elizabeth again.

"What aren't you telling me, Sophie?"

Sophie sighed. "If your mother did not have intense feelings for this man, I might not be able to tell you anything."

Elizabeth sat back against the chair. "What do you mean? My mother would have had strong feelings for this man. They made love!"

"Elizabeth," Sophie said quietly. "We both know that many women among the *ton* have affairs for nothing more than physical enjoyment."

She could not be speaking of her mother! "That

may be, but my mother was not one of them. She constantly warned me about the hazards of courtship. About the importance of finding a man who loved me, and whom I loved in return. She cautioned me against infidelities and the problems . . ." Elizabeth's voice trailed off as she realized that all her mother's warnings might have come from her own experiences.

Sophie nodded. "Elizabeth, we have no way of knowing how your mother felt for this man. She might have loved him with all her heart."

"Or she might not have loved him at all," Elizabeth muttered. "Will suggested I speak with some ladies close to her age."

"That is a wise idea."

"I thought I might try Lady Selby first. I know they were friends, but I'm not certain how close," Elizabeth said.

"Even if she wasn't close with your mother, she might know other women who were." Sophie stopped as her footman brought in a tray of tea. She poured the tea and handed Elizabeth a cup.

Elizabeth waited for the footman to leave before she asked the most pressing question. "What if it is true, Sophie?"

Sophie sat back and sipped her tea. "Then you must pray very hard that you are not with child. Because if you are, you will have no choice but to leave London, and most likely England as well."

Elizabeth's mouth gaped. She hadn't really thought about the consequences of being with child other than the gossip. Everyone would know he was the father and if the story became public, she would be completely disgraced. Sophie was right. Elizabeth would be forced to leave England forever. She would never see Will again, or her home or her friends. Where could she possibly go on her small allowance?

The sound of a cane hitting the marble floor made her look up. Lady Cantwell stopped at the doorway and looked in.

"Miss Reynard, thank you again for the reading and letting me rest."

Sophie rose and went to her client. She clasped the older lady's gnarled hands and held them tight. "You are most welcome, Lady Cantwell."

Lady Cantwell moved slightly and then walked into the salon. "And you, Lady Elizabeth."

"Me?" Elizabeth squeaked.

"I have told you before, when you are ready to learn about your family to come to me. But do not come alone. The duke needs to know his family history, too."

Elizabeth felt a bit confused. "I already know about my family."

Lady Cantwell leveled a disapproving look. "No, my dear, there is much you do not know."

"Are you speaking of my father?" Elizabeth whispered.

"And your mother." Lady Cantwell ambled out of the room and left the house. Elizabeth stood staring at the empty room. Could Lady Cantwell know who her father was?

"That woman is slightly mad," Sophie said.

"I think she might know who my father was," Elizabeth replied.

"Elizabeth, you know she is one of the worst gossips amongst the *ton*."

"I do know that." Elizabeth looked into her friend's gray eyes. "But what if she does know? She might be my only chance."

"Or she might be your complete and utter downfall."

Chapter 19

The door to her house slammed and Sophie immediately knew Somerton had arrived. She waited for him
to find her in the small receiving salon. She felt the
anger emanating from him even at this distance, and
used it as a warning. The footfalls of his boots pounded
the marbled floor almost shaking the house.

"What the bloody hell do you want now?" he demanded as soon as he saw her.

"We have a problem," Sophie said softly. While she
usually could manipulate him easily in his anger, today
was different.

"No, *you* have a problem." Somerton paced the room.

"They have been told a rumor, and I have no way of
knowing if it's true."

Somerton stopped and turned toward her. His hazel
eyes appeared almost completely green in the pale light
of the room. "What rumor, and how does it involve me?"

Right to the point. "Someone told them that they
might be brother and sister."

Somerton had the audacity to laugh and then just

as quickly stopped. He leaned over her chair and said, "Maybe you have this one wrong."

"What do you mean?" She hated how her voice quivered slightly. Somerton would never hurt her. His attempts to frighten her were nothing more than his way of taking control.

"Perhaps they are not meant to be together." He moved away from her and began pacing again.

"Do not doubt my powers, Anthony."

He spun around at her. "Powers? What powers? You throw two people together in a situation that would have anyone thinking about sex and love, and yet you believe you are the world's greatest matchmaker."

She decided it was best to ignore his outburst. "You need to find out if the rumor is true."

He laughed again. "So you want me to just walk up to people and ask them who Elizabeth's real father was. I am quite certain that will cause more than a little talk."

Sophie clenched her fists in frustration. "I believe you may have other ways of obtaining information rather then asking such a delicate question outright."

"Perhaps I do. But my patience is wearing thin, Sophie."

"We are almost there. She admitted they had been intimate. She wouldn't have made love with him if she wasn't already in love with the duke." Sophie paused and finally said what she knew he wanted to hear. "As soon as they are married, you will get the woman's name."

"No more games?"

"I promise," she replied, making a little cross over her heart.

"I will see what I can do. But this is a very delicate

situation and any information I discover could be disastrous if the wrong person figures out my motive."

"I understand, Anthony. Do your best."

With a shake of his head, he left.

Will waited for Elizabeth to return from her calls but dreaded seeing her again. Once more, he would have nothing but bad news for her. Seeing the constant agony on her face was killing him. A sense of futility filled him. He had never felt so worthless in his life.

Hearing the front door open and shut, he assumed she had returned. Her soft footfalls approached his study. He took the last sip of his whisky before looking over at her.

"No luck?" she said.

"I have no luck with anything," he muttered. No luck with women, no luck with love, and no luck with finding lost diaries. At least no luck finding the right diary.

"Sophie was of no assistance, either." Elizabeth sat in the chair across from him and removed her bonnet. Red curls rested on her forehead and one fell over her eye.

He longed to reach forward and gently move the curl from her eyesight. But he could not do that any longer. He had no right to touch her. No matter how hard the desire rode him. He might never be able to touch her again.

"Will," Elizabeth started.

"Yes."

"Lady Cantwell was at Sophie's today. She inferred that she had information about my parents."

Will frowned. "Why didn't she tell you?"

"She wants us both to call on her." Elizabeth glanced over at the clock on the mantel and shook her head. "It is too late now. We must get ready for the Hollingtons' ball."

"I think we should stay in tonight." He had no desire to go to a ball and pretend to have an enjoyable time. The idea of dancing with other women when all he wanted to do was take Elizabeth in his arms was driving him mad.

"Ellie and Lucy will be dreadfully disappointed if we don't attend."

"Elizabeth, we cannot pretend this didn't happen."

"I know, Will."

"I still want you," he whispered, leaning forward.

"I—I still want you, too," she said in such a quiet voice he barely heard her. She blinked several times.

He wanted to tell her he loved her, and take her into his arms and make love to her all night. Then he would wake up in the morning with her in his arms. But he could not do that.

For a moment, he did nothing but stare into her watery green eyes. He could lose himself in her depths. The last thing he wanted to do was go to a damned ball.

"We should get ready to leave," he heard himself say.

She wiped an errant tear and nodded. "Yes."

He rose slowly and held out his hand for her. "Elizabeth," he said, staring down at her. He had to tell her.

"Don't, Will."

"Don't what?"

"Don't say anything," she replied. "I cannot bear to think about this a moment longer. Tomorrow we will call on Lady Cantwell and perhaps our hell will be over."

"Or just beginning," he whispered.

* * *

Elizabeth watched Ellie and Lucy take their turns on the dance floor as melancholy enveloped her. She didn't want to be here but attended for the young women. With her closest friends unable to be here, and Will in the gaming room, Elizabeth felt terribly alone.

"Care to dance?"

Elizabeth turned her head to find Somerton standing next to her. She'd been so intent on her woolgathering that she never heard the sneaky devil approach.

"No, thank you," Elizabeth said honestly.

"It might do you some good."

She glanced over at his stoic face. "What do you mean?"

"I have heard a rumor. Personally, I do not believe it," he lowered his voice to a mere whisper.

Elizabeth grabbed the column she had been leaning on for support. He could not possibly know . . . unless Will talked to him after all. "What exactly did you hear?"

He gave her a smug smile. "A little bird told me you believe you have a brother."

"Which little bird told you that story?"

"A person who would not want to see you hurt." Somerton kept his head faced toward the dance floor. "And neither would I."

"I cannot trust you, Lord Somerton."

His lips moved upwards into a full smile. "I would not trust me, either. But I might be able to help you, and I am very good at keeping secrets."

"How could you help?" she asked softly and then glanced around to see if anyone had noticed them.

"When is your birthday?"

"My birthday?" she asked feeling more than a little perplexed.

"I need to determine the approximate month you were conceived. That way I can determine where your parents were that month. I can find out if any of that time overlapped with time his father might have been in the same location."

"Oh, that makes sense. I was born on April 29, 1791. And according to my mother, I was not early."

"Where?"

"At the estate in Kendal."

"Very good," he said with a nod. "Care for that dance now?"

"No, thank you."

"As you wish. When I discover something, I shall let you know." Somerton walked away and disappeared into the crowd.

What a strange man, she thought. Scanning the room, she found Will striding toward her with a scowl on his face.

"What did Somerton want?" Will asked as he reached her.

"You should know," Elizabeth replied in a flippant tone. She still wasn't happy that Will had gone to Somerton without her approval.

"How would I know?"

"You told him what happened. He came to ask me questions in order to help."

Will blew out a breath and raked his hands through his thick brown hair. "Elizabeth, I did not mention anything to Somerton about us."

"Then how did he know? I didn't tell him."

"But you did tell your friend Sophie."

Elizabeth looked over at him and shook her head.

"They don't even know each other. Perhaps Lady Cantwell overheard Sophie and I discussing the situation and talked to Somerton."

"Perhaps," Will drawled. "What did Somerton say?"

Elizabeth recounted the conversation. "Do you think he will be able to find anything?"

Will shrugged. "I have no idea. I thought you knew the man better than I."

"I know more of the rumors than anything about the actual man. Jennette swears Somerton helped her and her husband in their courtship but she never explained how."

"All we can do is wait and hope then." Will held out his arm. "Shall we?"

"We really should not dance tonight." Elizabeth wanted to dance but the consequences were far too high.

Will leaned in closer until she could smell the scent of his soap. The redolence seemed even more intoxicating to her this evening. She wanted to drown in it . . . in him.

"Haven't you ever wanted to do something you knew was wrong?" he whispered.

Not until she'd met him. "Very well, we shall dance before you say something you will regret."

"I have not regretted a single moment with you," he said in her ear as she looped her arm around his.

Her heart paused for a brief second. She wanted to stop and question him about his statement, but knew it was wrong. Until they knew for certain they were not related, nothing more could happen between them. And that thought made her heart ache with sadness.

She had never enjoyed being around a man as much

as she did Will. As the dance started, her thoughts remained on him. His brown eyes sparkled in the candlelight as they moved across the floor. His lips tilted upward when he smiled down at her. She wanted to move closer to him, closer to his lips. The desire she felt for him seemed overwhelming, and now that she couldn't act upon those desires, they burned her to the core.

"You really must stop looking at me that way," he whispered.

Elizabeth blinked and glanced away. "I beg your pardon?"

"You were looking at me as if you wanted to eat me up. While I would not mind that expression at home, here it appears a bit unseemly. Not to mention where it makes my thoughts go."

"Oh?" She could not believe Will was the one reminding her about her conduct at the ball. Perhaps she had taught him too well.

But being in his arms again felt glorious. Even through the silk of her gloves, she could feel the heat from his hands. If only she could take off her gloves and run her hands along his bare skin again.

"You are doing it again," he whispered.

She shook her head to clear her lascivious thoughts. She must gain some measure of control. As the dance ended, she walked off the dance floor with Will, and then made her excuse to him.

"I need to go to the ladies' retiring room," she said.

With a nod, he said, "Of course. Perhaps we can dance again later."

She couldn't help but smile at him. "Perhaps."

Elizabeth knew that she could not dance with him again tonight. Her mind seemed unable to think properly when he was near. And she needed no more ardent daydreams in his arms.

As she walked down the hall to the retiring room, she wondered if Somerton might actually find something about her family. She prayed he would, because the possibility of finding her mother's diary was getting smaller every day.

She walked in the ladies' retiring room to find it empty, save for Caroline.

"You do not take my warnings well, do you?" Caroline said, folding her arms over her extended belly.

"Warning? What warning?"

"About the duke. And you were just dancing with him. Have you no sense at all?"

"All you said is he might be my brother. I had not realized that meant I could not dance with him," Elizabeth moved slightly to get past Caroline.

Caroline placed a hand on Elizabeth's arm. "A dance is innocent enough, but anything more is highly suspect."

"It really is none of your concern, Caroline."

"It is my concern if you make a mockery of this family. Your sisters will be hurt, and Richard and I will be also. I will not allow it." Caroline released her arm but not before giving Elizabeth a tight squeeze.

A sense of fear raced through Elizabeth. She had never seen Caroline quite so venomous.

"You and my sisters have nothing to fear from my behavior."

"A rumor is a very hard thing to live down, Elizabeth."

Elizabeth had been about to walk out but she stopped and stared at Caroline. "Exactly what rumor, Caroline? The idea that perhaps the duke is my half brother? Hardly scandalous. Nearly half the *ton* has half siblings. I was born legally to the prior duke. He never repudiated me to the world and that is all that matters."

Caroline raised one blond eyebrow at her. "Is it?"

"Yes."

"Even if you have been intimate with the current duke?"

"That is a lie."

Caroline tilted her head and gave her a half smile. "Is it, my dear? We both know that many rumors are based in falsehoods, but that does not keep the tongues from wagging."

Will entered the gaming room and glanced around for a friendly face. Instead, he noticed Richard, once more deep in his cups and losing funds. The man looked old and weary. Perhaps that was what a much younger wife did to a man.

"We should talk," Somerton said next to him.

"You are the sneakiest man I have ever met. I did not hear you approach."

Somerton smirked. "That is the way I like it."

They walked toward the gardens and searched out a private spot. "I could not find anything on Richard other than his recent gambling issues. But that may be just to get away from the shrew he married."

"And Caroline?" Will asked.

"I would never turn my back on that woman. She will cut anyone down to get what she wants."

Will didn't doubt that. "And she wants to be duchess."

"True, but if she cannot manage that," Somerton

said, "then seeing one of her children become duke will do."

"And keeping me apart from Elizabeth might just help her gain one of her desires." Will had a terrible feeling about this. Caroline seemed just the type of woman who could start a false rumor about them.

"I need proof," Will quietly said aloud.

"I am working on that, too," Somerton replied.

"How did you know?"

Somerton shook his head. "A man like myself would never reveal his sources."

"Do you think you can help us?"

Somerton glanced away and stared at a rosebush. "I pray I can."

Chapter 20

Lady Cantwell lived in a large home on Cavendish Square, and as Will approached the house with Elizabeth, an unnerving sense of foreboding stretched across his body. Something about the older lady reminded him of his late grandmother. She was a forbidding lady with a temper far worse than his grandfather. While she died when he was only seven, Will had never forgotten her.

"Come along, Will," Elizabeth urged as they walked toward the door.

"You are in quite the hurry this afternoon."

"Don't you want to know what she has to say?"

A part of him did, but a bigger part didn't want to know if there was a possibility they were related. "I suppose I do," he said for her benefit.

Elizabeth glowed with anticipation. Her cheeks were rosy and her green eyes sparkled. Will hoped Lady Cantwell would not disappoint her.

A young footman opened the door as they approached it. "Good afternoon," he said.

Will handed the man a card and watched as the footman immediately stepped back to allow him entry.

"Please come in, Your Grace. Lady Cantwell is expecting you both."

"Very good." Will still didn't understand all the deference given him just because he was a duke. He took Elizabeth's arm and felt her tremble. "Are you all right?"

She nodded. "Suddenly I am a little nervous."

He patted her arm. "That's understandable."

They walked together up the steps to the countess's salon. When they arrived, they found Lady Cantwell waiting for them in a large green wingback chair.

"It is about time you both arrived. I have been waiting for hours."

Will glanced over at the clock and noticed it was only one in the afternoon. How long could the woman have been waiting?

"Your Grace, please sit down. I'm too old a woman to be craning my neck to see you."

Will chuckled at the older woman's demands. "Yes, ma'am."

He took the seat closest to Lady Cantwell on a large sofa, while Elizabeth sat next to him. "So you have information that might help Lady Elizabeth?"

"Tsk, tsk, Your Grace," she reprimanded. "Sidwell, close this door." Lady Cantwell waited until the salon door shut before continuing. "First we pour the tea. Lady Elizabeth, please pour a cup for us all."

"Yes, ma'am." Elizabeth poured tea for everyone before sitting back against the sofa.

"Now, Elizabeth," Lady Cantwell started slowly, "before we begin, you should know that I shall keep anything said here in my strictest confidence. I believe you are troubled by your heritage, is that correct?"

"Yes, ma'am. I fear I may not be my father's daughter."

Lady Cantwell laughed soundly. "Let us hope you are not. A more miserable man I have never met."

"We both thank you for your time, Lady Cantwell," Will spoke up. "Do you know anything about who might be Lady Elizabeth's true father?"

Lady Cantwell leaned back and closed her eyes. "There were many rumors regarding your parents, Lady Elizabeth. They tended to run with a very fast crowd, even as they progressed in age. After the duchess was delivered of your brother, God rest his soul, your mother became far more open with her affairs."

Will reached over and clasped Elizabeth's cold hand. Her face paled and she trembled. "It is all right, Elizabeth."

She only nodded and bit down on her lower lip. "Please go on, Lady Cantwell."

"As you wish, my dear." Lady Cantwell sipped her tea before continuing. "Your father allowed her infidelities most likely to salve his own guilt for having mistresses throughout their marriage."

Will glanced over at Elizabeth's face and almost requested Lady Cantwell stop. Elizabeth looked as if she might faint. He wondered if he should have shown her the late duke's journal.

"Shall I go on?" Lady Cantwell asked, staring at Elizabeth.

"Yes," Elizabeth replied. "I need to know this."

"I agree. Unfortunately, you might not enjoy the tale."

"Please, Lady Cantwell, I must know," Elizabeth said.

"Very well. The affairs became folly for the *ton*. People were making wagers at White's on the next person to take a turn in your mother's bed. I am sorry to say, your mother was not very discreet. As I was saying, in the summer of 1789, something changed between your mother and the duke. To all appearances, they had reconciled and were remaining faithful to each other."

Elizabeth frowned. "Then how . . . ?"

"I am getting to that, my dear. Slowly there came rumors that they were involved with a group of people who did not believe in fidelity in marriage."

"What do you mean, Lady Cantwell?" Elizabeth asked.

Will had a very bad feeling about this topic. Lady Cantwell glanced over at him as if to verify that she should go on. He gave her a quick nod.

"There were reports that at your mother's country parties, a room was set aside for groups of people to enter and have . . ."

"Have what?" Elizabeth asked.

"Sexual congress," Lady Cantwell whispered.

"I don't understand," Elizabeth said, shaking her head.

Lady Cantwell sent Will a pleading look.

"Elizabeth, I believe Lady Cantwell is trying to say that your parents may have set the room aside for groups of people to have sex at the same time. An orgy."

Elizabeth stood up and then reached for the sofa to steady herself. "You are wrong, Lady Cantwell. My mother would never do such a thing."

Will knew he had to speak up, but hated the idea of hurting her. "Elizabeth, I believe Lady Cantwell."

She turned her emerald eyes on him. "You what?"

"I didn't want to tell you this, but I found the late duke's journal in my bedroom."

Slowly, she sat back down on the sofa. "Why didn't you tell me?"

"Because there was nothing in there about your mother. And what was written was mostly about his affairs." Will turned and held her hands. "I am sorry. I didn't want to hurt you."

She pulled her hands away and began rubbing her temples. "I had always assumed they had both been unfaithful, but never could I have imagined something as depraved as this."

"Lady Cantwell, do you have any information regarding exactly who Elizabeth's father might be?" Will asked, suddenly tired of this conversation. More than anything, he wanted to hold Elizabeth and comfort her.

Lady Cantwell pulled out a few old journals of her own. She flipped through some pages before stopping and glancing up at them. "Based on Elizabeth's birth date, I would assume it was someone at the Langford country party. Unfortunately, the Langfords were much like the duke and duchess. They assumed everyone had only one thing on their mind—sex. Not that I approved or participated in such goings on, but I knew they happened. Let me read this for a moment."

The room went silent while Lady Cantwell read from her diary. "Ah, here it is. 'The party lasted for close to a month, starting in early July.'"

Something about that bothered Will. He couldn't put his finger on it, but a sense of unease filled him. "Lady Cantwell, would you happen to know if my father attended the party?"

She leveled him a strange look but then flipped through several pages rather quickly. "I do not mention him but that doesn't mean he wasn't there. Your father tended not to go to such frivolous things. He was a very serious man."

Will agreed. "Yes, he was." And he loved his wife far too much to have an affair with the duchess.

"So all we know is my father most likely attended a country party and that is where I was conceived," Elizabeth stated with no emotion.

"Elizabeth, I do have several men listed whom I know either had red hair or had red-haired children. Perhaps it might help if I made you a list of those gentlemen."

"Thank you, ma'am."

Somerton might find that list helpful, Will thought. Now that they knew where her mother was at the time of conception, perhaps Somerton would be able to discover his father's whereabouts, too. Then they could be done with this sordid mess.

Lady Cantwell wrote down the names of five gentlemen and handed it to Elizabeth. "I know this is hard on you, my dear. But to the world, you are the duke's daughter. He never denounced you. He accepted you as his own."

Even Will knew that was not true. The old duke made Elizabeth's life a nightmare by telling her the truth of her parentage.

"Thank you, Lady Cantwell," Elizabeth said, standing up.

"If I can think of anything else that might help you, I will let you know."

Elizabeth nodded.

They walked silently out to the carriage. As the door shut and the horses ambled away, the tears flowed down Elizabeth's cheeks. Will quickly shifted and pulled her into his arms. She clung to him as her tears told of her heartbreak.

"How could she have done this?" she sobbed.

"I don't know," Will replied. He didn't think there was anything he could say or do that would make her feel better. Only time would heal this wound.

"Will, I can't go home yet. Please, can we drive somewhere quiet?"

"Yes." Will pounded on the carriage roof to get the groomsman's attention and the carriage came to a stop. He ordered the driver to take a trip through Hyde Park, and they were off again.

"You should sit over there," Elizabeth said, pointing to the other seat. "It would look improper to be seen together like this."

"Of course." He moved back to his original seat across from her as she wiped her eyes.

"Will, I think I should leave the house."

"What?" he barely contained his voice.

"I have been thinking," she said, looking out the window as they drove into the park. "If this gets out, Ellie and Lucy will have no chance of a decent match. We will be scorned by the entire *ton*."

"You have no place to go."

"I can live with Sophie."

Impotent anger surged in him. "So it is better to go live with a woman who is a bastard?"

"That is dreadfully unkind," Elizabeth retorted.

"Yes, it is. But that is exactly what people will say. Leaving the house will only cause more talk, not less." He could not let her go. There had to be some way he could convince her to stay.

"I realize that, but I can say I am staying with her while her aunt goes to visit relatives."

"No."

Elizabeth frowned. "What do you mean, no?"

"I will not allow you to leave." After all, he was the duke and that had to mean something. Surely, he must have some power over her.

"You have no say in this."

He finally remembered the one thing that would make her stay. "If you leave the house, then I shall, too."

"What do you mean?"

"I will pack up the house and return to America. Immediately. I shall install Richard and Caroline to manage the estates and send me an allowance from the returns. They will control the properties."

"You would not dare!"

He leaned forward. "Oh, yes I would."

"I hate you," she whispered.

"No, you do not," he whispered back. "And that is the real problem, isn't it?"

Elizabeth refused to answer his question because she would never admit that he was right. At least, not now. If they ever got this disaster sorted out, then she would tell him the truth of how she felt about him. But not until then.

Sitting back against the velvet squabs, she crossed her arms over her chest. "Please take me home, Will."

"As you wish." He signaled the groomsman to return to the house. "What invitations do we have for this evening?"

"Only dinner at Lord Selby's home."

"Very well. I believe we should contact Somerton with the information from Lady Cantwell."

"Of course. He may be at the dinner tonight. He and Selby have become close since he acted as Selby's second last year." Elizabeth fidgeted with the decorative flowers on her skirts. She hated this distance between them, even if she knew it was necessary.

"Selby was in a duel?"

"Yes, a dreadful man hurt Avis, and Selby demanded satisfaction."

"Good for him," Will said.

"How can you say such a thing? He might have been killed."

"But he wasn't."

They arrived at the house and walked inside. Elizabeth followed Will up the stairs to his room.

"Are you coming in?" he asked in a seductive voice that almost made her consider it.

"I would like to read the late duke's journal."

Will breathed in deeply. "I don't think that is a good idea."

"Why not?"

"There are some entries not fit for an unmarried woman to read," he replied stiffly.

"I want the journal," she demanded. The infuriating man just stood there blocking the door.

"No. It is highly improper."

"So is what we did on the sofa in the music room. And what we did in my bedroom." Heat crossed her cheeks as she remembered exactly what happened in both those rooms.

He opened the door to his bedroom and pulled her inside. Shutting the door, he backed her against it until she was caught between the door and his hard body.

"Elizabeth," he murmured.

No matter how much she wanted him, it wasn't right. Until they knew the truth, one of them had to be the strong one and today it was her. She placed her hands on his chest and pushed him away.

"We cannot do this, Will."

"I know." He picked up a book from his desk and hurled it across the room. "I hate this, Elizabeth."

"So do I," she whispered. "Please let me have the book and I will leave your room."

"Very well, but I did warn you. This is a very sordid book." Will moved to the fireplace and slid open a panel. He removed a book and tossed it to her.

"Thank you, Will." Her hands shook as she stared down at the book. Apprehension crept around her. She had always assumed her father had kept a mistress but Will insinuated there was much worse in here.

"Elizabeth, if you need someone to talk to about it . . ."

"Thank you." Elizabeth left and walked into her room. After sitting in the chair by the window, she skimmed her fingers over the leather binding. With a deep breath, she slowly opened the book.

The first entry, dated January 1, 1790, spoke only of the daily routine. The duke had visited the tenants at Kendal and given small presents for the new year. There was no mention of her mother.

The next few entries were in a similar fashion, and Elizabeth wondered why Will thought this was so sordid. Then she understood when she came to the entry of January 12.

> *I finally spirited the new maid up the stairs to my room. The little slut put on quite the virginal act, until she saw my cock. Then there was no doubt I wasn't her first time. She begged me to take her from behind, so I gave her exactly what she wanted. I never expected Camille to return early. Nor did I think she would want me to keep fucking the little slut while she watched.*

Once the maid had come, I told her to strip off Camille's clothing and get her ready for me.

Camille stood there as the maid removed her gown and started to suckle her tits. I almost came right then. The slut forced Camille on the bed and licked her until she screamed her completion. After that, I took the maid's place and fucked Camille like I never had before.

Elizabeth closed the book and threw it on the floor. She felt dirty for reading something so depraved. How could her mother have allowed him to treat her like that? Why didn't she say no?

She sat in the chair, unable to move for nearly an hour. She had thought she would be able to handle anything written in the journal but the idea that her mother let a maid do those things to her disgusted Elizabeth. Based on Will's comments, Elizabeth doubted that what she'd read was even the worst of it.

She started at the sound of a knock on her door. "Yes?"

Her maid, Susan, peeked into the room. "Do you wish to get ready for the dinner party now?"

In her shocked stupor, she had forgotten about the dinner at Avis's home. "Yes, now would be fine."

Elizabeth quickly picked up the journal and placed it in her nightstand. The thought of reading more of it made her stomach churn with nausea. Maybe tomorrow she could bear it, but not tonight.

Susan picked out one of Elizabeth's favorite gowns for the dinner, a lovely pale blue silk with lace trim around the neckline. Maybe dinner with her friends would help her feel better, but somehow, she doubted it.

Chapter 21

Will enjoyed dinner with the Selbys. They had kept the guest list to less than twenty people so he knew everyone who attended. Unfortunately, the one person he wanted to speak with tonight did not come. Lady Selby had said Somerton accepted her invitation but she assumed something must have come up to detain him.

During dinner, Will had been able to keep his eye on Elizabeth, but now the ladies had removed to the salon while the men had brandies and cigars. He hated cigars but thankfully, only Lord Heatherstone decided to smoke.

"So, Kendal," Heatherstone said between puffs, "have you decided to stay?"

With all the men staring at him, he shrugged. "Haven't made up my mind yet."

Why couldn't he just admit he had decided to stay? Ellie and Lucy loved it here. The boys were settling in with their tutor, and even Michael seemed to like being here now.

"With all your visits to Parliament, I assumed you had made your decision," Selby commented.

"Time will tell," Will replied vaguely.

"Lord Somerton, milord," a footman announced.

Somerton sauntered through the door and took a seat next to Will. "Sorry I'm late."

"Somerton," Lord Heatherstone said, shaking his head. "Excuse me, Selby. I find I must be leaving."

Somerton smirked as Heatherstone ambled toward the door. "Interesting affect I have on some people," Somerton muttered. He leaned closer to Will. "I have only a bit of news."

"Where can we talk?"

"Selby's study is upstairs and past the salon. But we need to wait a few minutes."

"Very well." Will listened to the various conversations but did not participate in any of them. After what felt like an eternity, Selby announced that they should return to the salon with the ladies.

While the rest of the men entered the salon, Will and Somerton continued on to Selby's study. As soon as the door shut behind Somerton, Will turned and said, "Well? What information do you have for me?"

Somerton leaned against the closed door. "Your father spent most of his career on diplomatic missions for the king."

"I know that."

"What that means is I should be able to track his whereabouts during the time at issue."

"How long will it take, Somerton?"

"I am searching as fast as I can. Your father's general location should be documented. But I have papers to go through to discover his exact placement."

"I fear rumors will soon spread." Will turned away from Somerton. "It will kill her."

"I know."

Will turned around and Somerton was gone as silently as he'd appeared. Knowing his presence would soon be missed, Will walked to the salon.

Selby sauntered up to him with a grin. "So I hear Somerton met with you and left already. Is everything all right?"

"I asked him to do a little work for me. He had some pressing items to get back to," Will replied.

Selby chuckled. "I know exactly what type of pressing items Somerton might have at this hour. Usually blond and rather buxom."

"Some men have all the luck."

"Hmm," Selby muttered. "Seems to me an unmarried duke should have similar luck. Yet, the only time I see you with a woman, it is Lady Elizabeth."

Will sent his new friend a glare.

Selby chuckled again and walked toward his wife.

"Is everything all right?" Elizabeth asked as she reached him. "You were positively glaring at Lord Selby."

"Everything is all right. Go and enjoy yourself." Will picked up a glass of port from a passing footman.

Elizabeth inclined her head and walked toward Lady Jennette.

Will spent the next hour making inane conversation with some of the gentlemen while the ladies set up card games. He just wanted to leave. Catching sight of Lady Selby stifling a yawn, Will knew he had found his way out of this house. He walked up to Elizabeth and whispered, "I think we should leave soon. Lady Selby looks extremely tired and in her condition, she needs her sleep."

Elizabeth turned and smiled at him. "That is a very

fine thought, indeed. I will make our excuses. Perhaps if we leave, others will follow our lead."

Will felt a little guilty since he'd only seen Lady Selby yawn once. But she was quite heavy with child. Surely she needed her rest. He watched as Lady Selby protested Elizabeth's departure but finally nodded her agreement.

Elizabeth walked back toward him with a smile. "She tried to pretend she wasn't tired but I could tell she was."

"Shall we?" he asked, holding out his arm to her.

"Yes."

Will inhaled deeply and said another prayer that Somerton find that information quickly.

After two more tense days of waiting for Somerton to send him information, Will was about to give up and move out of the house. The strain at home was driving him mad. He could not stay in a room with Elizabeth for more than five minutes without fantasizing about her . . . and what he wanted to do with her. Now, she sat beside him in a small carriage as his sisters sat across from them. With each bump, her leg brushed against his, giving him more lecherous thoughts about kissing every inch of her body.

Thankfully, the ride to Lady Kingswood's home was only a short drive. He climbed out first and assisted Elizabeth and his sisters. They entered the ball together, but knowing he could not stand another moment of being in her company, he quickly left for the gaming room.

After a large glass of whisky, he decided to sit at one of the tables. A small measure of tension eased from his body as a second glass of whisky followed the first. He placed a few bets, not worried about losing a small amount of money.

Richard sat two tables away tonight, with Caroline watching over him. His wife didn't seem to give him any more good luck. Finally, she walked away with disgust written on her face.

Two hours later, Will had not moved and was down several pounds. He moved away from the table and headed to the ballroom to check on his sisters. After finding them both dancing with gentlemen, he scanned the room for Elizabeth. She was standing near her cousin Nicholas, deep in conversation. Nicholas noticed him and leveled him a glare. Her cousin did not seem to like him.

A large hand landed on Will's shoulder. "You really need to come with me."

"Please, tell me you have good news," Will said to Somerton.

"The best."

Somerton walked down a hall and turned into an empty receiving room. He pulled a piece of paper out of his pocket and held it up for Will to see.

Will plucked the paper out of Somerton's hand and quickly read the document. "You are absolutely certain of this?"

"He left in March and did not return until Christmas. So unless her mother went with him, there is no way you are her brother."

"Oh, thank God." Will relaxed for the first time all day. He folded the paper and placed it in his jacket. "How did you find the information out so quickly?"

"It's what I do," Somerton said with a grin. "Good night, Kendal."

"You're not staying?"

"Good Lord, no. I have a soft bed and a warm woman waiting for me." Somerton inclined his head and then left the house.

A soft bed and a warm woman, exactly what Will planned to have later, too. Now that he was certain Elizabeth wasn't his sister, there was no reason not to make love to her all night. Just thinking about her made him hard. He wanted to steal her from the room and leave this place now. But he knew she would never agree to leave this early. He waited a few moments before entering the salon.

He found her in the ballroom alone this time, and slowly approached her. "Did you save a dance for me?"

She looked up at him with a forced smile. "I do not believe that would be a good idea tonight."

"Hmm, I think it would be an excellent idea." Before she could refute him, he linked his arm with hers and led her to the dance floor.

"Will," she hissed. "Please, let me go back to the refreshment table."

"No," he said simply. The musicians started and he pulled her closer. "You will dance with me tonight."

"But I shall not like it."

He smiled at her. "You will love it."

Inhaling her rosy scent, he moved with her across the floor. Perhaps having her so close when all he wanted to do was secret her off to a secluded place was not a good idea after all. He could barely control the urges he felt tonight.

There was no denying that he needed her now. As the music ended, he said, "Elizabeth, I am not feeling terribly well. Would you mind if we left early?"

"Of course not," she replied with worry creasing

her brow. "Go wait for us in the front hall. I will get the girls."

"Very well."

As he waited for the carriage, his foot kept time with the small clock in the hallway.

"You really do not look very well," Elizabeth said once she and the girls found their way to the hall.

"I will be all right. I just need a good night's sleep." Will almost laughed. Sleep was the last thing on his mind tonight.

She shrugged, then walked to the waiting carriage.

Will clamored into the coach and was struck by the intimate setting. Darkness surrounded them and with the curtains drawn, it was as if the world had slipped away. He sat back against the seat and waited for the carriage to take them home.

Elizabeth had never been so thankful for Ellie and Lucy being with them. The dark enclosed carriage felt too intimate tonight. She was certain his leg had brushed against hers deliberately on the ride home. Each time she felt his leg next to hers, little shivers of desire spread throughout her body.

She climbed down from the carriage and strode past him. Distance was the answer. She had to get away from him before he wore down her defenses with another kiss.

"Good night," she said once they had walked into the house. She raced up the steps to her room. Once there, she breathed a sigh of relief to see Susan waiting for her.

"Good evening, Lady Elizabeth."

"Good evening, Susan."

While her maid pulled out a chemise for Elizabeth to wear for the night, Elizabeth pulled the pins out of her hair. She listened as his footfalls echoed up the stairs, closer to her room. Finally, she heard him close his door. She hoped he felt all right. Perhaps once Susan retired, she would check on him.

She relaxed as she dressed and Susan brushed out her hair. Seeing Susan yawn, Elizabeth said, "Go to bed. I can plait my own hair tonight."

"Thank you, miss." Susan picked up a few things before retiring for the night.

Elizabeth stared at her bedroom door. Going to him even to see if he was all right might give him the wrong idea. A sound from outside drew her to the windows. She looked out, only to see a wagon lumbering by. She was far too jumpy tonight.

She started to walk back to her mirror when the door opened quickly. "What are you doing in here?"

Will smiled in such a devilish way at her, and then turned and locked the door. "Why do you think I'm here?"

"Will, I will not play games with you tonight. Please leave my room." Elizabeth took a step back as he advanced on her. "Will, you told me you were ill!"

"I am perfectly fine." He continued to stalk her until she had backed herself up against her desk. He stared down at her with his dark eyes.

"Will, I asked you to leave!"

"No."

She swallowed and briefly wondered if he'd had too much to drink while in the gaming room with the men. He reached out and caressed her cheek with the back of his hand.

"Will, say something," she pleaded. If she could get him talking then everything would be all right.

Instead, he gently kissed her. This was not the kiss of a drunkard but a man out to pursue a woman. He deepened the kiss, brushing his tongue against the slit of her lips. Elizabeth knew she should be the strong one and resist the temptation, but she didn't want to be strong. She kissed him back, loving the feel of his tongue on hers.

His lips moved away from her and she moaned softly, missing the taste of persuasion. He kissed her jaw and then slipped her earlobe into the warm recesses of his mouth. She shivered with excitement and the allure of danger. But common sense finally eased its way back into her mind. Pulling away from him, she stared longingly at his face as if to memorize the look of passion on him.

"We must stop," she whispered.

He grinned at her like a madman. "No, we mustn't. I want you right here, right now, and nothing is going to stop me."

"Will," she groaned. "You know that there is a possibility that—" Damn the man for cutting her off with a passionate kiss. She wanted desperately to let go of her inhibitions but that would be so wrong. One of them had to remain strong.

This time, he pulled away and whispered in her ear, "You are not my sister."

"We don't know that."

He kissed her ear again, sending a new arrangement of shivers down her back. "My father was in Russia for six months that year."

Elizabeth pulled away and stared up at him. "How do you know this?"

Will yanked her back to him. "I am starting to truly appreciate what Somerton can do."

She pushed against his chest. "You are certain?"

"I have never been more certain of anything. The timing is right. There is no way my father could have been with your mother unless you were three months late or three months early."

Elizabeth held him back for a moment longer, gazing at him, loving the look of desire in his eyes. They didn't have to wait.

"I want you, too," she whispered. "Right here, right now."

Will growled softly and pulled her against him. He tore at the chemise until it ripped. As it dropped to the floor, Elizabeth wrenched his linen shirt out from his trousers and over his head. She wanted him as naked as she was, and she wanted it now. While she worked at the buttons of his trousers, he kissed her neck, then her shoulder, until finally he moved her hands and forced open the buttons.

He leaned her back on the desk until she was laying on it. Before she could protest, his mouth moved to her nipple. She arched upward as the heat of his mouth scalded her with desire. Moisture pooled between her thighs as his tongue raked her. On the edge of the desk, he split her thighs with his hips. He actually meant to do this here, she thought mindlessly.

Feeling his shaft at her entrance, she waited for the decadent pressure of him filling her. In one swift move, he pulled her toward him, thrusting himself into her depths. She watched as he stopped as if attempting to gain control. But she didn't want control, she wanted passion.

She moved against him, sliding her hips up and

down on him until he groaned. He grabbed her hips and thrust into her swiftly. Each plunge sent her higher, moaning in pleasure. Suddenly she realized it wasn't just her groaning. The desk moved and groaned with the driving force of their desire.

"Will, the desk—" she managed, just as its legs gave out.

Will grabbed her with a laugh as the desk crashed to the floor, and brought her to the bed. "Damn, that's a first."

Back on the softness of the bed, they clung to each other. Desire giving way to pressure, and pressure giving way to a shattering climax as she'd never experienced before. She cried out his name as he shook from his own pleasure. He rested on top of her, their hearts pounding in unison, their breathing uneven.

Slowly, he lifted his head and kissed her softly on the lips. She stared into his brown eyes and knew without a doubt that she loved him. But the words wouldn't come forth.

Will glanced away first as if uncomfortable with the intimacy of their embrace. Then, he started to chuckle.

Elizabeth looked where his gaze had landed. Her old desk lay in pieces on the floor. But something caught her eye. She had only kept a few papers in the desk, nothing of importance. Yet, there in the rubble of the oak was a leather-bound book.

"Will, what is that book?" she asked softly.

"I assumed it was one of your novels or poetry books," he answered with a shrug. Slowly, he moved off her and grabbed a cloth for them both. After cleaning up, he walked over to the remains of the desk and picked up the book.

He turned with a smile and held up the volume. "I believe this might be what you have been looking for."

"My mother's diary!" Elizabeth sat up, pulling the coverlet with her. "Let me see it."

He tossed it onto her lap and crawled back into bed with her.

Elizabeth touched the book with loving fingers. This was it. Her mother's journal. "How?" she whispered.

"The secret panel must have been in your desk all along."

Tears blurred her vision. "I checked this room twice and never found anything."

"Is that it?"

She blinked away the tears and opened the diary. Inside on the first page was her mother's name. "Mary Camille Kendal."

She looked up at Will, whose face went pale. "What is wrong?"

"Camille?"

"Yes, only my father called her that. He thought Mary was too common a name for her."

"Oh, dear God," he mumbled.

Chapter 22

Will stared at the book, unable to move. Her mother's name was Camille. The memory of the entry in the late duke's journal came back to him, A wager. They had wagered over bedding a servant. Camille had been his wife, not his mistress. This was going to hurt Elizabeth deeply.

"What is wrong, Will?"

"How far did you get in your father's journal?" he asked, hoping she hadn't discovered the truth.

She shrugged. "Not far. I found it quite disturbing."

"Elizabeth, you might not want to read your mother's diary."

Elizabeth frowned at him. "Of course I do. There might be mention of my real father in there."

He took the book out of her hand and kissed her knuckles. "Darling, perhaps you might find it more disturbing than your father's—I mean, the late duke's journal. Maybe even, you should give up this idea of discovering your real father. The duke never disavowed you. In the eyes of the law, you are the duke's daughter."

She smiled gently at him and then caressed his

cheek. "It is very kind of you to try to protect me from getting hurt. But I need to know."

"Elizabeth, it might not be good news."

She rolled her eyes at him. "Will, my mother probably had an affair with another titled gentleman. I most certainly will not seek out the man and claim to be his daughter. I just want to know for my own benefit."

"What if he's not a gentleman?"

"What do you mean?" she asked. "Even if he was a non-titled gentleman, the man must be from a well respected family. There is no one else they would have socialized with."

"But, what if the man is a servant, or a rogue?"

"Oh, please," she said with a laugh. "My mother would never have done such a . . ."

"What it is?"

She reached for her father's journal that rested on the nightstand. "Did you read this?"

"Only a few pages. Why?" Had she found the entry with the wager?

She opened the book and flipped the pages until she came to an entry for January 12. "Did you read this?"

"No, I don't believe I did."

She snatched it away before he could read the entire note. "I cannot let you see this. It's terribly embarrassing."

"It might not be as bad as some of the other entries," he said quietly.

"It gets worse?" she asked in a high tone.

"I don't know for certain, but what I read was not good. It was more than disturbing."

"Oh, God," she said, covering her face with her hands.

He drew her into his arms. "You don't have to face this right now."

"Yes, I do. I have to know. For years I have gone to balls and stared at all the gentlemen, wondering if one of them could be my father." She wiped away the tears streaming down her cheeks. "I have to know."

"All right. Do you want me to leave you alone?" The last thing he wanted to do was let her read these disgusting journals alone. But he also hated the idea that she would be embarrassed reading them with him.

Elizabeth stared at Will, and then at the books on her lap. He had already read some of her father's journal. He already knew some of what happened. And she didn't think she could handle reading the rest alone.

"No," she whispered. "Please stay with me."

He pulled her closer and kissed her softly. "I shall be right here for you. Nothing we read will ever cross my lips to another."

"Thank you."

She sat next to him with her head on his shoulder and opened her mother's diary first. As she did, she prayed she would find some admission that the duke had somehow forced her into his depraved ways. But reading the entries from the month of January made her realize that her own mother was just as dissolute as the duke.

January's entries discussed the affair she was having with a man referred to only as Lord M. By the end of the month, it appeared Lord M had broken off the affair.

Elizabeth's hands shook as she turned the page into February. Would she discover another man had taken Lord M's place? Her mother and the duke had attended a party at a nearby estate. Her mother's entry related the entertainment of the night, watching a seventeen-year-old virgin being deflowered by the lord of the manor. And then all the other men had their chance with the girl, as well as with the other women in the room.

"Oh, God," she cried. How could the woman she thought of as kind have been such an awful person?

"Maybe you should skip ahead to June and July," Will said.

She nodded, knowing she could not bear another minute of this wicked book. No wonder it had been so well hidden. She flipped the pages until she came to the entry for July 10.

> *John and I have finally found a way to break the boredom of this party. A wager! Whoever can bed the first servant shall win one hundred pounds. I have no doubt that I shall be victorious, and I know exactly what I will do with the money.*
>
> *This should be rather easy. I have had my eye on the young red-haired footman since we arrived. Now I just have to entice him.*

"Now they are wagering over servants!" Elizabeth shook her head in disgust.

"Red-haired footman," Will mumbled. "This only gets worse."

"How so?" Elizabeth had no idea how this could get any worse. The journal was nothing but wicked entries about who she had sexual congress with, and when.

He picked up the duke's journal and started turning pages while she continued reading. It wasn't until the entry for four days later that she gasped.

"What?" he asked.

"She won the wager."

"I know."

She glanced back at him with a frown. "How could you possibly have known?"

He blew out a breath and handed her the duke's journal, opened to the page he'd read yesterday. "When I read this I had never heard your mother being called Camille before. I assumed the woman he referred to was his mistress."

Elizabeth started to read the entry from the duke's journal. "He watched! How depraved were they?"

"Keep reading."

Elizabeth read the entry twice. "No, it's not possible. A footman! My father was a footman!"

She threw the book across the room with all her might. For years, she had imagined who her father might be, but never had she thought her mother would have bedded a servant. Elizabeth stared at the book on her lap. She wanted to burn them both and scorch the images from her head.

"We don't know for certain, Elizabeth," Will said quietly. "We are only assuming."

"Will! The man had red hair. The timing is right. Of course, he is my father. Some nameless footman. Neither of them even mentioned his name, as if he didn't matter." Elizabeth barely held back her tears. Rage and sadness warred inside her. She had never been so sickened in all her life.

"Darling, I think we should keep reading to see if there is any mention of another man."

"Very well." Elizabeth read through the rest of July's entries and discovered that her mother had taken ill soon after her night of debauchery with the footman. They had left the party as soon as she was well enough to travel.

She skimmed through the beginning of August, when she noticed a pattern of sickness every morning. Finally, toward the end of August, her mother mentioned it again.

> *There can be no doubt now. I am with child again. Damnation. The last thing I wanted was another baby. Now I will have to endure another month or two of sickness, and then I shall grow fat with child. If only I had the courage to be rid of it.*

Elizabeth gasped as Will muttered a foul curse.

> *But I cannot do such a thing. This child will be my penance for such dreadful behavior. John will be furious when he discovers the babe and realizes the timing of it. The only possible father of this child is that damned footman. Why could I not control myself? All of this happened because I wanted that new bonnet, and John wouldn't pay for it. I pray the babe is blond like the other children. If not, I fear for my life.*

She could not read another line. She had grown up believing her mother loved her, but it had all been a lie. Her mother had slept with another man to win the money to buy a bonnet. She had manipulated the man just to get what she wanted.

Elizabeth refused to look at Will and see the disgust she knew had to be written on his face. How could anyone look upon her and not see her shame. She would never be able to face Society again. After reading the diary, she was certain that many people knew she was nothing but the daughter of a servant and a whore.

Slowly, Will removed the book from her hand. "I think we should burn them both."

She had no idea what to think. Her entire world just turned upside down. If they burned the book no one could ever prove she wasn't who she said she was—the late duke's daughter. But if Caroline or Richard ever spread their hateful gossip about Elizabeth and Will being siblings, she might need proof.

"No, we cannot do that."

"Elizabeth, we must," Will insisted firmly. "No one can find out about this. It would ruin you."

"Hide them both in the panel of your fireplace. No one will find them there," she replied in a flat tone. She suddenly felt numb, as if someone had stolen all her emotions from her.

"Darling, everything will work out. No one will ever discover the truth, and you shall continue to be the daughter of the duke." He tried to pull her back into his arms but she resisted.

She shrugged out of his arms and moved to the side of the bed. "I know, Will."

He edged closer to her and put his warm hands on her shoulders. "I know, too. But it doesn't matter. No one else will ever know your true identity."

Elizabeth jumped out of bed and faced him. Fury raced through her. How could he not realize how much this meant to her?

"It does matter. It changes everything. My mother slept with a footman in order to win a wager. A wager! And why? Because she wanted an expensive bonnet that the duke refused to pay for."

Hearing the words aloud made her cringe. How could anyone do such a wicked thing? *Her mother.* Her mother had done it. All over a bonnet.

Elizabeth briefly wondered what other wicked things her mother had done to get what she wanted.

The ache in her heart became too much to bear any longer. She covered her face as hot tears burned down her cheeks. And once again, Will was there for her. He pulled her back into his arms and held her tightly. Caressing her hair, he murmured words of comfort to her but nothing could ease her anguish.

She clung to him, needing him more in that moment than she had ever needed another person. He kissed the top of her head. But she wanted more than comforting from him. She pressed her body closer to him and felt the instant reaction building between them. Tomorrow she would determine what to do with her life but tonight, she wanted to be in the safety of his arms again.

He brought her back to the bed and laid her against the pillows. Gently, he kissed her and she poured her love into every kiss. As he made love to her, she knew without a doubt that she loved him. He comprehended the truth of her background and still wanted her.

Will awoke before dawn and stared at the beautiful woman in the bed next to him. He should leave her now and get back to his room before the servants started their day. Instead, he watched the gentle rise and fall of her breasts as she slept.

Making love with her a second time had been the most incredibly loving thing he had ever experienced. His only thought had been to help her through her pain. But everything felt different that second time. It was as if she couldn't get enough of him.

Almost as if she were saying good-bye.

He shook his head to clear himself of such morose

thoughts. Elizabeth wasn't going anywhere. He would make certain of that. As he lay in her bed watching her, he made his decision. He would ask her to marry him this evening after dinner. And he would tell her that he was staying in England.

Slowly, he slipped out of bed so as not to wake her. He picked up the clothing scattered across the room and placed her chemise by her pillow so she could find it before her maid walked into the room. After pulling on his trousers, he crept to the door like a thief. He paused and glanced back at her once more before leaving the room.

Tonight, she would become his betrothed. His sisters would be ecstatic to learn that Elizabeth would be their new sister. Here in England, he would build his new life. And he would make certain he did whatever possible to ease the sufferings of the less fortunate. That way he would still be living up to his stepmother's ideals, but he could do it with the power of his name and fortune.

A few hours later, he was finally rested and ready to face the day. After dressing, he left his room and crept to the door of Elizabeth's bedroom. He peered inside and discovered she had already gone downstairs.

As he reached the bottom step, he stopped and asked the footman, "Have you seen Lady Elizabeth?"

"She left a few moments ago for Miss Reynard's home, Your Grace."

Damn. He wanted to find out how she was feeling. Perhaps she needed to talk with her friends. Hopefully, she wouldn't tell them too much information. Keeping this a secret was necessary for her reputation.

"Your Grace," the footman said as Will started toward the morning room.

"Yes, Kenneth?"

"A missive was delivered an hour ago. I left it on the desk in your study."

A missive? Curiosity forced him to walk to the study. He found the note in the center of his desk and picked it up. He didn't recognize the seal.

After breaking the seal, he opened the letter and read it. "No," he whispered. "How could it be possible?"

I have made the most important decision of my life. I defied my father and refused to marry Josiah Harwood. I am in England and ready to be your wife. I shall call upon you later today.

With all my love,
Abigail

Chapter 23

"Perhaps we should go to Gunter's for some ices," Sophie suggested.

"Ices! How is that going to help?" Elizabeth said. Had Sophie completely lost her mind?

"We need to get you out of the house. And something is telling me we need to go to Gunter's." Sophie gave her a weak smile and a little shrug.

Elizabeth waved her hand around her. "I did get out of my house. I came to your home. And the last thing I want to do is go out for ices."

Sophie tilted her head back and sighed. "You need to be in public. You need to see that just because you discovered who your father is makes no difference. No one else knows."

"Now you sound like Will," Elizabeth mumbled. After waking this morning alone, she had sat in her room and thought about her future.

"Good, I personally like the man. He has a sound mind and I think he loves you," Sophie said in a soft tone.

"It matters not." Elizabeth realized this morning

that she would have to leave the house. Whether she loved Will or not, she could not stay. She wasn't one of them any longer.

"Of course it matters. Assuming you love him," Sophie drawled. "You do, don't you?"

Exasperation crept up her skin. "Yes, I love him."

"Good, then we are off to the booksellers."

Elizabeth blinked and shook her head. "I thought you wanted ices?"

Sophie pursed her lips and shook her head. "I was wrong. I must look for a book."

Never in all the years that Elizabeth had known Sophie had she seen her friend in such an odd mood. As much as she had no need to go to the booksellers, Elizabeth decided she had better accompany Sophie today. There was just no telling what her friend might do.

"All right, we shall go find your book," Elizabeth said.

"Very good," Sophie said with a self-satisfied smile. "I shall order the carriage."

As Sophie left to speak with her footman, Elizabeth sat in the chair, bemused. Sophie was up to something, Elizabeth determined. But she had no idea what.

Elizabeth had come over to talk about what happened last night, knowing she could trust Sophie with such a private subject. Not that Elizabeth had given Sophie the lurid details in the diaries. Only that they had discovered Elizabeth's father. But Sophie had barely listened to her. Perhaps Elizabeth should have gone to Victoria for guidance. Although, Elizabeth had never been certain about Victoria. There was always an air of quiet mystery surrounding her friend.

None of that mattered any more. Tonight Elizabeth would pack her belongings and tomorrow she would move in with Sophie. Sophie's aunt had agreed that she could stay with them and her small allowance would help offset the rising costs. Everything would be perfect.

Except she would not see Will any longer. And she would never kiss him again. And what if she was with child? Elizabeth rubbed her temples to keep the agonizing pain away. She had been such a fool to let him make love to her again last night. But if they hadn't, she might never have found the diary. Still, the idea of having a child out of wedlock terrified her. She didn't have the means to take care of a child on her own.

"Elizabeth, stop this nonsense right now. I know what you are thinking."

"What are you speaking of?" Sophie could not know what Elizabeth was thinking. Could she? Perhaps her friend's powers were stronger than Elizabeth ever realized.

Sophie glared at her. "You are not with child. You will not be out on the streets. You have friends who love you and will help you in any manner possible. So no more self-pity!"

Elizabeth almost laughed at Sophie's angry tone. Never had her friend spoken in such a way to her. "Very well, Sophie. I shall have to trust you in this matter."

"Yes, you shall at that," Sophie said. "Now come along, the carriage awaits."

"As you wish." Perhaps Sophie could tell with her powers that everything would work out all right. Elizabeth wondered if Sophie knew for certain that she wasn't with child. As much as she loved children, and would be pleased to have a baby when she married, having one now would be a disaster.

They traveled to the bookstore in relative silence.

Elizabeth didn't mind as she was still lost in her own thoughts. Will would not be pleased when she told him that she was leaving. It was her fault. She should have left as soon as he arrived. Then she never would have fallen in love with him. She never would have found those disgusting journals and discovered just how depraved her parents were.

But now she had to move forward. Decide on a path for her future. Something that would involve never seeing Will again. No matter how much that hurt. The future Duchess of Kendal could not be the daughter of a footman.

They finally arrived at the bookshop and climbed down from the carriage. "What book are you looking for, Sophie?"

Sophie paused. "I am not quite certain. I shall know when we enter the store."

Elizabeth shook her head as frustration with her friend overcame her again. "I cannot help you if I do not know what you are looking for."

"Help me? We are here to help you, not me," Sophie said elusively.

"Help me with what?"

"Will, of course." Sophie walked toward the store, leaving Elizabeth standing behind her with her mouth gaping.

She followed quickly behind Sophie as her friend walked around the store. "Over here," she whispered to Elizabeth.

"Why are you whispering?"

Sophie put her finger to her lips to hush her. Elizabeth had no idea what they were doing sneaking around a bookshop but she followed her friend anyway.

Sophie stopped by a selection of poetry and pulled

out a book. She inclined her head to let Elizabeth know to do the same. Elizabeth found a volume of sonnets and pretended to peruse it. As she did, voices carried from the stack of books on the other side of the shelves.

"Everything is set," the woman said with confidence. "I sent him the note this afternoon."

"Excellent, my dear. You will soon be the Duchess of Kendal," the man said in a soft tone.

Elizabeth reached for the shelf in support. Who was on the other side of the bookshelf? She attempted to glance through the spaces but could only see a blue gown that looked slightly outdated.

"Do you honestly think this will work, Father?"

"Abigail, remember, he must believe you defied me by coming to England. He must believe you love him and this was all your idea. If he ever discovers the truth, he will never marry you and all our plans will be for naught."

"I understand, Father. Everything will go exactly as we planned. He will marry me and I will become the duchess."

Abigail. The Abigail? The woman he loved and begged to defy her father by marrying him? She was in London. And obviously planning to marry Will.

There was no chance of that happening. Elizabeth started to move toward the aisle when Sophie stopped her.

"Not now," Sophie whispered.

"What do you mean, not now?" Elizabeth frantically tried to pull her arm out of Sophie's grip.

"They are leaving. Will must make the decision, Elizabeth."

"You heard them. They are planning to trap him."

Elizabeth finally broke free and strode to the aisle just in time to see them leave. "I have to stop them."

"Do you?"

She turned back to Sophie. "What do you mean? I must warn Will that she is coming. And she lied about defying her father."

"Indeed?"

Elizabeth hated it when Sophie arched one brow at her in such a condescending manner. It made her feel like a naughty child. "Of course I do."

"Is it not his decision to make?"

Slowly they walked out of the store, having bought nothing. "I don't understand."

"Has he told you he loves you?"

Elizabeth shook her head. "No," she admitted.

"If he is still in love with Abigail, shouldn't he be allowed to make his own decisions?"

"But it would be a dreadful mistake, Sophie. There is something iniquitous about what they are planning."

"Perhaps," Sophie drawled. "It should still be his decision, not yours."

"I cannot believe you are saying this to me!" Elizabeth climbed up into the carriage. "You are the one who told me to seduce him."

Sophie had the grace to blush. "At the time, I never imagined the woman would come to London to chase after him."

"But she doesn't love him."

"From the conversation, I would have to agree," Sophie said. "But you don't know if he loves you, either."

Elizabeth didn't know if Will loved her. He acted as if he did. He held her when she needed comfort and helped her find the diaries. If breaking a desk during intercourse could be called helping. Still, he could have asked her to leave as soon as he arrived, and he hadn't. He must have some feelings for her.

And even if he didn't love her, he should not be stuck with a conniving little witch for a bride. He needed to learn the truth about Abigail.

"Sophie, I think I need someone else's help with this." Sophie's mouth drew downward. "Who?"

"Lord Somerton. He can find out what they are up to and then I can tell Will the truth."

Sophie groaned. "Very well. When we return home, I shall send him a note."

"No," Elizabeth said. "We must go to his home now."

"We cannot do that."

"Either you come with me or I shall do it by myself."

"All right." Sophie glanced out the window and mumbled, "He is going to hate this."

Anthony fell back against the pillows, breathing hard. The woman next to him appeared to be falling asleep already. That was not about to happen.

"Wake up," he said, shaking her shoulder. What the devil was her name again? "Annette, wake up."

The blonde blinked her eyes slowly at him and then leisurely licked her lips. Her attempts to entice him would not work this time. He'd had his pleasure, and now it was time for her to leave.

A knock sounded on his door. "Lord Somerton, there are two ladies here to see you."

"Hell, Busby. I already have one in here."

"They don't appear to be that sort of lady, milord."

Annette sat up. "What did he mean by that?"

"Annette, get dressed and Busby will see that you are delivered to your home." Anthony threw off the coverlet and grabbed his trousers. "Who the bloody hell is calling on me at this time of day?"

He glanced over at his clock to see it was only three in the afternoon. "It had better be important, and not two old ladies looking for charitable donations."

"Somerton," Annette whined prettily. "Can't I stay here and wait for you to be done? Then we could take another go at it."

"Go home." He left the room before she could argue with him. He hadn't even bothered with his neckcloth. Maybe his inappropriate attire will scare the ladies off.

"Where are they?" he asked once he reached the bottom step.

"In the receiving salon, milord."

"Take Mrs. Haddon home."

"Yes, sir."

Anthony walked into the salon as casually as he could when all he wanted to do was wring someone's neck. He noticed Sophie sitting in the floral chair and his anger rose to a boiling point.

"You are the reason I am out of bed this afternoon? I happened to have a lovely woman up there with me."

A small gasp from the couch brought his attention to Lady Elizabeth. *Damn.* "Excuse me, Lady Elizabeth. I did not realize you were here."

"Lord Somerton, Miss Reynard is only here because of me," she said in a timid voice.

He glared back at Sophie, who merely smirked at him. "And why are you here?"

"I need your help."

He was bloody sick of helping people. "What do you need?"

Lady Elizabeth quickly explained her need as her cheeks reddened with every word. He did like the woman, and thought she would make Kendal a good wife. Why would he doubt it? Sophie was always right about her matches.

"Very well, Lady Elizabeth," he said slowly. "I will do my best. But it could take a few days to get all the information you may require. *If* I can discover their true intent at all."

"I understand, Lord Somerton. I shall pray that you find the information quickly. I am not sure how long we have before she tries to see him."

"Elizabeth, go out to the carriage. I will join you in a moment. I need a word in private with Lord Somerton," Sophie said with a smile.

"Of course," Elizabeth replied, eying them both carefully.

Anthony waited for the door to close before attacking Sophie. "Why did you bring her here?" he demanded.

"I did not bring her here. She insisted we come to your house to make this request. I tried to stop her."

Sophie stood and paced the room. "I do not like this development. I had everything under control."

Anthony laughed caustically. "You mean you didn't *see* them coming?"

"No," Sophie bit out. "I never thought Abigail would come all this way. Out of the blue today, I realized something was happening. Luckily, I was able to sense that Elizabeth and I needed to go to the bookshop. Why is Abigail here?"

"Perhaps if you didn't sense this until today, you are losing your powers," he said with a smirk.

She narrowed her eyes on him until he tensed. "You had best hope I haven't lost my powers, or you will never get the name you are seeking."

Damn her for making him wait this long already. All

he needed was one girl's name. How hard could that be? "Why didn't you sense them?"

Sophie paced the small room with a worried frown. "I wish I knew." She suddenly stopped and looked at him with a slight smile. "Perhaps it is because the duke really doesn't love Abigail, so her presence here is meaningless."

"And if he does love her?"

"Then all may be lost."

Bloody hell, he would never get that girl's name.

Chapter 24

Will paced the study from his desk to the fireplace and back. What would he say to Abigail? How could he tell her that she had wasted her time and money, and quite possibly ruined her reputation by chasing after him? He didn't love her any longer.

He loved Elizabeth and wanted to marry her.

But the idea of hurting Abigail was killing him. He'd waited years for her to come to her senses and defy her father. She would never want to stay in England with him. Perhaps if she had come over weeks ago, before he became involved with Elizabeth, things might have been different. But he was thankful she hadn't. Otherwise, he might never have fallen so deeply in love with Elizabeth.

He didn't know how to tell Abigail that he didn't love her. Had he ever? He sank into a chair closer to the fireplace. Had he ever loved Abigail? Or was she simply something he thought he wanted. Marrying her would have given him the excuse to stay in America and not face his duties in England. If she had defied her father, then he would have been forced to do the same and reject the title.

After returning to England, and seeing the possibilities for changes he could make, he started to enjoy the place. But it was Elizabeth that helped him see all those things. She made London feel like home to him.

He could not give it up. And he would not marry Abigail. He would put her on the first ship heading back to America.

A knock sounded from the outside of his door. "Yes?"

Kenneth walked inside. "Your Grace, there is a lady here to see you." He lowered his voice to a whisper. "She came without a chaperone or maid. Should I tell her you are not at home?"

"No, Kenneth. I believe it is an old friend from America. I will see her in the small salon. Bring refreshments." Like a bottle of whisky for him.

As the footman left, Will rose from his seat and adjusted his cravat. Where was Elizabeth when he needed her support? He walked to the door. Breaking a woman's heart was not an easy thing to do.

The stroll down the hall to the small salon seemed endless today. The dread in his heart slowed him to a snail's pace. He needed to get this over with now.

He stood at the threshold and stared at her. She hadn't noticed his presence yet. Her blond hair was swept up into a loose chignon, and she held a green velvet bonnet in her lap. He must have made some small noise because she suddenly turned her head to look at him. Her sparkling blue eyes filled with tears as she sat there gazing at him.

"Will!" She quickly launched herself into his arms.

Backing away, she apologized softly, "I am dreadfully sorry. That was very wrong of me."

"Abigail, how are you?"

"Wonderful now," she said with a sigh.

"Have a seat and we shall have tea," Will said. He waited for Abigail to take her chair, and then moved to the chair across from her.

Abigail poured tea while Will watched her every move. Her hands trembled as if nervous around him, something she'd never been before. She handed him a teacup with a weak smile.

"So, Abigail, how did you arrive in London?" he asked to make conversation and put her more at ease.

"I sold my grandmother's necklace for passage," she replied, then sipped her tea. "I had just enough money for the trip and a night or two in London. I hoped you would help me find other accommodations until we can be married."

Married. She had not even waited for him to bring up the subject. "I will make sure you are taken care of," he said softly.

"Oh, Will, I have missed you terribly," she said stiffly.

"Abigail, what changed your mind about defying your father and coming over here?"

She smiled at him. "I missed you. I met Josiah Harwood and immediately knew he was not the right man for me."

Will sat back and sipped his tea. "Why not? I knew Josiah in Virginia. He is a good man."

"Oh, Will," she said coyly. "He is so much older than I."

"He is thirty, Abigail. Only two years older than me."

"But he seems much older than that. His hair is

almost all gray. And he already has two children from his first marriage. And he owns a farm, Will."

What was it that seemed different about her? It was almost as if her conversation was scripted. "While I don't have the gray hair, I do still have seven siblings to care for, and I own four estates."

"Yes, estates," Abigail commented. "With servants."

So that was it. Josiah did not have enough money for her. Although, her father had enough money and would have assisted them if needed. Something didn't seem right. Could she possibly have planned this all along? Had she been rejecting his offers of marriage until he actually inherited the title?

No, that made no sense. If that had been the case, she would have agreed to marry him before he left for England. He had written to her about the trip five months before he left. She had plenty of time to let him know she wanted to marry him and come along with him.

"Tell me more about your estates, Will."

Will glanced over at Abigail and could have sworn there was a gleam of satisfaction in her eyes. "I really don't know too much about the estates yet. Elizabeth thought it best if we stayed in London for the Season before venturing off to the country."

Abigail's blue eyes widened. "Elizabeth?"

"She is—"

"Standing right here, Will."

Will turned his head to the doorway where Elizabeth stood with her arms folded over her chest and a look of fury burning in her eyes.

"Elizabeth, come in," he offered. "Meet Abigail."

Elizabeth smiled tightly while her heart raced in

her chest. Now she had no time to discover what they were up to. She had to come up with a plan. She could never let Will marry that deceitful Abigail.

"I am sorry," Abigail said slowly, "how do you two know each other?"

"I am his cousin. The former duke's daughter." She said the lie easily.

"Oh, I see," Abigail said in a relieved tone. She leaned back against the chair and smiled at Elizabeth.

"Do you?" Elizabeth asked, using her haughtiest voice.

Abigail blinked as if she realized her mistake.

Seeing the look in Will's eyes, Elizabeth wondered again how he felt about Abigail. Perhaps she should leave the room and let them talk. But she didn't want to see him hurt by Abigail again.

"Abigail, back to our conversation," Will said, "why did you wait five years to defy your father? You had the perfect opportunity when I was leaving for London with the children. I would have married you before we left. I would have paid your passage so you wouldn't have been forced to sell your grandmother's pendant."

Abigail blinked as if holding back tears. "I did not realize how much I loved you until you were gone."

"Oh, for pity sake, he'd been in Canada for five years," Elizabeth mumbled. She looked away as both Will and Abigail glanced over at her.

"Are you all right, Elizabeth?" Will asked softly.

"Perfectly fine," she bit out.

Will appeared to be suppressing a smile. "Abigail, we have been apart for five years. Why this sudden rush of feelings?"

Abigail looked away as her face turned white. "I have always loved you, Will. But the idea of marrying

Josiah made me realize just how strong those feelings were. I realized that I could not live without you."

Elizabeth bit her tongue so as not to interfere with their conversation. All the while, her anger rose. She wanted to scoff at Abigail and chase her from this house. But that was for Will to decide, not her.

"Why did you write that letter to me stating you agreed with your father to marry Josiah?" Will asked.

"Oh, Will," she cried. "My father made me write that letter. He sat at the table next to me and forced me to write every word. I had no choice."

Oh, dear God, Elizabeth thought. Will was starting to believe the charlatan. "Why did you not send a second letter, written in private, of course, explaining the situation?"

"Elizabeth," Will warned. "This is my business."

"Yes, Will," Abigail complained. "Why is she here for our private conversation?"

"That is enough, Abigail. Elizabeth is my cousin, and as such, she has a right to be here."

Abigail narrowed her gaze on Elizabeth. "It seems a little inappropriate, if you ask me."

"I do not think anyone asked you." Elizabeth wanted to reach over and strangle the woman.

Abigail stood up and crossed her arms over her chest. "Will, I believe our conversation is finished as long as she is in the room."

Will shook his head. "Elizabeth, leave us. I will speak with you when we are done."

Abigail sent Elizabeth a smug smile. "Now we can plan our wedding, Will."

Wedding! Elizabeth's head spun. She couldn't let him marry Abigail. There had to be some way she could stop them. The comment sent Elizabeth over a great precipice, and the words tumbled out before she could stop them.

"Will, you cannot marry her. I am with child." Elizabeth clapped her hand over her mouth. How could she have said that?

"What!" Will exclaimed, rising from his chair and staring at her.

"Will! You did . . . that . . . with her!" Abigail shrieked.

"Elizabeth, go up to your room. We will talk in a little while. I must speak with Abigail." Will slowly sat back into his chair.

"Will!" Abigail exclaimed again.

"Sit down, Abigail."

Elizabeth walked out of the room with leaden feet. How could she have blurted out such a lie? She would not know for weeks if she was with child. What made her say such a thing?

She sat on her bed and noticed the diaries still on her nightstand. They had both forgotten to hide them again. As she sat there staring at those books, Elizabeth's mind wandered back to what her mother had done. She had manipulated that footman to get what she wanted.

Elizabeth cringed as she grabbed the diary off the table and opened it up again. She scanned through the entries and found numerous examples of her mother using sex to get what she wanted. She had wanted to refurbish the house in Hampshire, so she agreed to let the duke watch her have sexual congress with another man. When she wanted a new oil painting for the great hall in Kendal, she agreed to have sex with the duke and four other men at the same time.

The entries only served to sadden Elizabeth. Her mother must have hated what she had done. But as Elizabeth continued to read, she could find no entries showing her mother's feelings about it. On one day, her mother expressed how much she enjoyed a visit from Lord H because he was so much bigger than the duke. Perhaps her mother hadn't minded at all.

Elizabeth put the book down and thought about her own actions. Guilt filled her as she remembered being flirtatious with Will in order to continue to stay in this house. Then there was that dreadful thought that she had first made love in the music room to get him to stay in England. Had that been the reason she had done such a thing?

No. She could not be as manipulative as her mother. But if that was the case, why had she blurted out that she was with child? Perhaps she did it only to keep Will from marrying Abigail, but it was still manipulation.

Sophie had told her that he had to make the decision regarding Abigail, but Elizabeth refused to listen. She sank deep into her pillows and let her tears fall. She had done it to control the situation to get what she wanted. Just like her mother.

But Elizabeth knew she couldn't let Abigail marry Will. The woman had deliberately lied to him. Elizabeth pounded the pillow in frustration.

None of it mattered any longer. After all she had done to get her way, and then discovering who her father was, she could never marry Will. He deserved far better than a woman who used her wiles to get something out of him. Her heart ached with the love she had for him.

She wanted to be the one to show him the importance of being duke. She had wanted to be the one to celebrate a victory in Parliament with him. Or visit the tenants with him.

Or watch his face when he saw his heir for the first time.

Now, because of her actions, and the actions of her mother, Elizabeth would never have those things. Instead, she would go live with Sophie until she could determine a path for her future. A bleak future, indeed.

"You were actually with that . . . that woman!" Abigail exclaimed once Elizabeth left the room.

"Yes," Will answered honestly. He did not care if Abigail learned the truth. With Elizabeth's pregnancy, they would have to be married as quickly as possible. Abigail knew no one in London, so she would not be gossiping.

"I cannot believe it. She must have tricked you into her bed."

"Why would she have to do such a thing?"

Disbelief showed on her face. "She has red hair . . . and freckles!"

And was one of the most beautiful women Will had ever known. "What does that have to do with anything?"

"Oh, Will, she enticed you into her bed so she could become the next duchess," Abigail said with a slight sob. "She wanted to take you away from me."

"Abigail, nothing happened until after you sent me that note stating you were going to marry Josiah. I had been completely faithful to you for all those years, waiting for you to realize how much I loved you."

"Then you do still love me." Abigail brushed away a tear. "Then everything will be fine. You can pay her money to have the baby in the country, or even in another country. I am sure we can make up a lie for her, such as she is a widow—"

"Abigail, no." Will could not believe the woman he thought he once loved would be so heartless.

"What do you mean, no?"

"I am not about to give Elizabeth money to go have my child alone."

Abigail shook her head with a pitiful look upon her face. "Will, you do not even know that baby is yours."

Will clenched his fists. "Yes, I do know."

"Oh," she whispered.

"I am sorry, Abigail. But I am marrying Elizabeth." Will stood and held his hand out to her. "I will see to your passage back to Virginia."

"I cannot return. I will be a laughingstock. I have ruined all chances of a decent marriage."

"No, you have not. People will understand that I married another," Will replied.

Abigail thrust his hand away from her and stood. "You are a fool, William Atherton. That woman is just trying to become your duchess. She has no love for you."

"Indeed," Will said softly. "How is that any different from what you have been doing?"

"How dare you! I have never thought about being your duchess, only your wife. I love you, Will." Abigail appeared to force out more tears. "I could not disobey my father."

Remembering Elizabeth's words from when he first arrived in London, he said, "If you truly loved me, your father's wishes would not have mattered."

She stiffened and held her head high. "When that

little strumpet shows her true colors, I will be waiting for you."

"Before you leave, give my footman the name of the inn where you are staying."

"Why?"

"So I can send your ship passage there." Will started toward the doorway. He turned at the last minute and looked at her again. "Good-bye, Abigail."

Chapter 25

Will had never felt so relieved as when the door shut behind Abigail. He waited in the back hallway to make certain she left. She was gone. The woman he once thought he loved had come to him, defying her father, and he'd rejected her. When he thought about it like that, he felt a twinge of guilt. But something did not seem right about Abigail's sudden arrival.

It just wasn't like Abigail to do something quite so rash. There had to be a better reason for why she could not marry him earlier. Not that it mattered any longer. The most important thing was to speak with Elizabeth.

They had a wedding to plan and a baby to think about now. He walked up the steps and down the hall to her room. He knocked softly on her bedroom door, waiting for a reply.

"Go away, Will."

"We need to talk, Elizabeth," he replied to the door.

"No, I cannot talk right now. I need some time to think."

Think? "About what?" He tried the knob but found it locked. She had locked him out.

"Us."

He barely heard her whispered reply. "Elizabeth, let me in now."

"No."

"Very well, I shall be in my study." Will strode to his study and then stood in the room. It seemed very empty today with Ellie and Lucy making calls to some of their new friends and the boys off riding in the park. The only other person left was Sarah. And she was probably upstairs with her governess learning her letters.

He didn't like it when the house was this quiet. Especially when Elizabeth was home and probably crying in her room. He wanted to go to her again. Make her understand that everything would be all right. They would marry and love each other. They would not behave like her parents.

Will believed in love and marriage. After watching his father attempting to recover from his mother's death, there was never a doubt in Will's mind how much his father loved her. And if it hadn't been for Betsy, his stepmother, his father might have lost his mind. She was the person who helped him through his grief. She taught him to love again.

And Will was certain he loved Elizabeth in the same manner. He never wanted to see her hurt and as pained as she was now. If she would just let him explain. She might not even know that Abigail was gone for good.

He was done waiting for Elizabeth to talk with him. He walked back up the steps again, determined to speak with her this time. Pounding on her bedroom door, he said, "Elizabeth, let me in now. We need to talk."

"Yes, we do," she said from behind the closed door. "But not here. I will be downstairs presently."

"Very well."

* * *

Elizabeth stared at the door to her bedroom and then to the valise she had packed. After spending the past hour reflecting upon her actions, she was certain there was only one outcome. Once she told him everything, he would want her to leave. She expected it.

She inhaled sharply, trying to ignore the pain in her heart. As she walked down the steps, she looked at the house that had been her home for twenty-six years. She'd always loved this house more than the estates. It was smaller and more intimate.

Her heels clicked softly on the marble floor as she walked to his study. Every step brought her closer to him, and closer to leaving. She could do this, she told herself. The time spent in her room had been an attempt to gain her confidence and tell him the truth. The awful truth. The sordid truth. At least once she left, he could dedicate the rest of the Season to finding a wife worthy of being the next duchess.

She knocked on the door and then entered quietly. He stood near the window looking out until he heard her cross the threshold.

"Elizabeth," he whispered.

The look of love in his eyes almost forced her to retreat. Once she told him what she'd done, he would hate her for it. Almost as much as she hated herself.

"Will, sit down so we can talk."

"Of course." Will sat down in the chair closest to the fireplace. "Come sit close to me."

"No. I need to stand." Elizabeth closed her eyes for a moment, and then blinked them open. "Will, I am not with child. At least not that I know of."

Will frowned, his gaze moving from her face to her

belly. "I do not understand. Why would you announce such a thing in front of Abigail if you were not with child?"

This was more difficult than she even imagined. "Sophie and I were at the bookshop today, and by chance, so was Abigail. And her father."

"Her father is in Virginia, Elizabeth. The man despises England and never would have allowed her to come, much less come here himself."

"Will, I was standing in the aisle next to them. I heard them both."

"You never met Abigail until she arrived here today. How could you possibly have known it was her?" His voice grew deeper with anger as he spoke.

He didn't believe her. She hadn't thought it possible. He must still love Abigail after all. "The man called her Abigail, she called him Father, and he talked about her becoming the Duchess of Kendal. That could only mean marrying you."

"Even if she did, that doesn't excuse your actions today. Why did you lie to me?"

"I felt I had no choice. I was certain you wouldn't believe me over Abigail, and I knew she was lying to you." Elizabeth wrung her hands in despair. She wanted desperately for him to believe her. "I blurted it out to protect you," she whispered.

"Elizabeth," Will said, then paused, staring down at his clenched hands. "Did you tell me you were pregnant to get me to marry you?"

"Yes, no, I don't know!" Elizabeth tried to blink away the tears but they continued to fill her eyes. "It doesn't matter anyway. You cannot marry me."

"And why is that?"

She didn't want to tell him everything, but he did

have a right to know. "This wasn't the first time I've manipulated you. I have been as awful as Abigail."

He looked over at her sharply. "What are you talking about?" he asked slowly.

She licked her lips and then pressed them together. "I flirted with you to convince you to let me stay in the house. I made love with you to get you to stay in England. I read almost all of my mother's journal. She did terrible things just to get her way. I'm no better than she was."

Will rose from his seat and stalked her. With each step closer, she could feel the anger emanating from him.

"You made love with me only to get me to stay here?"

She looked away from him and nodded. "I wanted you to stay so I could continue to look for the journal."

"And that was the only reason you let me touch you?"

She should tell him the truth but it didn't matter at this point. She was a terrible person, and he deserved so much more than her.

"Yes," she whispered.

"Get out of this house," he said in a menacing tone. "I don't want to see you here again."

Elizabeth closed her eyes and nodded. "I will send for my things."

"Do that." He strode from the room and slammed the door behind him.

She dropped into the chair and wept for all that she had lost. Everything she ever wanted had just stormed out of the room, leaving her behind. She had nothing now . . . except her heartache.

Slowly, she stood and wiped away her tears. She had to leave now before she went up to his room and begged him to let her stay with him. To tell him that she loved him. And that the other times they had made love were what counted, not the first time. But she couldn't do such a thing. He did not want her any longer, and she couldn't blame him.

She was a terrible person who had used her wiles for her own gain. Just like her mother.

Walking down the hall, she gathered her courage and asked for a carriage to be brought around. Then she waited. She could hear the boys upstairs and wanted to say good-bye, but she didn't think Will would want her to do it. She wondered if Ellie and Lucy were upstairs, too. They might not have returned from their morning calls yet.

"The carriage is ready, miss."

"Thank you."

She walked out to the carriage just as Ellie and Lucy arrived home.

"Elizabeth, where are you going at this time of day?" Ellie asked. "It will be dinner soon."

She couldn't tell them. They would never understand. "I am dining with my friend Sophie tonight."

She barely got the words out of her mouth before her eyes filled with tears again.

"What is wrong?" Lucy demanded. She always reminded Elizabeth so much of Will.

"I'm sorry. I must go." Elizabeth climbed into the carriage and then glanced back at the young women. Both looked shocked by her abrupt departure. As the carriage rolled away, Elizabeth stared back through watery eyes at the house that had been her home forever.

"What have you done to her?" Ellie demanded as soon as Will entered the salon.

After spending the rest of the afternoon in his room, his anger had only grown. "I did nothing to her."

"She left here in tears. Susan told me Elizabeth took a valise and that she wanted the rest of her things packed and sent to Miss Reynard's home." Ellie crossed her arms over her chest. "That does not sound like nothing."

"Elizabeth is gone?" squeaked Sarah. "Where did she go? When is she coming back? She promised to read me a story tonight."

Seeing Sarah's face crumble, he said, "I'm sorry, Sarah. I am certain Ellie will read to you tonight."

Sarah ran from the room in tears.

Will glanced around the room to see everyone looking expectantly at him. "She decided to leave. It has nothing to do with any of you."

"But it does have something to do with you," Ellie said.

His sister's unusual anger only spurred his own. "Maybe it does. Maybe I discovered that Elizabeth is not the person I thought she was."

"This was her home," Lucy said, entering the debate. "How could you force her to leave? That is cruel."

"And she loved you," Ellie added.

Will turned on his sister. "No, she did not. All she did was use me to get what she wanted."

"That does not sound like the Elizabeth I know," Lucy said quietly.

"Because she lied to us all," Will said.

Ellie glared at him. "I highly doubt that. *You* did something to hurt her. You are the reason she left us all."

Will clenched his fists into tight balls. "I did nothing. But since none of you want to believe me, I shall get my supper elsewhere."

"Will," Ellie yelled as he reached the hall. "This is not over. You will apologize for what you did."

"I did nothing, Ellie. Absolutely nothing." He hurled the front door open and slammed it behind him.

He did nothing, except fall in love with the wrong woman. Which he realized was the same thing he had done with Abigail. So why didn't he feel this much anger at Abigail? She had used him for years.

Because he did not love Abigail.

He had to know if Elizabeth told him the truth about Abigail. Not that he wanted to return to her. But because he needed to know the extent of Elizabeth's deceptions. He turned back to the house and ordered the coach.

After a short drive, he arrived at the inn where Abigail had told him she was staying.

"I'm here to see Miss Mason," he said to the innkeeper.

The innkeeper eyed him from head to toe. "Do they expect you?"

They? Every now and then, Will truly enjoyed being a duke, and this was one of those occasions. He handed the innkeeper his card.

"Your Grace, I apologize." The innkeeper bowed. "Miss Mason and her father are in the dining room. I will tell them you are here."

"No, wait," Will said, grabbing the man's arm. "I will announce myself."

"Very well, Your Grace."

"When did they arrive?" Will asked.

"Yesterday morning, Your Grace."

"And they arrived together?"

"Yes."

Perhaps Elizabeth was right. "Is there a private room we might use?"

"Yes, Your Grace. The room behind you will be cleared in a moment. The dining room is down that hall," the innkeeper said, pointing toward the main hallway.

"Thank you." Will walked down the hall and stopped at the threshold. He scanned the room until he found Abigail and her father. As he strolled toward them, Abigail glanced up and her eyes widened. She glanced around as if looking for an escape route.

He reached their table and placed his hands on the back of both chairs. "Good evening, Miss Mason, Mr. Mason. What a surprise to find you *both* here."

Mr. Mason glared back at him. "I just arrived here this evening. I came to collect my little girl before she made a huge mistake."

"Indeed? Why don't we remove ourselves to a more private accommodation?" Will released the two chairs and stepped back, allowing them to stand.

"Will"—Abigail started but then stopped when he shot her a glare.

"Come along," he said hoarsely.

They followed him to the private room the innkeeper had provided. Will sat in a wood chair and waited for the others to follow. "You might want to close the door, Mr. Mason."

Mr. Mason hesitantly shut the door. "What is this about, Atherton?"

"Oh, but it's Kendal now. As in, the Duke of Kendal."

Mr. Mason turned up his lip. "What does that matter? You were nothing but a farmer in Virginia."

"True, but we are not in Virginia any longer, are we?"

"Just tell me why you are here," Mr. Mason demanded.

Will smiled at him. "That is exactly what I want to know. Why are you here? Both of you."

"Will, I already told you that this afternoon," Abigail said sweetly. "At least I did until that little strumpet interrupted us."

Will clenched his jaw. "Do not ever call her that." Even if that was an appropriate description of Elizabeth.

Abigail sat down in a huff. "I still cannot believe you bedded that awful woman, Will."

"We have been through that, Abigail. I would like to know why you are both here. Especially you, Mr. Mason."

"I told you. I arrived late this afternoon."

"Indeed? Then how is it that my cousin overheard you and Abigail in a bookshop early this afternoon?" Will laced his fingers behind his head in a casual demeanor even though tension knotted his muscles.

"Is this the same cousin who is carrying your child?" Abigail questioned.

"Yes," Will replied.

"Will, you are so infatuated with this girl you cannot see when she is lying. My father arrived late this afternoon. Your cousin was purely looking out for her own interests."

Will pondered that for a moment until he remembered the innkeeper's words. "And yet the innkeeper swears you both arrived yesterday."

Abigail's face drew pale as she glanced over at her father for support.

"Well played, Atherton. We did arrive yesterday. My daughter was bound to get to London and I wasn't about to let her go alone."

That he could almost believe, Will thought. "Why now? I offered for her several times over the past five years. Every time, you both rejected my proposals."

"Because you aren't good enough for my daughter, Atherton. Being a duke doesn't mean a damned thing to me." Mr. Mason grabbed his daughter's hand. "We will leave now."

Something was not right about their behavior. They were still hiding something. "Wait. My cousin said she heard you," he said, looking at Mr. Mason, "talking about Abigail becoming the next Duchess of Kendal. I shall give you one thousand pounds for an honest answer. Was she right?"

"Will, I thought we already decided your cousin did not see us there," Abigail said.

"I was speaking with your father, Abigail. And I would like him to answer."

Mr. Mason's face turned red. "Yes, I did say that this afternoon. Because my daughter would make a perfect duchess. It is exactly what she should be."

Will raked his hand through his hair. "You hated me and the fact that I was to become a duke."

"No, I only wanted you to think that," Mr. Mason replied. "If you had married her before you inherited, you never would have returned to England to claim your title and inheritance. If you had thought there was no chance of obtaining Abigail, you would stay here. Then Abigail could come a month later to surprise you. By then you would be settled here."

"But you told me how much you hated the British."

Mr. Mason gave him a smug smile. "Of course, I did. You had to believe you would never have a chance with my daughter. Good God, man, do you have any idea how hard it is to make a decent living in America? Abigail deserves more than just a small, filthy house."

Will shook his head in confusion. "But you had money. From how you lived, I believed you had a good deal of money. More than enough to support your daughter should she need it."

"All an illusion. Abigail's mother had the money. Once she died, her family stopped sending money over. I knew the next best thing was to marry her off to you once you decided to remain here as the duke."

Will could not believe what he was hearing. "Abigail, how were you involved with this?"

"I—I knew all along," she finally admitted, staring at the wood floor.

They had both been manipulating him. For years! They were no different from Elizabeth. Except she admitted her mistakes to him freely, unlike either of them. He only had to pay with his heart to get Elizabeth to tell him the truth.

"Get out of my sight," he said in a low voice. "In fact, get out of my country."

Chapter 26

"What are you doing here?"

Elizabeth looked at Sophie, dropped her valise, and hugged her friend for support. "I left him, Sophie."

Sophie pulled away and stared at her. Then she slowly led her into the receiving salon and closed the door behind them. "What happened?"

Elizabeth explained how Abigail had arrived at the house by the time Elizabeth returned home. "I did the most dreadful thing," she whispered.

"What?"

"I told them I was pregnant with Will's child."

"But you are not with child." Sophie grabbed her hand and held it tightly for a moment. "You are not."

"No, I am not." A wave of disappointment shot through her. She wanted to have Will's child and watch his face as he held their baby for the first time.

"Then why did you say such a thing?" Sophie asked.

"I don't know. I guess I thought it was the surest way to keep them apart. I acted horribly, Sophie."

Sophie drew her hand away and back to her lap. "Did it work?"

"I have no idea. Will dismissed me to my room like a child."

"Was he angry?"

Elizabeth shrugged. "He is now."

Sophie rubbed her temples. "Then why are you here?"

"Sophie, I lied to him."

"And did you tell him the truth after Abigail left?"

Elizabeth nodded. "But there is more."

"How much more?"

"We found my mother's diary last night," Elizabeth said quietly.

"Elizabeth, you are talking in circles. What does finding your mother's diary have to do with you being here instead of at home?"

"Everything," Elizabeth whispered, sensing Sophie's frustration. "It was awful, Sophie. The things my mother did."

Elizabeth related the events in the journal, including the section regarding the wager and the red-headed footman.

Sophie hugged her again. "I am sorry, Elizabeth. I know how much you had wanted to know the truth. And how you expected your father would turn out to be a peer."

Elizabeth sat back and stared at the rug. "I would be able to accept what she'd done if she loved him. But she did not love him. She only wanted to win the wager and buy a bonnet."

Elizabeth buried her face in her hands as tears tracked down her cheeks. "He watched," she whispered.

"Who? The footman? That isn't very unusual, Elizabeth. Most men like to watch as they make love."

"Not the footman. My father watched them.

There was a peephole, and he watched them have sexual congress."

"Oh, my," Sophie muttered. "But how did you end up here because of that?"

Elizabeth explained how she realized that she had been manipulating Will with her wiles. Then she told Sophie about her conversation with Will in the study.

"You told him you only made love with him in order to get him to stay in England?" Sophie almost shouted. "Have you lost your mind?"

"I think I have," Elizabeth replied. "What am I to do?"

"I am not really certain," Sophie admitted. "Stay here tonight, and we will figure what to do in the morning."

Caroline sighed as she walked to the salon. Whoever could be calling at this dreadful hour of the morning? Anyone with sense knows calls begin in the afternoon. She had been at the Howards' party until one in the morning. With a baby due in a few months, she needed her sleep.

"Who is in the salon, Rogers?"

The handsome footman turned with a smile that made her knees go weak. This baby had better be a boy because she wanted to get that man in her bed and couldn't until Richard had his heir.

"A Mr. Mason and his daughter Abigail. They are recently from America."

Americans, she thought with distaste. She might have known they would not know about proper etiquette. She walked into the salon with a forced smile.

"Good morning," she offered.

Mr. Mason stood quickly, and then nudged his

daughter until she did the same. "Good morning, Baroness. I hope this wasn't too early to call on you?"

"Not at all," Caroline bit out. She took a seat by the window. "I do not believe we know each other, do we?"

"No, ma'am," Mr. Mason said. "I was discussing my problem with a man at the inn, and he suggested I speak with you."

"And what problem is that?"

"I want to be the next Duchess of Kendal," Abigail blurted out.

Caroline rolled her eyes. This insignificant girl believed she could be a duchess. *Americans,* she thought again. "I am not quite sure how I can be of assistance with that."

"I was told that your husband was next in line," Mr. Mason said.

"Yes, he is the heir presumptive. However, if the new duke has any boys, the eldest will be the heir assumptive." Caroline wondered what these two were about this morning. Had the duke sent them to discover what she and Richard were doing?

"My daughter will promise to never have children if you can help her become the duchess." Mr. Mason's cheeks blotted red.

Caroline eyed both Mr. Mason and his daughter. Suspicion remained deep in her heart but curiosity won out. "Why?"

"I want to be duchess," Abigail whined. "I was supposed to be the duchess but my father's plan went awry."

Mr. Mason explained what his plan had been until the duke's cousin ruined everything.

"Elizabeth is with child?" Caroline almost shouted. "Yes."

As much as she dreaded the idea, Caroline knew she had no choice in the matter now. She had to keep William from marrying Elizabeth and unfortunately, these two minions would have to assist her.

"How will you keep your daughter from getting with child? The new duke is a young and lusty man. He will demand his husbandly rights."

Abigail's face drew pale.

"The man at the inn told me of a surgeon who says he can make a woman barren," Mr. Mason said.

Caroline winced. What kind of father would subject his daughter to something so horrible? It mattered not to her. They obviously wanted the money and position so desperately it would not be Caroline who stopped them.

"I can get us what we both desire. However," she said, holding her hand up to stop him from interrupting her, "I will do nothing to assist you until the surgeon guarantees me that the surgery was a success. I will take no chances that she will become with child and have his heir."

The young girl's face turned white but she said nothing.

"Do we have an agreement?" Caroline asked impatiently.

Mr. Mason glanced over at his daughter, then nodded. "Yes. We will do whatever it takes to make my daughter duchess."

"Very well, then. We shall start today. Call for your surgeon."

Will glanced out the window as the coach rolled toward his home. The last two days had been hell.

He'd barely slept, drunk far too much whisky, and did not care about anything. After sending money and passage to Mr. Mason, he was glad to be done with them. With any luck, they would be sailing out of his life in the next few days.

Now, if only he could get over his anger at Elizabeth. A part of him did not believe she only made love with him to get him to stay. He loved Elizabeth. He had wanted to build his life with her. Instead, she had used him. Broke his heart and ripped it to shreds.

Will glanced out the window of the coach as his driver turned down Maddox Street to get around some commotion ahead. He knocked on the roof to gain the groomsman's attention.

"Yes, Your Grace?" the man said as the carriage stopped.

"I shall get out here."

"Are you certain, Your Grace?"

"Yes, I am." Will had one thing on his mind: getting Elizabeth out of his head once and for all. A tumble with a prostitute might be just the thing to do it.

He clamored onto the street and glanced around for the right house. After finding it, he walked toward the home with all the candles blazing from the interior rooms. He opened the door and the sweet aroma of women enveloped him. A few of the women stared at him. Several gentlemen inclined their heads in greeting but didn't say a thing. And why would they? Most of them were here when they could be spending the evening with their wives.

"Good evening, Your Grace," a soft, feminine voice sounded from behind him.

Will turned around to see Lady Whitely smiling at him. "Good evening."

"Is there something I can assist you with?" She took his arm and led him back to the room where he and Somerton had had drinks. "Sit here and I shall bring you some whisky. That is your drink, is it not?"

"Yes."

She walked to the bar, whispered something in a footman's ear, and then quickly returned a moment later with a bottle and one glass. After pouring it to the rim, she carefully handed it to him.

"So tell me, Your Grace," she purred. "Do you know how this works?"

Will sipped his whisky and then laughed coarsely. "I believe I do."

Lady Whitely smiled at him. "No. How this establishment works."

"Why don't you tell me?" Will leaned back and downed the rest of his whisky.

She refilled his glass and said, "The first time you enter my establishment and desire to be with one of my girls, I help you decide which girl is right for you."

"Any of them will do," he said. The whisky tasted far too good tonight.

"We do not work that way. You tell me everything you want in a woman, and I do my best to fulfill your fantasy. So tell me, what do you like in a woman?"

Will shut his eyes and imagined Elizabeth. "Red hair and green eyes. Taller than average but not a giant. Slim figure and perfectly rounded breasts with rosy nipples."

He blinked his eyes open. Had he said that aloud?

"Hmm," Lady Whitely said. "I only have one redhead, and honestly, I do not know her eye color. It might be blue. Is that a problem?"

Damn, he had described Elizabeth. He gulped

his second glass of whisky down fast. "No, it's not a problem."

"Do you like your women submissive? Domineering? Or maybe playful is your desire."

"Whatever you feel is best for me," Will replied, wanting this process to be over. He just wanted to thrust inside a pretty woman and get Elizabeth out of his head.

"All right, if you do decide submissive is your preferred way, there are ties attached to all the beds."

"Wonderful," Will remarked.

"Very well, then. I shall check to see if she is occupied yet." Lady Whitely rose and gracefully walked out of the room.

Will glanced around the garish room and wondered what the other men in the place were doing here. He chuckled softly. He knew exactly why they were here. The same reason he was—to forget someone.

He poured another glass of whisky, hoping the alcohol would numb his mind and heart to the ache he felt. Forgetting Elizabeth was the only option. She had lied to him, manipulated him, and never loved him. Everything she had done had only been for herself.

Or had it?

She had attempted to flirt with him in order to stay in the house, but he'd seen right through her. He'd known what she was doing and never stopped her. She also insisted his sisters have a Season, something he never would have allowed. She hadn't used her wiles to get him to agree. She used logic. And she had been right that in order for them to be accepted, they needed to make their bow and join in the festivities.

Elizabeth had also asserted the boys needs for a tutor to keep them up with their studies. Again, she was right. And every night they were home, she read to Sarah before bed. Those didn't seem to be the actions of a selfish woman. He couldn't imagine Abigail doing any of those things for his siblings.

He sipped his whisky, noticing the first affects of the drink. His mind felt slightly fuzzy. Had she really manipulated him?

Thinking back to that day in the music room, he only remembered her pain at telling him about her father. If she had truly wanted him to stay, she could have insisted on marriage after they had finished. His honor should have insisted upon marriage, regardless of her misgivings. Why did she think she'd manipulated him?

He drank down the rest of his whisky. He wanted nothing more than to slip into a stupor for the night.

Lady Whitely walked back and sat down next to him with a smile. "She needs a few minutes to ready herself."

This was a foolish idea. He should leave, return home, and attempt to get sober.

Elizabeth and Sophie enjoyed a small dinner and then returned to the salon to talk. For two days now, Elizabeth barely touched her food, her stomach tied up in knots all the time. She had not heard from Will but truly hadn't expected to. Her real disappointment was that Ellie and Lucy had not tried to contact her. Perhaps Will had convinced them that she was a horrible person.

All she wanted to do was go to bed and forget about this day. But Sophie insisted on talking . . . again.

"Elizabeth, do you honestly believe you only slept with the duke to keep him in England."

"Must we discuss this again?"

"Yes. I just don't believe it," Sophie said.

"What do you mean?"

"I have been thinking about this. Is there a chance you decided there must be a reason you succumbed to his charms, so you invented this excuse?"

Elizabeth relived that day. She'd been so distraught about her family and the late duke, and being with Will felt so wonderful. "I was scared, Sophie. If he returned to Canada or America, I would have been left alone . . . again."

"You have been alone before," Sophie commented.

"Not like this. After falling in love with him and his family, I feel so lost not being with them."

Suddenly the front door hurled open and Lord Somerton stepped inside. "Sophie! Where the bloody hell are you?"

Sophie rolled her eyes. "In here, Somerton."

Lord Somerton raced into the room and looked over at Elizabeth. "Thank God."

He strode toward her and pulled her out of her seat.

"What are you doing?" Sophie exclaimed.

"She needs to come with me."

"Why?" Elizabeth and Sophie said in unison.

Somerton stared at Sophie. "He is at Lady Whitely's."

Sophie's eyes widened. "Oh, my. How did you find out?"

"She sent a footman to inform me." He looked over at Elizabeth again.

"This must be her decision," Sophie said to him.

"Dammit, we don't have time for this. Lady Elizabeth, do you love Will?"

"Yes," she admitted quietly.

"Will you do whatever it takes to get him back?" Somerton demanded.

Get him back? Did she ever have him to begin with? She had no idea. Maybe this would help her find out.

"Elizabeth, you will always be considered the duke's daughter. No matter what happened," Sophie said, "you love him. Go get him."

Somerton stared at her as if his patience had just about run its course. "Will you do whatever it takes to win him?"

"Yes." Elizabeth felt as if they were speaking another language, yet they seemed to understand each other perfectly. "Please, what are you both talking about?"

"The duke is at Lady Whitely's," Sophie started.

"Who is Lady Whitely? I have never heard of her before," Elizabeth said.

"Lady Whitely runs a . . . a . . ." Sophie looked over at Somerton for assistance.

"She runs a brothel," he said simply. "And Will is there right now. If you don't get over there, he might make a huge mistake."

A brothel. Will was at a brothel. "Why?"

"I shall explain in the carriage," Somerton said. He looked at Sophie. "You owe me far more than a name for this one."

"You might be right," Sophie said.

Elizabeth picked up her bonnet and walked out to the carriage with Somerton. A ripple of fear stopped her cold. She knew so little about the man she was about to be alone with in the carriage.

"What is wrong now?" Somerton asked in an impatient tone.

"I . . . I should not be alone in the carriage with you."

Somerton laughed soundly. "That is the least of

your problems, Lady Elizabeth. You just agreed to enter a brothel, and you are worried about being in a coach with me."

She had not thought about it that way. "I actually have to go inside the brothel?"

Somerton held out his hand to help her inside the carriage. "Yes, my dear. Assuming you wish to save him from making a huge mistake."

"I do," she answered.

"All right, then. Lady Whitely is currently keeping him occupied with a little whisky and conversation. You will enter through the servants' entrance and someone will escort you up to a private room."

"What am I supposed to do?"

Somerton groaned. "I really don't need to tell you *that*, do I?"

Elizabeth looked at him and shrugged.

"Seduce the man. Please tell me you know how to do that."

Heat crossed her cheeks. Hopefully in the dark carriage, Somerton would not notice. "Of course."

"Damn. You don't know what to do." Somerton leaned his head back and stared at the ceiling of the carriage. "Entice him, Elizabeth. Make him want you so desperately, he'll tell you anything."

She didn't rebuke him using her given name when she knew she should. "How?"

"Lady Whitely will provide a very revealing gown. Flaunt your assets. Let him see what he is missing."

"But he will know it's me. He's so angry with me that he will most likely dash from the room once he sees me."

"Good point. I will make certain Lady Whitely provides a mask for you to wear. Keep only a few candles lit so the room is dark. Do not let him take off the mask until he realizes what a huge mistake he has made. Let him grovel at your feet for forgiveness."

Groveling is what she should be doing, not Will. "What if this does not work?"

"Would you rather not try? Go back to Sophie's never knowing if you could have made this work?"

The carriage slowed to a stop and as Elizabeth glanced out, she realized they had come to a standstill directly in front of Victoria's home. Her friend had never spoken of a brothel being next door. Perhaps Victoria did not know about it. This wasn't an area normally filled with brothels.

"I will continue with this plan," Elizabeth finally answered.

"Good," Somerton said, then climbed down. He held out his hand for her. "I will make sure one of the girls tells you the best way to seduce him."

"Wonderful," she replied as she walked alongside him. Now she would be getting lessons from a strumpet. How had her life gotten to this point?

She kept her head down as they walked to the servants' entrance. Hopefully Victoria would not glance outside and notice her. They walked inside a warm building with the sound of voices coming from upstairs.

"Welcome, Lord Somerton."

Elizabeth turned to look at the woman who had called Somerton's name in such a seductive voice. Her mouth gaped. The woman's red gown had a slit up to her mid-thigh that opened wide with every step.

"Good evening, Venus," Somerton said.

He knew this woman? The man was more depraved than she had ever realized.

"Lady Whitely asked me to assist you in any manner necessary," the woman said.

"My friend might need some womanly advice on the art of seduction." Somerton stepped toward Venus with a smile.

"I do not think that will be a problem," Venus replied with a coy smile. "Come along with me."

Elizabeth walked toward the woman and then glanced back at Somerton. He gave her an encouraging smile.

"Win him over, Elizabeth," he said. "Make him grovel."

She had no idea how to manage that feat. She followed Venus up to the third floor where there were only three rooms. As she walked past one room, she could hear the moans of a man, and a woman urging him on. When they reached the next room, Venus stopped and opened the door.

Elizabeth entered the room expecting to see it covered in gaudy red velvet. Instead, the bed was covered in a white lace coverlet, the two chairs were pale blue velvet, and the rug a collection of blue and green flowers. It did not look much different from any lady's bedroom.

"This is the virginal room," Venus said with a laugh.

"Virginal?"

"It is for the young men who come here for their first time, or couples who need to put a little excitement back in their marriage. They can be two different people here."

"Oh," Elizabeth answered, trying to sound more worldly than she felt.

"It's not your first time, is it?" Venus ambled to a linen press and opened the doors.

"No."

"Good. Do you prefer white, black, or red?"

"For what?" Elizabeth asked as she walked over to the linen press.

"Your gown." Venus's gaze roamed from Elizabeth's head to her toes. "Personally, I think the white would make you fade away. The red is too garish, but the black is perfect."

"Very well, the black one."

Venus pulled out a gown much like the one she wore. Elizabeth stared at the fabric, wondering what would be used to make it so sheer.

"Turn around, and let me help you."

Elizabeth waited while Venus helped her undress and put the daring gown on.

"Oh, my," Elizabeth exclaimed as she caught sight of herself in the cheval mirror. The bodice fell into a V shape, exposing more of her breasts than anything she had ever worn. A slit raced up to her hip, showing all of her leg as she walked.

Venus stared at her. "You need something more," she decided. "It's your hair."

Elizabeth's hand went to her head. "What's wrong with it?"

"It's far too formal for such an occasion." Venus walked toward her and pulled a few pins from Elizabeth's upswept style. Then Venus drew a few strands down around her face and neck. "Now the mask, and you shall be all set."

Elizabeth closed her eyes as Venus placed the mask over her face. When she opened them, she could not believe her eyes. If she didn't know it was her reflection, she would not have recognized herself.

"So, how do I seduce him?" she asked aloud.

"That, my dear, is the easy part." Venus went to the

chairs and placed a bottle of something on the table in between them. "He drinks whisky. When he comes in, have him sit there while you pour. As you do, make certain the neckline of your gown gapes open a little more, so he can see the merchandise."

"The merchandise?"

"Your tits," Venus said with a laugh. She cupped her own and said, "These are your best assets in this business. They determine if you are a Covent Garden whore, or an earl's mistress."

But Elizabeth did not want to be a mistress. She wanted to be a wife. Will's wife. "Any other advice?"

"When you sit across from him, let him see your privates. It drives men mad."

With the slit in her gown, that would not be hard. She imagined the slit would easily slide to the right and open up in front of him.

"Don't look so pale. Perhaps you should have a little rouge."

"No. I shall be fine."

"You will be great," Venus said with a smile. "Just remember, make him grovel."

Chapter 27

"I believe it is time to go upstairs," Lady Whitely said seductively.

Oh, hell. Will hoped she wasn't thinking he was interested in her. At this point, he really wasn't interested in anyone. He should return home and forget about this day. Maybe in time, he could forgive Elizabeth. And if not, he would have to forget about her.

Not that it would ever be possible. Forgetting Elizabeth would be as hard as forgetting his own name.

Suddenly, Lady Whitely was pulling on his hands to get him to his feet. He should protest but the whisky seemed to have addled his mind. He followed her like a puppy dog up two flights of stairs.

She opened the second door and whispered, "Enjoy."

Will walked into the room and blinked. After all the red furnishings, this room was a welcome surprise. The scent from the room vaguely reminded him of Elizabeth.

A small sound alerted him to someone standing behind a blue chair. Slowly she walked forward, her entire body silhouetted by the candles behind her. She was dressed in a sheer black gown that could never be worn outside. Even from this distance, he could see the round globes of her breasts, her nipples erect and waiting for his mouth. Between the room smelling like her and this beautiful woman looking like her, he realized he was in too deep.

A seductive smile lifted her lips upward and a part of him lifted, too. He could not want her. She wasn't Elizabeth. But she looked so much like her that his body didn't seem to care.

"Take off the mask," Will ordered. He knew seeing her fully would finally dampen his desire. And he really did not want to want her.

"No. Lady Whitely told me the mask stays on the first time I'm with a customer. Why don't you come over here and sit down. I shall pour you a whisky."

Her alluring voice was like a siren's call to him. He seemed unable to stop his feet from moving across the rug. Her gaze ran the length of him but paused as she noticed his erection.

As soon as he sat, she bent over the decanter and her full breasts bounced forward. He groaned softly. She handed him a crystal glass with whisky.

"How did you know I drink this?" he asked.

She laughed softly. "Lady Whitely knows her customers' preferences."

"What is your name?" That would do it. Hearing her name would stop him cold.

"What do you want it to be?" she replied coyly. "I can be whomever you desire tonight."

Will gulped his whisky down. "Elizabeth," he whispered.

"What?" She sounded surprised.

He should never have said that aloud. Calling her Elizabeth was almost as bad as being here in the first place. He placed his hands on the arms of the chair to lift himself up. "I should go."

"No."

Since when did he listen to prostitutes? But he quickly sat back down.

"Why don't you tell me why you want to call me Elizabeth?" she whispered.

Even her voice reminded him of her. What did he have to lose by telling her this? "I love her."

In the dim room, he barely noticed that her eyes widened behind the mask.

"You do? Then why are you not with her?"

"We argued," he said. They hadn't really argued. She had been trying to explain what she had done.

"Do you want her back?" The enchantress let her legs slip apart, allowing him a view of her damp folds.

He gripped the arms of the chair, trying not to embarrass himself. "No," he lied.

She stood up and walked behind his chair. Her soft lips kissed the sensitive spot right behind his ear. She skimmed her hands down the front of his jacket. He clasped her hands with his.

"Do you think she wants you back?" the woman whispered in his ear. "She might be dreadfully sorry for whatever she said."

"You do not know anything about it." Damn. Why did he drink that last glass of whisky?

Her hand went to his cravat and slowly untied the knot. Unraveling the linen from around his neck, she let her breasts rub against his shoulders.

"How badly do you want her back?"

"I already told you, I don't want . . ." his voice trailed

off as her hands unbuttoned his shirt. Her warm, soft hands slid down his chest until she reached his nipples.

"Are you certain you don't want her back?" She kissed his neck. "I am sensing that you do."

Her fingers rubbed and pulled slightly on his nipples, driving him mad. How was he supposed to think about anything when she was doing that to him?

"Do you want her back?" she asked insistently.

"Yes. I want her back," he admitted. "But I highly doubt she wants me."

He held her arms to stop her from moving any farther down. His desire was almost out of control. And he did not want this woman. He wanted Elizabeth. His Elizabeth. The woman who made love with him on the sofa and on the desk. The one who was so damned good to him and his siblings. His resolve strengthened.

"I am leaving now." He moved away from her and picked up his cravat.

"Where are you going?" she whispered.

"To find Elizabeth. My Elizabeth." He moved toward the door, but she was blocking it with her body. Of course, he had forgotten to pay her. He reached into his pocket and pulled out more than enough for her spending time talking to him.

"What are you going to do when you find her?" the woman asked.

"Apologize and beg her forgiveness for my dreadful behavior. Make her understand that what she did has nothing to do with her mother. And ask her to be my wife."

Elizabeth had heard more than enough. She did not need groveling, especially when she was the one at fault, not him. Lifting her hands, she trailed her fingers up his arm.

He caught her right arm and stared at the small mole just above her elbow. "Elizabeth?"

He could not have realized it was her based on a mole. Elizabeth was the name he'd wanted to call her. "That is my name for tonight."

His eyes stared at her as if he was seeing her for the first time. "I have decided to stay."

"What?"

"I want you to seduce me." His head moved toward her ear and he whispered what he wanted her to do.

Why was he staying? Somerton had told her that once Will figured out that he truly wanted to be with her, he would leave. Not stay and make love to her. Or rather, she make love to him.

If she backed out of this now, he would know it was her.

"What are you waiting for?" He pulled off his jacket and threw it towards the chair.

"I thought you wanted to go beg for her forgiveness."

His eyes narrowed on her. "I decided I would rather stay here for awhile longer."

It suddenly occurred to her that he knew. He must have noticed the mole on her arm was heart-shaped before today. He was playing with her. And she wanted to play along.

"As you wish," she said. She reached for his linen shirt and pulled it out of his trousers.

"Allow me," he said, whisking the garment over his head.

She moved her hands to the buttons on his trousers. Quickly they fell to his knees, stuck there by his boots. He carefully walked backwards until he found the bed. He sat on the edge and waited.

"The boots are next," he said.

She moved to his feet, yanked on the boots, and then tossed them aside. Full naked, he stood back up. His erection rose proudly from the patch of curling hair.

"What are you waiting for?" he asked.

Remembering what he had requested she do, Elizabeth knelt down and skimmed her fingernails up the length of his shaft. She brought the tip of him to her mouth and let her tongue glide across him. Hearing his moan, she brought him into her mouth. Sliding down the length of him, she heard him hiss.

She brought her fingernails down the hard muscles of his buttocks and then moved to his thighs. The sound of his groans increased as she moved along his length. Moisture pooled between her folds as desire raced along her veins. She wanted him now.

As if he sensed her yearning, he pushed her away and led her to the bed. Still wearing her gown, she laid back against the pillows. He covered her body with his own and he brought her hands over her head. Quickly, he bound her hands with a cloth attached to the bed. The silky fabric rubbed against her wrists.

"What are you doing?" she asked.

"Don't tell me you haven't been tied to the bed before."

"No," she whispered.

His mouth moved to the base of her neck. "How is that possible?" he asked between kisses.

"I haven't been here long," she panted as his lips trailed down her chest.

"I never would have guessed," he said.

Her breasts rubbed against him as she arched her back to be closer to him. With excruciating slowness, he slid the V of her neckline apart until it would go no more. He smiled down at her and ripped the fabric, exposing her nipples to his gaze.

"You are so beautiful," he whispered before circling his tongue around one hard nipple. He drew it into his mouth, suckling her.

Her hips bucked under him as he moved to her other breast. He chuckled softly. He lifted off her and then tore at the rest of the gown, stripping it from her. Completely naked and bound, she never felt so exposed before.

He spread her legs apart and moved in between them. His tongue lashed against her nub.

"Oh, God," she moaned.

He continued to tease her, bring her to the brink of desire . . . only to stop. As he started to brush his tongue against her again, desire sped through her. He inserted one finger deep inside her. She closed her eyes, certain this time he would let her reach the apex.

"Please don't stop," she begged him.

But just as quickly, he halted again.

She groaned in frustrated desire. As her body started to calm down, his mouth was on her again. Her heart pounded as hot passion flowed through her body.

"Will, please don't stop this time," she begged again.

"Do you love me?" he whispered, pausing only a second before resuming with his mouth on her.

"Yes," she cried out. "Please don't stop again."

Slowly, he circled her clitoris with his tongue. Tension curled her toes as the pressure grew within her.

"Did you love me the first time we did this?" he demanded and then moved his tongue over her again.

"I don't know." She felt as if she could barely breathe with the pleasure building so quickly. "I wanted you so desperately that day. I wanted your comfort, your love. I wanted you to be there for me. I wanted you and only you."

"What do you want me to do?"

"Love me . . . forever."

Suddenly he moved over her and thrust deeply inside her moist depths. In seconds, she clung to the ties that bound her wrists and cried out in passion. Just as quickly, he followed her over the edge of the abyss.

He rested his body on top of hers as they returned to the reality of what they had done. He had forced her to confess, made her grovel, and she had done so willingly. She didn't want to be without him. The idea of losing him made her heart go cold.

Slowly, he moved his hands to hers and untied them. He reached for her mask and slid it up off her face. After kissing her gently, he whispered, "I am sorry."

"For what?"

"Getting angry with you for lying when all you did was attempt to protect me from Abigail."

"I'm sorry, too, Will." She brought her hands up to his face and kissed him with all the love she had in her heart.

"As much as I love that, we do need to talk."

Elizabeth nodded.

Will moved off her to lie next to her. "Elizabeth, do you honestly believe that everything you did was only to manipulate me?"

"Not everything," she answered. "Oh, Will, I read the majority of my mother's diary. It was dreadful. If she wanted something done, she would offer to do disgusting things for the duke."

"And have you ever done that?"

She looked at him. "Of course not."

"What about a few minutes ago when I asked you to do that to me? Did you do it willingly or because you thought it would get me to marry you?"

Thinking about having him in her mouth made her smile. "I did it because you asked me to and I wanted to. I wanted to give you pleasure. No other reason than that."

"Then why would you think you are manipulating me?" Will asked. "I felt as if I had taken advantage of your pain when we made love the first time."

"You most certainly did not," she said.

"Then why do you think . . ." He paused, and then said, "You were ashamed."

"Oh, Will, I made love to you and honestly, at that point, I did not love you." Elizabeth curled closer to him and skimmed her fingers through the dark hairs on his chest. "I could not understand why after twenty-six years, I would do something like that with a man I did not love."

His lips lifted upwards. "So you assumed you must have had an ulterior motive."

She nodded against his chest. "I had never experienced desire like I do with you. Sophie told me a few times to seduce you, but I could not go through with it until that day."

"Sophie told you to seduce me?"

"Yes. She is a bit of a matchmaker. I don't think she had any reason other than wanting to see me happy."

"And are you?" he whispered.

Elizabeth moved over him and smiled as she felt the rough hairs on his chest. "Very happy. At least, I think I am. Are you angry about tonight?"

"How exactly did you plan this? I had no intention

of coming here tonight. My carriage took a detour and I decided to come in for a drink."

"A drink? I thought this was a brothel."

"True. So how did you get here?" he asked, caressing her cheek with the palm of his hand.

She explained Somerton's sudden appearance at Sophie's house.

"But how did . . . never mind, I think I know," Will muttered.

"How?"

"He seems rather close with Lady Whitely. I presume she sent him a note stating I was here."

"Why would she care?" Elizabeth asked.

Will shrugged. "I do not understand half of what Somerton does."

"He told me I was to come here to keep you from making a big mistake. What mistake was he talking about?" Elizabeth asked, caressing his jaw.

"I believe he thought I was going to use one of Lady Whitely's girls."

"Were you?" she whispered.

Will closed his eyes. "I don't know. I planned on leaving and tried a few times. But I never seemed to make it out the door. And when I saw this," he said, kissing her heart-shaped mole, "I knew it was you all along."

"Were you mad?"

"Only for a moment. I realized you must love me quite a bit if you were willing to sacrifice your reputation to come here for me."

"I do, Will."

"I love you, too, Elizabeth."

"What about my father?" she mumbled. "I really am no one. Just the daughter of a footman."

He pulled her up and kissed her softly. "It doesn't

matter to me who you are. The *ton* considers you the daughter of the Duke of Kendal. No one but us needs to know the truth."

Elizabeth stared at him, knowing in her heart that everything would be all right.

Chapter 28

"Elizabeth!" Sarah raced into her arms and clung to her.

Elizabeth walked into the salon with Sarah wrapped around her. "I missed you, Sarah."

"I missed you so much. Please don't ever leave again."

Elizabeth looked over at Will and said, "I do not plan to."

"Sarah, run upstairs and have your sisters and the boys come down here," Will said, removing Sarah from Elizabeth's arms.

Sarah raced off with a look of glee.

Elizabeth sat on the sofa with her heart pounding. They had decided to tell the children of their plans before announcing it to the world. She heard the boys running down the stairs and smiled. She still had some work to do to turn them into young gentlemen.

"Elizabeth," Michael said with a look of surprise on his face. "I thought you left."

"I have decided to return," she answered.

"Elizabeth!" Ellie and Lucy said in unison.

"Sit down, everyone," Will said loudly as the volume in the room continued to grow.

"Oh, my!" Ellie whispered and stared at Elizabeth.

"Elizabeth and I have decided to marry."

Elizabeth braced herself for a mix of emotions. She knew the girls would be happy but wondered about the boys, especially Michael. A loud shout erupted from the room and suddenly everyone, except Michael, enveloped Elizabeth in a hug.

Slowly, she broke away from the crowd and walked over to Will's stepbrother. Sitting next to him, she asked, "Are you all right with this?"

Michael shrugged. "This means we are never going home, doesn't it?"

"I do not know, Michael. Will and I have not discussed where we shall live."

"Would you come to America?"

Elizabeth nodded with a smile. "If that is where Will wants to live, then yes."

"And what if Will wants to live here?" Will asked in a gruff tone. There was a look of delight on his face like she had never seen before.

"I will live wherever my husband chooses to live." Elizabeth patted Michael's hand. "But how do you feel about it?"

"Honestly?" he asked.

Elizabeth nodded and then Will sat down next to her.

"I don't mind too much. I've met a couple of friends while Mr. Smith takes us on walks in the park."

"And you will make plenty more in the next year," Elizabeth said.

Michael put his arms around Elizabeth and whispered in her ear, "Thank you for marrying Will. Abigail was an awful person. And we all love you."

Elizabeth's heart swelled with love. She had gone from feeling completely alone to having a large family around her.

"Excuse me, Lady Elizabeth," Kenneth said from the doorway. "Lady Selby and Lady Blackburn are here to see you. Shall I tell them you are at home?"

"Yes, place them in the receiving salon. I will be there presently." Elizabeth squeezed Michael once more and then detangled herself from his grip.

"Did you tell them already?" Will asked.

"No. I have no idea why they are here. They are both due in a matter of weeks. They should be home in bed." Elizabeth took Will's hand. "Why don't you come with me? We can tell them together."

"I would enjoy that," Will said.

They entered the room hand in hand, and both Avis and Jennette gasped.

"What is the matter?" Elizabeth asked.

"It's true." Avis's face grew pale.

"What is true?" Elizabeth demanded.

Jennette cleared her throat. Never one to mince words, she blurted out, "Last night at the Dorchester ball, a rumor made its way through the crowd. The rumor said that you and the duke are actually siblings, and have been having an incestuous affair."

"Oh, my Lord," Elizabeth whispered, feeling faint. She dropped to the chair and attempted to swallow. "It is not true, Jennette."

"The rumor also said you are with child from the relationship," Avis added quietly.

"Caroline," Will spat. "I think we need to have a talk with my cousin and his wife."

"Wait, Will." Elizabeth caught her breath. "I am not Will's sister. We have proof that Will's father was in

Russia during the month of my conception." Elizabeth blew out a long breath. "And my father was a footman for the Langfords."

Avis and Jennette both sat back in the chairs, looking relieved. "Oh, thank God," Avis whispered.

"But are you with child?" Jennette asked with a smile.

Elizabeth shook her head. "No."

"But perhaps rather quickly after the wedding," Will added with a wink.

Will stormed up the steps of his cousin's home and flung the door open without waiting for the butler. "Richard! Caroline!"

"Will, do try to have a little patience," Elizabeth said, placing her hand on his arm.

Richard walked down the hall with a look of confusion on his weathered face. "Your Grace, what are you doing here?"

"Who is making that noise? There is a sick young woman up—" Caroline stopped when she noticed them in the hallway. Slowly, she walked down the steps. "To what do we owe this honor?"

"As if you did not know," Will muttered.

"Your Grace, what is this about?" Richard asked.

"A rumor regarding my relationship with Elizabeth," Will said. "A very untrue rumor, I might add."

Caroline scoffed. "I highly doubt that. You two cannot seem to keep your eyes off each other."

"I was speaking of the rumor regarding her father," Will said.

"No one knows who her father is. It could just as easily have been your father," Caroline replied, walking into the parlor.

"Except my father was in Russia for six months at the time, making the possibility nonexistent." Will led Elizabeth into the room with Caroline as Richard followed silently behind.

"So you say," Caroline rebuffed.

"No, so this official document says." Will pulled out the document that Somerton had given him.

Caroline pressed her lips together. "This only proves that he was not here. She might have been with him."

"She was at the Langford country party. And my father happened to be one of the Langfords' footmen," Elizabeth said proudly.

Will squeezed her hand. He'd told her she should not feel compelled to tell anyone about her father as long as they had the document from Somerton.

She looked at Will and said, "I am sick of the lies. If you do not care who my father is, then why should I?"

Will smiled as love filled his heart almost to bursting.

"Call for the surgeon!" A voice shouted from the top of the stairs. "Hurry! She's bleeding again. She might not make it."

Will knew that voice. Why would Mr. Mason be here? "What the hell is going on?"

"Nothing that concerns you." Caroline tried to get up but her bulging belly hindered her progress.

Will took Elizabeth's hand and they raced out of the parlor. He looked up to see Mr. Mason's face paler than a piece of linen.

"What is wrong?" Will asked.

"Abigail is bleeding. It's everywhere."

Will turned to the footman. "Get the surgeon now."

He released Elizabeth's hand and took the steps two at a time. He followed Mr. Mason into Abigail's room. The dark room held the stench of death. Will looked at Abigail's gray face and was certain there was nothing the surgeon could do.

"What happened to her?" Will demanded.

"It is none of your concern." Mr. Mason clutched his daughter's hand.

Blood seeped from between her legs, soaking through the sheets. Elizabeth entered the room and gasped.

Abigail blinked her eyes open for a minute. She focused on Will. "I'm sorry," she whispered. "I did this for you."

After one last shuttering breath, she closed her eyes for good. Will stared at her still body wondering what she might have meant by her words.

Mr. Mason turned on him. "This is all your fault!" he screamed.

"What did you do to her?" Will demanded.

"She only wanted to be your wife. She made a deal with the devil just to be a duchess," Mr. Mason ranted.

"What happened?"

Richard entered the room with a look of disgust. "She got what she deserved. They both did."

Richard quickly explained the scheme Mr. Mason had planned in order for his daughter to become duchess. Caroline stood there, staring at the body.

"Richard, get out of London. Take your wife to your estate and do not let her out of your sight." Will turned to Mr. Mason. "I am quite certain the constable will want some words with you."

Unable to stand any more, Will escorted Elizabeth out of the house. Once in the carriage, the reality of what they had done sank in.

"Why?" he mumbled.

Elizabeth was there, holding him. "Do you remember

I told you that some women would do anything to become duchess?"

Will nodded slowly, remembering her lessons.

"Abigail was one of them."

Three weeks after Abigail's death, Elizabeth became the Duchess of Kendal in a very private wedding. With only Will's siblings and Elizabeth's friends attending, they held the ceremony at the house.

"To the happy couple," Lord Selby said, holding his glass of champagne.

Elizabeth sipped her champagne slowly. The nerves of the wedding had made her stomach a little off the past few days. Will reached over, grabbed her hand, and gave it a little kiss.

Finally, their lives were at peace. Richard did as Will suggested and left for the country house before Caroline could not travel. Mr. Mason, personally escorted to the docks by Somerton, left for New York.

"Your Grace, there is a Mr. Lewis here to see you. He said you would see him."

"Thank you, Kenneth."

Elizabeth looked over at her new husband with a smile. "Could your business not wait this morning, Will?"

Will pulled back her chair. "No. And you will meet him, too."

"What is this about, Will?"

They walked together to the salon where Mr. Lewis awaited them. Elizabeth stopped at the doorway when she realized exactly why Will wanted her here. Mr. Lewis stood and bowed to them both.

"Your Graces."

"Oh, my Lord," Elizabeth whispered as she looked at the man. His red hair was streaked with gray but his green eyes sparkled.

"Mr. Lewis, I believe you have yet to meet your daughter, Elizabeth, Duchess of Kendal."

Mr. Lewis stood there as if not knowing what to do. Elizabeth turned to her husband. "How?"

Will smiled. "I truly appreciate Somerton's talents."

"I love you!"

Will hugged her and kissed her quickly on the lips. "I was hoping he could get here before the wedding but he was detained. Talk with your father. I will tell everyone why you left the breakfast."

Elizabeth watched her husband leave them alone, and knew for certain, this time everything would be all right.

Epilogue

Anthony Somerton walked into Selby's house quietly. While he had been invited to join the festivities, there was only one reason to be here. The cold November air had chilled him to the bone, but the house was warm and filled with people. He handed his greatcoat to the butler and walked into the room. After a journey that took him to France for five months, he was exhausted and done playing matchmaker.

Although, glancing around the room, he realized he'd done a good job. Avis held her daughter, Isabel, while Selby looked on. Jennette and Blackburn watched as Elizabeth held their son, Christian. Kendal gave his wife a quick peck on the cheek. Anthony wondered if they were keeping a little secret about a baby.

"Lord Somerton, welcome," Avis said, coming to greet him. "It is a shame you could not make it to the church for the christening."

"The roof might have fallen in if I should happen to set foot in a church," he replied. "Your daughter is beautiful, just like her mother."

With her father's raven hair and blue eyes and her

mother's heart-shaped face, Isabel would grow up to be a beauty.

"Your charms don't work on me," Avis said with a grin. "Get some refreshments."

Kendal and Elizabeth walked up to him before he could sneak away.

"Thank you again, Somerton," Kendal said.

"And thank you for finding my father," Elizabeth said quietly. "He is thoroughly enjoying his new life at the estate in Kendal."

He kissed the new duchess's hand. "You are very welcome."

Pleasantries out of the way, he searched for the only reason for attending. Sophie arched a brow at him and then inclined her head toward the hall. He waited while she walked out of the room before joining her in Selby's study.

"Welcome back, Anthony."

"Enough, Sophie. I have waited an additional five months to get her name. I want it now."

Sophie laughed softly. "Very well, I shall keep my promise. Her name is Anne Smith."

Anthony waited for some sign of recognition, but her name was as common as she had been. Just an orange seller. "Do you know if she is still alive? It's been ten years."

"She is alive."

Anthony frowned, seeing the way Sophie looked down when she answered. "What are you keeping from me?"

Sophie smiled and patted his cheek. "Why would I keep anything from you, my dearest brother? The woman you are searching for is in the room you just left."

ABOUT THE AUTHOR

Christie Kelley was born and raised in upstate New York. As a child, she always had a vivid imagination, but never thought about writing. After receiving a Bachelor's degree in Business Management, she worked for American Express, JPMorgan Bank, and Accenture Consulting. An avid romance reader, she finally turned to writing in January 2000. She sold her first book, *Every Night I'm Yours,* to Kensington Books, and has never looked back.

Christie lives in Maryland with her husband and two boys. You can visit her at www.christiekelley.com.

More by Bestselling Author
Hannah Howell

__Highland Angel	978-1-4201-0864-4	$6.99US/$8.99CAN
__If He's Sinful	978-1-4201-0461-5	$6.99US/$8.99CAN
__Wild Conquest	978-1-4201-0464-6	$6.99US/$8.99CAN
__If He's Wicked	978-1-4201-0460-8	$6.99US/$8.49CAN
__My Lady Captor	978-0-8217-7430-4	$6.99US/$8.49CAN
__Highland Sinner	978-0-8217-8001-5	$6.99US/$8.49CAN
__Highland Captive	978-0-8217-8003-9	$6.99US/$8.49CAN
__Nature of the Beast	978-1-4201-0435-6	$6.99US/$8.49CAN
__Highland Fire	978-0-8217-7429-8	$6.99US/$8.49CAN
__Silver Flame	978-1-4201-0107-2	$6.99US/$8.49CAN
__Highland Wolf	978-0-8217-8000-8	$6.99US/$9.99CAN
__Highland Wedding	978-0-8217-8002-2	$4.99US/$6.99CAN
__Highland Destiny	978-1-4201-0259-8	$4.99US/$6.99CAN
__Only for You	978-0-8217-8151-7	$6.99US/$8.99CAN
__Highland Promise	978-1-4201-0261-1	$4.99US/$6.99CAN
__Highland Vow	978-1-4201-0260-4	$4.99US/$6.99CAN
__Highland Savage	978-0-8217-7999-6	$6.99US/$9.99CAN
__Beauty and the Beast	978-0-8217-8004-6	$4.99US/$6.99CAN
__Unconquered	978-0-8217-8088-6	$4.99US/$6.99CAN
__Highland Barbarian	978-0-8217-7998-9	$6.99US/$9.99CAN
__Highland Conqueror	978-0-8217-8148-7	$6.99US/$9.99CAN
__Conqueror's Kiss	978-0-8217-8005-3	$4.99US/$6.99CAN
__A Stockingful of Joy	978-1-4201-0018-1	$4.99US/$6.99CAN
__Highland Bride	978-0-8217-7995-8	$4.99US/$6.99CAN
__Highland Lover	978-0-8217-7759-6	$6.99US/$9.99CAN

Available Wherever Books Are Sold!

Check out our website at
http://www.kensingtonbooks.com

Romantic Suspense from
Lisa Jackson

See How She Dies	0-8217-7605-3	$6.99US/$9.99CAN
Final Scream	0-8217-7712-2	$7.99US/$10.99CAN
Wishes	0-8217-6309-1	$5.99US/$7.99CAN
Whispers	0-8217-7603-7	$6.99US/$9.99CAN
Twice Kissed	0-8217-6038-6	$5.99US/$7.99CAN
Unspoken	0-8217-6402-0	$6.50US/$8.50CAN
If She Only Knew	0-8217-6708-9	$6.50US/$8.50CAN
Hot Blooded	0-8217-6841-7	$6.99US/$9.99CAN
Cold Blooded	0-8217-6934-0	$6.99US/$9.99CAN
The Night Before	0-8217-6936-7	$6.99US/$9.99CAN
The Morning After	0-8217-7295-3	$6.99US/$9.99CAN
Deep Freeze	0-8217-7296-1	$7.99US/$10.99CAN
Fatal Burn	0-8217-7577-4	$7.99US/$10.99CAN
Shiver	0-8217-7578-2	$7.99US/$10.99CAN
Most Likely to Die	0-8217-7576-6	$7.99US/$10.99CAN
Absolute Fear	0-8217-7936-2	$7.99US/$9.49CAN
Almost Dead	0-8217-7579-0	$7.99US/$10.99CAN
Lost Souls	0-8217-7938-9	$7.99US/$10.99CAN
Left to Die	1-4201-0276-1	$7.99US/$10.99CAN
Wicked Game	1-4201-0338-5	$7.99US/$9.99CAN
Malice	0-8217-7940-0	$7.99US/$9.49CAN

Available Wherever Books Are Sold!
Visit our website at **www.kensingtonbooks.com**